seventh day

BOOK SEVEN

A.D. CHRONICLES®

seventh
day

Tyndale House Publishers, Inc.
Carol Stream, Illinois

BODIE & BROCK
THOENE

Visit Tyndale's exciting Web site at www.tyndale.com

TYNDALE and Tyndale's quill logo are registered trademarks of Tyndale House Publishers, Inc.

A.D. Chronicles and the fish design are registered trademarks of Bodie Thoene.

Seventh Day

A.D. Chronicles series designed by Rule 29, www.rule29.com

Interior designed by Dean H. Renninger

Edited by Ramona Cramer Tucker

Library of Congress Cataloging-in-Publication Data

Thoene, Bodie, date.
  Seventh day / Bodie & Brock Thoene.
    p. cm. — (A.D. chronicles ; bk. 7)
    ISBN-13: 978-0-8423-7524-5
    ISBN-10: 0-8423-7524-4
    ISBN-13: 978-0-8423-7526-9 (pbk.)
    ISBN-10: 0-8423-7526-0 (pbk.)
    1. Jesus Christ—Fiction.   2. Bible. N.T.—History of Biblical events—Fiction.
I. Thoene, Brock, date.   II. Title.   III. Title: 7th day.
  PS3570.H46545 2007
  813′.54—dc22   2007028593

Printed in the United States of America

14   13   12   11   10   09   08
 7   6   5   4   3   2   1

With love to our sixth and seventh grandkids—
Turner Graham Thoene and
Wilke Lynn Thoene—
Psalm 139

the middle east

FIRST CENTURY A.D.

Mount Hermon +

Mediterranean Sea

GALILEE

• Caesarea Philippi

Chorazin •
Capernaum •
Magdala •

• Bethsaida

Sea of Galilee

• Tiberias

Jordan River

SAMARIA

Jericho •

Jerusalem • + Mount of Olives

• Bethany

Bethlehem •

• Herodium

PEREA

JUDEA

Dead Sea

IDUMEA

N

← to Alexandria, Egypt

Prologue*

Dimming twilight stained the sky above Jerusalem. Night seeped into the Old City house where Moshe and Rachel Sachar had once lived. Jacob and Lori Kalner were the last of the old friends to leave after the Jerusalem memorial service of Professor Sachar. Old Alfie embraced the frail couple in a giant bear hug and they wept together in the foyer of Moshe's home.

Thirty-nine-year-old Shimon Sachar hung back in the doorway of his father's study and observed the farewell of the three who had been childhood friends in Berlin since before the days of Hitler. Shimon had not seen Jacob and Lori since the death of Rachel and Shimon's wife, Susan, in a Palestinian suicide bombing. Lori's sight had been failing even then. Her vision was completely gone now. A muscled black lab named Romeo served as Lori's eyes. Tears streamed from beneath her dark glasses. Dressed in a heavy black coat, she nevertheless wore a bright red scarf over her head. Lori leaned heavily on Jacob's arm. Jacob, as ramrod straight and distinguished as ever, was professor emeritus of archaeology at a major university in England. He ran a hand through his

---

* For more of the story, read the Zion Chronicles series and the Zion Legacy series by Bodie and Brock Thoene.

thick thatch of silver hair and patted Alfie on his broad back. Though German was the common childhood language of the three, they had refused to converse in their native tongue ever since they fled the Nazis. They spoke in heavily accented English, making Shimon smile as he listened.

Lori placed her hand on Alfie's cheek. "Alf, dearest. We come soon as a flight was got."

"Soon enough. Seven days since Moshe flew away," Alfie remarked, brushing Lori's tears away with his thumb. "Almost we're the only ones, eh? Only ones left, eh?"

Jacob embraced Alfie again. "This new generation. The young Israelis are getting visas to go to Germany or Poland in case things get bad in Israel."

"They have forgot." Alfie spread his palms. "If there had been Israel in 1936 . . . yes? If only. How many then would be alive?"

Thus was the wisdom of the world confounded by the simple, Shimon mused.

Alfie, the gentle old man who had calmly survived wars and persecutions for eight decades knew well enough why Israel must survive. Alfie, Lori, and Jacob were the last who could tell the tale.

Lori presented Alfie with a thick file sealed in plastic. "For Shimon, yes? Jacob's letters. My journals. Our story. The three of us. Something now to add to the other memories. Someday. Someday. Yes, someone will read our words and know what it was to live in such days."

Alfie raised the packet to his lips. "Sure. The boy keeps them all safe. Many brung them . . . sent them. Shimon keeps them all safe, you know. Don't know if we'll meet again, eh? Not here, maybe."

"Only apart a short while, I think." Lori smiled. "I am blind, but I will see. And the first face I will see . . ."

"*Ja*. The Light. All the days of Shiva from all the mourning of this life . . . they will come to an end," Jacob added.

Shimon turned away from this final farewell of the trio who had been through so much together. Retreating to his father's study, he lay down on the cracked leather sofa. Closing his eyes, he slept instantly.

It may have been hours before Alfie noiselessly entered the room. Shimon felt the old giant's presence hovering over him. He opened his eyes.

Alfie's compassionate face gazed down at him. The old man placed the packet from Lori and Jacob on the desk. "Their story. Our story. Mine too with theirs. Everybody gone now."

Shimon sat up and cradled his head in his hands. "I fell asleep."

"Sure. It's good to sleep when you're sad. I brung you something else too." Alfie removed a letter from his pocket. "From your papa. He says to me that when he is gone, you should have this."

Shimon gazed at the familiar handwriting on the clean white envelope. "He knew."

"Sure. Like I said, if we live long enough, we're all gonna die. Read. He left the best for last."

Shimon sighed as he broke the seal and began to read.

Dearest Shimon,

It is the seventh day. The end of Shiva. For seven days I have been again with my beloved Rachel, your mother. Do not grieve for us after this morning. The time for sorrow is over. In other letters which you and your brothers and sister have read since my death, I have shared how much your mother and I love you all. I have left instructions for Alfie to give you alone this letter on the seventh day after our parting. Alfie will lead you alone to the final gift. In this gift is the future. Present Time grows short. There is hope only for those who grasp the sleeve of Truth as He passes by. Alfie will show you the way.

All my love,

Baruch atem b'shem Yeshua,

Papa

Shimon raised his eyes to see that Alfie had already opened the hidden entrance that led down to the Chamber of Scrolls.

"Ah, Shimon. Your good papa, he saved the best for last. He saw this day coming, and he set them aside these last years until now. He knew you would need to read them when he was gone. Put your nosh in your pocket." The old man grinned as he slung a backpack over his shoulder. "I brung enough food for later too. A new branch tonight. Hold to my shirt. It isn't far."

The two men descended the narrow steps into what seemed to be a cistern. Alfie pushed the pattern carved into the stone. A whoosh of wind announced the opening to the passageway.

"Don't ask no questions." Alfie held up two fingers, which he placed into a groove in the ceiling. "Hold on. It's different, all right."

A lump of apprehension in his throat, Shimon clung to the belt of old Alfie as they wound through the darkness. The tunnel that led to the Chamber of Scrolls seemed familiar and yet, midway, the old man's voice whispered, "Right to left we read the words now, eh, Moshe? Not left to right." Then he turned abruptly to the left.

Shuffling downward, Shimon remembered the many times he had asked his father where other passages led. The answer was always the same: "When you need to know, you will be shown the way."

Minutes passed. Alfie spoke again. "Don't move." There followed the sound of slow counting; then the old man repeated the Shema: "*Hear, O Israel . . .*"

The clank of a latch, the groan of ancient hinges, and the scrape of moving stone assaulted Shimon's senses. A dim light radiated from a low, narrow portal. Alfie struck a match and lit a candle. Tugging Shimon's sleeve, Alfie commanded him not to bump his head as he entered. The stone chamber seemed to be a perfect cube of about thirty feet on every side. In the exact center was a smooth marble slab of perfect geometric proportions to the room. It was flanked by two stone benches. On the slab were six clay jars matching those Shimon had seen in the much larger Chamber of Scrolls.

Alfie blew out the candle, but the room did not darken. "Look up," he instructed.

Painted stars on the ceiling of the secret chamber seemed to glisten with a new light. Shimon traced the stellar signs of Messiah's birth as they were viewed in the stars by the Magi and recorded in the journals of Peniel two thousand years before.

Three planets—Mars, Jupiter, and Saturn—formed a close conjunction within Israel's constellation of The Two Fish. Gold Hebrew letters identified the proper name of the heavenly lights:

Mars was Ma'Adim, The Adam
Jupiter was Tzadik, The Righteous
Saturn was Shabbatai, The Lord of the Sabbath

"The heavens declare the glory of God . . . and the birth of Messiah," Shimon whispered quietly. "What is this place?"

Alfie spread his hands as if offering a banquet in the cold chamber beneath the place where Solomon's Temple had once stood. "A miracle."

Shimon peered upward as he spoke in hushed tones. "I went online, you know? To verify the account of Peniel's journals against scientific details about the conjunctions of the stars the year Jesus was born. E-mailed Tom Wickersham, a friend of Susan's at NASA. He e-mailed me a series of photos from an astronomical program—the skies above Jerusalem in 7 and 6 B.C. And there they were. The conjunctions. This . . . this ceiling . . . it's like a planetarium, you know?" Shimon raised his arms as if to embrace the stars.

"Yes. Full of treasures. Your great-grandpapa used to say, 'Everything means something.'"

"More than that, Alfie." Shimon turned his face toward the walls, where Hebrew letters carved in smooth stone identified the words of the prophet Zechariah. "Everything . . . has meaning."

Alfie placed the backpack on the floor. He ran his finger around the rim of a first-century clay jar to check the seal. "Of all the boys your papa wanted you to know. So much more."

Shimon cleared his throat. "After Susan and Mama were killed? The intifada? No peace in Jerusalem. No life for Israel, I thought. All the dreams of you and the others coming here . . . struggling, dying . . . the rebirth of Israel as a nation. It seemed to amount to nothing. I didn't want to live without Susan and the baby."

He touched the jar containing the first scroll of Peniel. "Then you and Papa brought me here. I read the scrolls and saw myself for the first time. I knew I was blind like Peniel. I was a leper like Lily. Bitter like Alexander. Afraid like Yosef. And then, Yeshua was born in my heart. Now when I'm outside, I walk through the streets in a different century. I go to the Pool of Siloam, where Peniel washed clay from his eyes and gained his vision. I search the faces of everyone as I pass by, thinking I'll see Peniel. Hoping I will round a corner and find Yeshua teaching his talmidim. I drink a cup of coffee at Starbucks—and count the hours. Can't wait to come back here. To read. To learn. To know Yeshua better."

Alfie replied, "Yes. Truth is like food, nu? Such stories. Warms the bones of an old man. Like a good cup of tea. Yes, tea. I brung enough for a while. Your papa said you should start with Peniel's Seventh Day. It tells the future. Everything they say they want to know in the outside world, but they don't really want to know. They see it, but they don't know what it means."

Shimon placed six scrolls in the correct order, marked with the name of *Peniel: Face of God.* In the large library Shimon had seen thousands of other containers. Each jar contained a personal eyewitness account recording Jerusalem's long history. This small chamber denoted a portent of something greater than all the other stories combined.

Shimon could hardly speak. His thoughts tumbled out in a rush. "How will we ever . . . how will I ever read them all? All of them. Papa told me each scroll represents a life. An event. A miracle. So much more Yeshua did. So much never recorded. All the books in all the world can't hold everything.[1] They were real, these people. More than just names in a story, eh?"

The knuckles of Alfie's hands were swollen. He fumbled through a leather briefcase before removing a single sheet of paper. "Here. The list where your papa and me started in 1948. Your papa. These was his favorite." Alfie's voice echoed in the room. "Here it is. Here. You read. This was his most favorite. He saved it for you because he knew you would need it most. And I brung tea. A fresh pot. No more biscuits. We should bring biscuits and apricot jam and bread down tomorrow. Your mama always made good scones to send along. And sandwiches. We was never hungry when Rachel was alive."

The slope-shouldered old giant lumbered toward the study table. He grasped the pottery jar marked in Hebrew *Seventh Day*. It was sealed with Peniel's mark. Alfie grinned. "Ah! I like this one best too."

Shimon frowned. "So, the man born blind. What else did he see?"

"You'll see. Best so far."

"You like them all."

Alfie nodded. "Peniel's stories, yes. This one? Proof."

"Proof of what?"

"Your papa said, this one . . . a time machine."

Shimon studied the painted stars that had glowed in the night sky above Jerusalem two thousand years before. "It was a winter sky?"

Alfie's faded eyes glistened with pleasure. "Almost Hanukkah. The baby in the manger's grown up. A man. Hanukkah's coming. They're in the Galil. All afraid, but . . . he's not afraid. Me neither. Hanukkah. I like the lights. The best for our last journey, I say."

"Last?"

Alfie nodded. "Almost home. Almost the end. But you won't be alone. They'll always come to hear you read."

"They?" Shimon asked the old man.

"Sure, Shimon. Them." Alfie jerked his thumb toward the portal. "Always watching over us."

Shimon raised his eyes, hoping to see the angels Alfie spoke to with such certainty. There was no one there.

"So?" Alfie nodded eagerly at Shimon, indicating that he should open the seal and remove the seventh scroll of Peniel. The document was tied with scarlet cloth and wrapped in linen like that used for a shroud. It was smaller and lighter than the other scrolls.

Shimon carefully unwound the covering. The sheepskin had more than survived two thousand years. It seemed as fresh and supple as it had when it was new.

Alfie clapped his hands and chuckled as if someone had spoken to him. "Come on, then! It's beginning! Hurry, Shimon. See? They're coming. Shining. Bright. Sent! Coming . . . joy calls to them. Just there!" He inclined his head toward the end of the table as Shimon opened the document. A sprig of pressed lavender fell from the scroll, and suddenly the chamber was filled with its sweet aroma. "Shalom," Alfie cried, greeting unseen guests with joy. "So many of you today! Shimon, golden ones! Tall! Come to hear you read Peniel's story like your papa."

Shimon blinked at the place where Alfie said angels had gathered. Was there a glimmer of unexpected light? the faint rustle of wings?

Shimon raised his hand in greeting, just in case what the old man saw was more than imagination. "Shalom."

Suddenly Alfie bowed and addressed the empty air. "Shalom! Yes, you'll have to stay with Shimon when I go. Today is Peniel's Seventh Day. Thanks. Thanks." He sat down, propped his head in his hands, and confided in a whisper to Shimon, "Read good, boy. They come a long way to hear it. Want to hear it again. What Peniel seen that day! Sad, sad story. A friend . . . dies. But happy too, though. Don't worry. Best ever, I said when he read it to me first. 1948. Above us demons danced in the streets . . . burned down the Jewish Quarter. Synagogues burning and burning above our heads. So many good friends died. Haj Amin Husseini told the world there weren't no Jews left in Old City Jerusalem. Said there never would be no Jews here again. Didn't know about us two down here, or the angels with us. Moshe and me down here under the Temple Mount. This is where the stones of Jerusalem wait for him to come. Where Israel lives. Your papa opened the books and read and read. Best story in heaven and earth since the day one brother first killed the other. Seventh Day it was—the future. Never such a day. . . ."

PART I

THE LORD'S SEVENFOLD COVENANT WITH ISRAEL

I will bring you out of Egypt.

I will rid you of their bondage.

I will redeem you.

I will take you to Me for a people.

I will be to you your God.

I will bring you into the land.

I will give it to you.

EXODUS 6:6-8

Journal of Peniel the Scribe
Blind Beggar of Nicanor Gate Healed by Yeshua HaMashiach

This account of the works of Yeshua is set down by the hand of Peniel, the beggar of Nicanor Gate. Blind from birth, I first received my sight from Yeshua HaMashiach, the Eternal Potter who formed man from the red clay of the earth.

Yeshua, who created everything seen and unseen, came to dwell among men in the time appointed. Conceived in the womb of a virgin in Nazareth, He was born in Beth-lehem and grew to be a great teacher and miracle worker known by all the world.

Men ask me how a man born blind became a scribe.

In Jerusalem I sat in darkness, incomplete, unable to comprehend the glory of The One who created the stars. And though I heard the psalms that spoke of the beauty HaShem had created, I could not understand.

One day Yeshua saw me in the Temple Gate, and His compassion was warmed for me. Then He who is the Great Potter, forming all creation with His hand, knelt beside me. He spit into the dust of stones King Solomon had raised. He made clay from the dust of Israel's fallen greatness. This dust of Jerusalem, beloved by God, still bears witness to the covenant power of HaShem to forgive and heal the land and the people.

The truth of God's love and mercy is recorded in Torah, the Prophets, and the Writings. Everything in Scripture means something. Every story written about an individual or the whole nation of Israel is meant to teach us to trust God. Even my blindness, such a grief to my father and mother, was meant to prove to Israel that "nothing is impossible for God!"[2]

In my darkness I longed for The Light of the World, as did all of Israel.

Yeshua, The One Sent from Olam Haba, anointed my unformed eyes with the clay of glory He made. Then the Anointed One sent me to wash in the pool called "Sent." When I washed, I could see as well as any man born with vision. In this way Yeshua created eyes for me to receive the light.

I was blind and now I see. By this miracle God strove to prove the identity of His Son and awaken faith in the hearts of His beloved people.

I am only one among a multitude who have been forever changed by a touch or a word from Yeshua. There are miracles beyond counting in the lives of men and women I know well.

Those close disciples who walked with Yeshua from the beginning have set down the true facts as they witnessed them. These chronicles set the standard of all stories about Yeshua that follow. There can be no disagreement with these first accounts, which are purest truth.

These are stories beyond counting, as the great disciple John says. Your own life is a story written by the very hand of the Lord. Every event in your life is meant to teach you to trust that God loves you. Perhaps it is easier to believe what God has done for others.

I will attempt to share these with you as you have asked me. I pray with trembling that the words I set down may be acceptable to the Most High.

I am Peniel the Scribe. Once I was blind, but now I have seen His face and The Light shines brightly in my heart.

Even so, there were those who witnessed my miracle with their own eyes who refused to believe Yeshua gave me sight. Instead they sought to dishonor and kill The One who is my Light, The Light of Israel.

Yeshua, The Light of the World.

Yeshua, proof that God's covenant promises are Truth.

There was a time at the campfire in Perea when I looked at His face and saw that His heart was consumed with grief at their rejection of God's mercy. Unbelief betrayed Him.

"This is not meant to end in death. . . . You will yet see the glory and power of God."

Even now He grieves for those who will not trust Him.

"Only believe me and you will see. . . ."

But the rejection of the power of the Holy Spirit and the salvation of

Yeshua the Messiah began long ago. The rejection of Yeshua's gift of mercy began with those among whom He had grown up.

I, Peniel, man born blind, scribe of the Way, record these memories for generations who will be born after us.

Is it still true in your day that those who should trust Him with the faithfulness of a child are instead the very ones who deny the glory, might, and power of The One Sent to open the eyes of the blind?

1

It was some time after the death of Yosef, His earthly father, that Yeshua returned to Nazareth to reveal the secret—to plainly share the testimony of His true paternity, as prophesied in Torah.

Though certain they had known Him all their lives, the people of Nazareth had no idea who Yeshua was or where He had come from. Nor could they imagine the eons that had passed since this moment of divine revelation had been planned.

Despite the fact that every detail of Messiah's life and mission was revealed within the text of ancient law and prophets, the good people of Nazareth did not comprehend.

Not surprising.

After all, could Messiah live next door?

"Yeshua, my mother wonders, please, could she borrow two eggs?"

Was it possible that The Lord of All the Angel Armies, El Olam, and Ancient of Days, had descended to earth from His throne and was singing in the carpenter's workshop?

Could the descendant of David—Prophet, Priest, and King—be more than a metaphor? Could He truly be Immanu'el, God-with-us?

They had heard of Yeshua's miracles, yes, but even then, few in Nazareth believed.

"Messiah, remember me? I gave you water when you were building new stairs to my roof. So . . . just give me a sign."

One particular Shabbat, Yeshua stood among His neighbors.

It was in the autumn. The fifty-first week of the cycle of Torah portions. The reading for that Shabbat was Nitzavim, which means in Hebrew, "Standing."

Certain men of the congregation, including Yeshua, were chosen to make aliyah, to ascend the bema to read. One section of the Parashah was recited by an old man with a quavering voice. It was taken from the last chapters of the book of Deuteronomy:

"Today you are standing, all of you, in the presence of Adonai, your God . . . in order to enter into a covenant with Adonai, your God; a covenant Adonai is making with you today and sealing with an oath."[3]

Taken literally, the verse informed the congregation plainly that they were in the presence of the Lord, that He was physically there.

Yet the hearers did not hear.

Those who saw Him did not see.

Another read:

"But I am not making this covenant and this oath only with you. Rather I am making it both with him who is standing here with us today before Adonai our God and also with him who is not here with us today; those of future generations. See, I have set before you today life and prosperity, death and destruction. Now choose life."[4]

The truth of the message escaped them. After all, Scripture was just Scripture. Familiar. Boring. An obligation. They studied it, read a different Parashah every week, memorized it, and talked about it all the time. It never meant anything literal, did it?

That the Lord Himself was standing in their midst?

Torah readings completed, the congregation recited the blessings:

"King, Helper, Savior, and Shield! Blessed are You, O Eternal! Reviving the dead; You are all powerful to save! He sustains the living in

mercy, and reanimates the dead in abundant compassion; supports the fallen, heals the sick, releases those who are bound! Who is like You, Lord of mighty deeds?"

Praise was on their lips, but what was in their hearts?

Then their Redeemer, Messiah, Adonai, Immanu'el, God-with-us, stood before them at the bema of the little synagogue.

If only!

Yeshua's deep brown eyes, flecked with gold, searched each familiar face, knew every unspoken thought and secret.

The scroll of the prophet Isaias was presented to Him. Unrolling it, He found the appointed place and began to read:

"The Spirit of Adonai is upon me, because He has anointed me to preach good news to the poor. He has sent me to bind up the brokenhearted, to proclaim freedom for the prisoners and recovery of sight for the blind, to release the oppressed, to proclaim the year of the favor of Adonai."[5]

Yeshua rolled up the scroll, gave it back to the shammash, and sat down. The eyes of everyone were fastened on Him, and He said to them, "Today this passage of the Tanakh is fulfilled in your hearing."

"What?"

"Fulfilled?"

"You don't say?"

The congregants eyed each other in consternation.

Yeshua's earthly father was dead, His mother left a widow.

"If you are truly the Messiah, why did Yosef die?"

Broken hearts in Nazareth were still broken. The poor were still poor. Blind were still blind. The oppressed were still burdened. If Yeshua *was* Messiah, He had not done them any favors!

"Today the Scripture is fulfilled, he said? Who does he think he is?"

"Isn't this Yosef's son?" an old man asked.

Yeshua said to them, "Surely you'll say to me, 'Doctor, heal yourself! Do here in your hometown what we have heard you did in Capernaum.' I tell you the truth, no prophet is accepted in his hometown. There were many widows in Israel in Elijah's time, when the sky was shut for three and a half years and there was a severe famine in the land. Yet Elijah was not sent to any of them, but to a widow in Zarephath."[6]

"*Elijah was sent to outsiders, he means!*"

"*Is he comparing himself to Elijah? Saying he can raise the dead, is he?*"

If only they had let Yeshua speak, He would have taught them how Elijah raised the widow's son from the dead and miraculously provided flour and oil enough for her and her son to eat while all the rest of the country hovered near starvation.

If only they had opened their hearts, they might have understood that Yeshua was The One Sent from heaven to lavish Yahweh's endless *chesed*, mercy, on all who called out to Him.

If only!

But the people of His hometown were in no mood to listen.

"*He's a nobody, this son of a carpenter!*"

"*Yet now he declares he meets the criteria to be Messiah!*"

"*Heal the sick and raise the dead? To cleanse the Temple of corruption and set up a kingdom? And bring the exiles home?*"

"*Yeshua claims he is the fulfillment of all the writings of Torah and the prophets?*"

"*He's a madman! Or worse!*"

It was a mob comprised of old friends and good neighbors who dragged Him outside the town with the goal of hurtling Him over a cliff.

The Sovereign Lord of the Universe, the Anointed Messiah promised by the prophets, had indeed lived next door. And they drove Him away.

The Parashah proclaimed, *Listen! Today you stand before Adonai! He has come to you personally to seal the covenant He made with Abraham, Isaac, and Jacob! Choose life!*

They chose, instead, to try to kill Him.

Yeshua never returned to Nazareth. Not ever. There were other towns, other needs, others who hoped He would come to them . . . and His time to live as a man among mortal men was growing very short.

☖

His name was Abel. Abel begins with *alef*, the first letter of the alphabet. He was Eve's first and only son—her miracle, her joy. He was her life. He was everything . . . the substance of every hope.

Like Isaac, the baby was a miracle child—a gift from God, his father, Absalom, said. So they named him Abel, meaning "God is my Father."

Circumcised into the covenant of Abraham at eight days, Abel was the lone offspring of Eve and Absalom the Scribe.

Perhaps her dreams for him were unrealistic, her love for him too extravagant. Much later the people of Nain would say she should have known better, should have been more cautious with her love.

After all, nothing ever turns out the way it should.

Eve, daughter of the innkeeper, was a homely girl with a kind spirit. Married off to the childless and much older scribe after his second wife died, she was a good match for him. Absalom treated her kindly. When she became pregnant, he was pleased and felt young again, though friends in the synagogue jokingly called him "Father Avraham."

Like the original Father Abraham, Absalom was proud to have a son learn his craft and carry on his trade.

A sign bearing the image of a writing case and a quill pen hung above the door of their house near the center of the town.

Letters and deeds and sales documents were the bread and butter of his business. However, Absalom the Scribe was best known as a *ketubah* artist. Famous throughout the Galil, he drew up marriage contracts that were works of art.

Ordinary legal terms for matrimony—bride price, dowry, and the like—were set down on scraped and bleached lambskin. Perfectly formed Hebrew letters were intertwined with a garden of gold leaf vines and flowers created from the rare purple ink of a sea snail.

No matter if the bride was homely or the groom a dolt, a *ketubah* drawn by Absalom was fit for the wedding of King Solomon and the queen of Sheba. It was said that arranged marriages, if sealed by a document drawn up by the Scribe of Nain, were sure to be blessed with many strong, healthy sons.

For some, this may have been true, but Eve, the wife of Absalom, had only one son. Abel was neither strong nor healthy. Even so, his mother widely proclaimed that Abel was better to her than ten sons. She thanked Adonai daily for the gift of Abel's life.

As befitting the son of a scribe, Abel learned his alef-bet easily and could read and write his name before his fourth year.

It was whispered that if he lived, Abel would inherit the writing case of his father, along with his father's reputation.

If he lived? The issue was indeed a matter of concern. Almost from the beginning Abel's hold on life was tenuous. He could not run and play like other boys in the village of Nain. When the winds blew in from the fields and orchards, he was put to bed and ordered not to venture out. The boy sat beside his aged father in the doorway and wheezed worse than the old man as they watched the world pass by.

Though Abel did not have the breath to sing, his mother sang to him constantly. He knew and loved the psalms and could write the words by heart before he was seven.

Abel was only eight when his father suddenly died. And just that suddenly the boy was the lone remaining joy in his mother's life. She clung to him and thanked Adonai that at least she had this one reason for living, so her life was not over!

Even then people whispered that she should hold something back— be cautious in her dreams. After all, nothing ever turned out the way it should . . . not on this side of *olam haba*, the world to come.

Abel mourned for his old father seven days. In the silence of his grief it was as though the boy was old and wise beyond his years. When he rose from the ashes, he whispered aloud a thought that was surely a prophecy about his future.

He told Adonai how very much he longed to be with his father one day. When Abel became very ill, he told Adonai he wouldn't mind dying, except for the fact that his mother needed him.

He was only thirteen years old when the life that had begun with such joy moved inexorably toward its end.

Much later, perhaps, Eve would say she knew all along there was something greater, something eternally necessary, some purpose more important than the suffering she endured for the sake of loving her child.

But not now.

Not yet! He's so young!

Not in this terrible hour when night fell heavy and crushed out the only light left to her.

There is no dawn for me without him!

Not as she sat helpless at his bed and bargained with a silent God for the life of the only one who loved her in all the world.

Please! My life for his!

Not as she held her son in her arms and watched him die.

Don't leave me all alone! Hazak! Be strong!

Help for her only child had been a mere twenty-five miles away from the tiny house, yet she knew now that help might as well have been at the other end of the world.

If only!

Vain hopes for his healing had killed him. She was responsible.

She would have to live with that guilt.

If only. If only we had stayed home. If only we had not set out in search of a miracle! If only!

No one else in the village would blame her for trying, except perhaps the doctor. After all, was there anyone—anyone—in Galilee and Judea who had not heard about Yeshua, the wonder worker of Nazareth?

Mired in hopelessness before Yeshua came, the *am ha aretz*, the common folk, were resigned to suffering. Bitterness was a kind of opiate that numbed the pain of living and the inevitability of death. Beaten down by unrelieved despair, they accepted the fact that life was brutal and unmerciful, and they made the best of it.

Then rumors stirred the watch fires of Israel. The quiet whisper was passed from one to another as water was drawn from the village wells.

"They say the Deliverer is alive! His name is Yeshua!"

Hadn't Yeshua healed someone who knew someone who told someone who told everyone?

Yeshua, a descendant of King David, restored health to the sick, gave galaxies and sunsets to the blind!

Poetry and song poured from the throats of the mute!

Music and laughter tickled the ears of the deaf!

Cripples danced at the Temple gates!

Lepers were made whole again!

There was free bread for all who were hungry!

Messiah!

Tenuous roots of possibility sank deep into hearts and minds with every new report. Then suddenly it was not enough simply to hear about Him anymore. Those who were most desperate for an answer lay in bed and stared into the darkness at night.

If only!

With trembling hands they constructed an image of their savior out of the very stones that weighed them down. But it was a false image, nothing like the truth of Who and What He Was and Is.

They plotted ways they might meet Him personally. Imagining

themselves close enough to touch Him, they rehearsed what they would say to Him if only.

If only . . .

"You are the Messiah? I've been waiting for you to come. You see, I want a lot! But I've heard you can do everything for me. Health, first of all. Yes. You haven't got anything if you don't have your health. Heal me. And after you make me healthy, please make me be happy always! I heard you can arrange everything. I want to be loved. I want my children always content around me, appreciating me, honoring me. I want my problem solved right now. You can do it if you're really the Messiah. I want to be right, and I want everyone to know how right I am. I want to win. I want those who hurt me to be punished. I want guaranteed success. Prosperity for my business. Always. I want you to thank me for being so righteous. I want . . . I want . . . I want. . . ."

Everyone wanted something. Few made the journey simply to meet Yeshua face-to-face. Tens of thousands of the *am ha aretz* took up the pilgrim staff, drawn to Him as the baker of endless bread, the panacea for every problem. Searching, longing for a personal miracle, they swept in like the tide.

"His name is Yeshua! Where can I find him?"

So many glutted the roads and camped in the fields that year that it was impossible to count them or know their names or ask why they had come.

They sought him in cities and in desolate places.

"Yeshua. Have you seen him? You're looking too? Do you know where he camps? I have a favor I must ask him."

Here and there pilgrims who had set out too late in life ended the quest as they were carried to their graves.

Families turned back, disappointed, with new reasons for bitterness.

"If only he had been here! Where is he? The journey was too much! If only! Why didn't he come? Why? If he is the Messiah, why did this happen?"

So it had been that morning when the widow and her thirteen-year-old son set out in search of Yeshua. Their need was as great as anyone's need. Perhaps Yeshua would answer their request, and life would forever be different for them!

The wonder worker was in Capernaum. Only a day's walk for a healthy person. Surely the boy could survive the journey. Mother and son would take it slow. Camp early. Make the trip in two or even three days if necessary.

It was spring. The flowers of Galilee bloomed. Hills were a vibrant green. The tendrils of vines grew strong in the sunlight. Orchards blossomed. In the ultimate irony, this season was the most dangerous for Eve's son. Normally he would be confined to his bed in the corner of the one-room house. The Greek physician had decreed that the boy must never inhale the scent of flowers or ever, ever attempt to run across the fields with other boys on pain of death. Travel beyond the city walls in the spring was strictly forbidden.

And yet . . . perhaps a miracle waited in Capernaum. Wasn't it worth a try?

"Mother, remember . . . remember . . . the Parashah of my bar mitzvah? Maybe the Torah portion was a sign."

How could she forget? Every night Abel had recited the words of Deuteronomy until he fell asleep in midsentence:

"All of you are standing today in the presence of Adonai . . . in order to enter into a covenant with the Lord your God. . . . See, I have set before you life and death. . . . Choose life!"[7]

The boy believed the Scripture so completely. *Choose life!* He was certain he would breathe and live even in a place where there was no breath! The Lord would be with them when they traveled in spite of the danger. Yes! Yeshua of Nazareth was just over the hills in Capernaum!

"Hazak! Mother! Be strong!" he had said to her.

To be so near and not go?

If only!

So mother and son joined the surging tide of pilgrims.

On the verge of the orange grove less than a mile from home the boy's lungs closed as though the sea had swept over his head. Where was the Lord? Where was the promise? Abel gasped and collapsed, clawing his throat for air. Two young men from the local synagogue carried him back home. The doctor was sent for.

"What have you done to him, woman? I warned you! Warned you! Your son can hardly draw a breath to walk across the room, let alone go all the way to Capernaum to meet some trickster! What have you done? Your son may well die of your foolishness!"

Guilty, ashamed, Eve turned away and wept silently. What, indeed, had she done? Daring to hope? Willing to believe that a miracle could be in the future of her only son? Freedom? Release from the unseen plague that strangled him every year? What had she been thinking of?

If only it would rain! Her thought was half a prayer as she gazed out the window at the cloudless sky. *Oh! Wash the world with my tears and let him breathe!*

It was not supposed to be like this. It was unnatural in the order of life. A mother was not meant to outlive her child. No, not ever. Such a tragedy would crack the still-beating heart of any woman into so many pieces that it would never properly heal.

She reminded the One God of Israel of this fact as the doctor toiled to save the boy that afternoon.

Take my life instead. Anything! Please. Only let him live.

At last the gray-haired Greek physician rummaged through his leather satchel, then held up a bottle of amber liquid in his right hand as he extended his left for payment. "Nothing more to be done. Four drops of this twice a day mixed with honey and wine for the cough. Half-shekel." He wagged the medicine over the boy temptingly. "And you'll pay every penny of it as a reminder to obey my instructions."

Eve frowned at the upturned palm for a moment before fumbling for the money pouch hidden in the nearly empty flour sack. Two copper coins and one silver half-shekel coin were lodged in the leather purse. She had saved the half-shekel for the boy's first payment of the required Temple tax. His bar mitzvah had been celebrated only two months ago. The rite formally initiated him into the responsibilities of Jewish manhood in spite of the pale skin and fragile frame that made him appear much younger than his thirteen years.

The doctor's fist snapped shut around the coin. He extended the medicine.

She clutched the vial to her heart. "Spring. Every year since he was a baby. I only wanted . . . I hoped, maybe . . ."

"There's no hope for this, woman. Haven't I told you? *Anhelitus*, it is called in Latin. The gasping disease. *Asthma* in my own language. I don't know what you Jews call it in Hebrew. A curse from your God, I suppose. Galilee. The orchards. The fields. Everything in bloom." He packed the bleeding lance, tourniquet, and cup into the bag. Bloodletting had finally relaxed the spasm of coughing that had given the boy's skin and lips a faintly blue pallor.

"Will he get well?"

"Give him the dose as prescribed. Care for him as best you're able. A warm damp cloth over his nose and mouth with a few drops of camphor oil will help him breathe when he begins to cough again. If he survives the spring, he'll improve after the summer months. My advice? Instead of chasing after prophets and holy men for a cure, move away from here. Move to the sea."

"The sea."

"If he comes round, feed him oxtail broth and bread every day until he can eat meat."

"Oxtail. Broth." Eve repeated the instruction. She would find a way to buy the ingredients. Somehow. There had to be a way.

For a time, Abel seemed to be at rest, breathing easier. Eve inhaled and exhaled each breath with him, willing him to get well. *Hazak! Be strong!*

It was nearly evening when Abel stirred and opened his eyes. There was a moment, a look, when Eve knew he had forgiven her for failing. The miracle they had both longed for was too far from reach now.

The cough and rattle deep in his chest began again. Almost immediately his throat constricted. Panic gripped his face.

Her hands trembled. She fumbled as she prepared the medicine. Four drops in a mixture of wine and honey. Holding it to his lips, she promised him this would help him breathe. He could not swallow it . . . shoved it away. She rushed to fetch the damp cloth treated with camphor and placed it over his nose and mouth. He clutched at his chest and shook his head. No good. No use. Lips tinged with blue. Skin pale as milk. Eyes grew wild, frantic for want of air! Then he convulsed and, as if drowning on dry land, went limp in her arms.

Silence fell like a thunderclap, deafening her to everything as she stroked his hair and kissed his brow in the gloom of a single candle flame.

Don't leave! Please! Speak to me! Speak to me!

At last the flame guttered, and with the darkness her quiet pleading came to an end. She did not call out for help or rend the fabric of her garment as finally she accepted his death. No. A few hours more of this night and the women from the synagogue would come and wash the body and bind him in the winding sheet and carry him away from her forever.

Forever!

For now, only in these last few hours before their parting, he still belonged to her. Her boy. Her only . . . only son. The one true treasure.

She lay her cheek against his head and silently rocked him. Sleeping in her arms for this last time, he was once again her baby, toddler, little boy, youth, young man proudly wrapped in his prayer shawl and standing at the bema. She remembered how he had struggled to read the Scripture portion on the day of his bar mitzvah. He had closed his eyes briefly to pray and ask Adonai to give him breath enough to speak. She had watched from the Women's Gallery and prayed for his strength. *Hazak! Hazak! V'nit'chazak! Be strong, be strong, and let us be strengthened!*

In a sort of miracle Abel's lungs were charged with air, and his voice was suddenly strong. Later that day he said to her, "Mama, I couldn't sing with the other boys, but I felt the angels singing for me. And maybe Papa watching me from heaven too."

Yes. And your grandfather would have been proud.

Maybe one day she would be content to live only with memories of her son's unfinished life. Perhaps in a time to come she would think of Abel singing in heaven and be comforted by songs she could not hear.

But not now. Not tonight. No.

As if he could hear her whisper, she rehearsed details of his short life and thanked him, *thanked him*, for the love he had given her.

And then their time alone came to an end. She would have to give him up.

The pastels of dawn lightened the sky. A rooster crowed. One final kiss good-bye. His lips were curved in a peaceful smile.

Eve laid his body on the bed. Crossed hands over chest. Smoothed back the still-damp curls for the last time. Turned her back and tore her garment.

Stepping outside into the morning, she inhaled deeply and caught the scent of star jasmine, thick and fragrant on the air. Strange that something so beautiful and perfect as a flower had been her enemy, its very fragrance warring over the life of her child for so long.

Sun rose over the plain, illuminating the snowy peak of Hermon far to the north before all else. To the west were the hills that enclosed Nazareth. Northeast was Capernaum, where Yeshua of Nazareth was probably just waking up. If only they could have reached Him! Everything might have been changed . . . if only.

If only!

Across the narrow road, she heard children stirring in the neighbor's house. Shuffling toward the sound, she knocked three times.

A woman's voice called out, "In a minute."

Could she make herself say the terrible words? She focused on the mezuzah on the doorpost and tried to believe the unbelievable.

He is dead. Dead. Last night. My boy is dead.

Inside five small children babbled happily over breakfast. The door groaned open slowly, revealing the porridge-covered face of the five-year-old daughter. The sweet voice piped, "Shalom, Eve. Good morning! Come in. We're all eating."

She trembled, gasped. "Please. Elizabeth, will you fetch your mother. . . . Please . . . I need . . . your mother."

The child's eyes latched onto the rent fabric. Comprehension flooded her young face. Wide-eyed, the little girl cried, "Mama, something's happened! Eve looks ill. Mama! Come quick!"

And so began a day Eve imagined only in her worst nightmares. Had she always lived in fear of losing him?

"Last night. It's Abel! Last night . . . he's . . . flown away. Gone. Oh, help me! Yahweh has turned his back on me. My son . . . my boy is dead!"

With that admission, every action was beyond her control. A child was sent to the synagogue with the news. Within minutes the solemn blast of the shofar announced to all that death had visited their congregation.

The who and the how and the why of it spread through the community like a fire.

"They were on their way to find Yeshua!"

"They hoped he would be healed!"

"The doctor commanded her to keep him in bed!"

"She was so full of hope when they set out!"

"If only! If only they could have found the miracle worker in time!"

Returning to her house, she did not look at the corpse. She moaned and sank to the floor. The room was suddenly engulfed with women, each of whom had some predesignated role to play.

Closing her eyes, Eve rocked back and forth and did not speak as the ritual of preparation swirled around her.

The street outside quivered with shrill cries of mourning. *"Alas, the lion of death devours her only son! Alas, the hero who might have given her hope for her old age is fallen!"*

Sparse furnishings were turned to the wall.

The boy's hair and nails were clipped. Washed, anointed, and bound in linen wrappings provided through the charity of the synagogue, his body was then placed onto a wicker bier and covered with a thin sprinkling of salt. The two remaining copper coins from his mother's purse sealed his eyes.

All was bustle and matter-of-fact preparations. Actions substituted for thought, motion for emotion. Movement fended off crippling reality.

There was no money for incense or aloe, so men left their shops to gather myrtle boughs. Women wove the sweet-smelling branches into the wickerwork frame.

The synagogue's charity did not extend far enough to include a canopy to be carried above the body. Palm branches hastily slashed from trees in the Plain of Jezreel took its place.

Murmured words of sympathy and condolence replaced full sentences.

"Hazak! Be strong!"

The unspoken question foremost in every mind asked how the widow would survive her own advancing years without at least one child to support her. Who would marry a woman on whom The Eternal had frowned twice with such severity?

"Her husband taken. She has no other living relatives. Now he only son cut off."

Surely this was a judgment of Adonai against some hidden sin in her life.

Voices played around Eve like the hum of a beehive . . . like the susurration of wind in oak leaves. Present, but not decipherable.

Occasionally other noises penetrated her consciousness. A breeze from the sea freshened the land, bringing the scent of rain. Where had the clean air been twelve hours earlier? Why did it come now when her boy could not, would never, feel it?

It was late afternoon. Nearly time for the burial. The rabbi, who would give the funeral oration at the graveside, waited for the procession to begin. He could not enter the house or come near the body, lest he be defiled.

"It is time, my dear Eve." The elderly matron who directed funerals for the congregation bent low to mutter a question. "Eve, what will you place beside Abel's body?"

"My son's life is over before it was lived. What can I give that will speak of my love for him? Can I place my heart in his grave?"

"Think on it, dear. Something to honor him."

When a man past bar mitzvah age died unmarried and childless, he had no one to carry on after him. In such a case, tradition dictated that some token of his profession accompany the coffin to the grave, lest all memory of who he was be lost.

But her son had no trade. What, then, could she send with him in death to define who and what he had been in life? Eve closed her eyes and prayed, *O Lord, only you and I know what he was. His life was your greatest gift to me. My only son. Beyond value. And you alone, Lord, know what he might have been if only he had lived. If only! How will he be remembered?*

The answer came to her as strongly as if a voice had spoken aloud: *Remember his testimony at the bema on the day he was sealed in the covenant as a man of Israel before all the congregation? All men are appointed to die. Though flesh become dust and a name be erased from stone, Adonai will not forget him. His name is written in the eternal book. Adonai will not forget your grief.*

The old woman placed a hand gently on Eve's shoulder and urged, "Offer something he valued. *Zevadatha*, provision for the journey. It is tradition, my dear Eve. We cannot carry him to the grave until you offer a gift. Place it on the bier beside his body. The rabbi is outside waiting."

Eve nodded, silently acquiescing. She fixed her eyes on the pale cold cocoon that had been her child. Rising stiffly from the floor, she made her way to a plain wooden chest containing all her possessions. Silence rippled outward from the interior of the room and into the crowded street.

She felt the eyes of the mourners on her back and knew what they were thinking. *Poor thing. What will she choose to send with the boy on his journey?*

Hinges groaned as she raised the lid. Inside was the scribe's belt Absalom had worn in the marketplace. A leather pouch contained red sealing wax, pen and ink, and a sheaf of parchment for the preparation of business contracts and marriage *ketubot*. Only two months ago the boy had proudly used his father's writing instruments as he copied out the Amidah, the blessings he had recited at his bar mitzvah. The scroll containing blessings was then wrapped in linen and sealed as a memento of the accomplishment.

Remembering how the rabbi had praised the boy's perfect formation of the Hebrew letters, Eve held the package gently in her open hands, then touched it to her cheek. How proud Abel had been of his work.

Hazak! Be strong!

But today in Eve's eyes, the parchment, in its white shroud, resembled a miniature corpse. Where were the promises her son had chosen for his personal Scripture and practiced every day? For months he had prayed so earnestly to sing correctly before the congregation. How many times had she awakened in the night to hear him rehearsing the blessings in his sleep? *"Blessed are you . . . O Adonai. . . ."* He who had been barely able to take a breath wheezed out the passages as though his very life depended on it.

"Blessed are you, O Adonai, who gives sight to the blind! You who keep your covenant with those who sleep in the dust!"

Yet the river of death had swept over him. And she was drowning after him.

Drowning!

If only! *Where were you, Lord, when we called out for your help? When we sought you in our need, why did you hide yourself? Why didn't I lie down and die with him?*

Fumbling, she retrieved the writing stylus from its slot on the belt. Like bloodstains congealed on the blade of a sword, the nib was blackened with ink from broken promises.

Pen in right hand, scroll in left, she turned to face the bier.

Many crowded into the room to witness what the widow would do and say in this final farewell before the procession began. Would she remain stoic, strong?

Hazak, hazak, v'nit'chazak! Be strong, be strong! And let us be strengthened!

Her voice trembled. Emotion threatened to choke her into silence. She remembered how her son had spoken even when each breath was an agony. She forced herself to emulate his courage.

"These are the tools of a scribe. They belonged to his father. A thousand years the line of scribes was unbroken in this family . . . till now. My only son, my Abel, used this pen. If Abel had only lived, he would've been . . . he was . . . a scribe like his father and grandfathers before him. Here is the proof. Here is the Parashah he copied down for his bar mitzvah. These things—pen, ink, and parchment—bear witness to my son's life. Though he is dust, remember him. This is my only son, my beloved boy . . . my Abel."

She bowed low, touching her forehead to the edge of the wicker bier. Placing pen and parchment beside the corpse she broke the silence with a cry that pierced the hearts of all who gathered to console her. Like a stone thrown into a still pond, the ripples of opinion spread out from the center of her anguish.

"Poor creature. She loved him, though he was always a burden."

"Aye. Poor thing. But she's better off now he's gone. Maybe now she can sell herself as a bondservant. Have a roof over her head and food to eat. Couldn't do that as long as he was alive."

"It was meant to be. They're both better off now he's gone. Suffering ended. Better off, they are."

"Aye. Anyone could see by looking what a sickly boy he was."

"And as for him ever giving her grandchildren? He never would have married anyway."

"Cursed by poverty and illness. Who would marry such a one?"

"And what did she expect? They say Yeshua and his talmidim often steal away to the hills or across the waters to escape the crowds. Many have gone in search of him and he's not there."

"Take the lad twenty-five miles to find a miracle worker? What was she thinking?"

"Blessed are they who do not hope, for they shall never be disappointed."

The shofar sounded again, marking the imminent beginning of the procession to the cemetery and beckoning all members of the synagogue. Tradition dictated that refusing to follow the dead to their resting place mocked Yahweh. Nearly eight hundred members of the community, barefoot as a sign of respect, milled around outside. All in all, the late afternoon was very pleasant and cool since the little cloud-burst. A good day for a funeral.

"*Hazak*, be strong, Eve, dear." The funeral director's voice was kind but firm in her instruction. After all, the ritual must all be played out according to a strict code. "Rabbi D'varim is ready. He will lead out the procession. As he goes he will announce your son's good deeds. He asks if there's anything you want him to say?"

"Abel was kind to me always. Never a burden."

"I'll tell him. You'll walk after the rabbi and directly in front of the bier since, you know, it was woman who first introduced death to the world."

Eve nodded once, certain that she, like the first Eve, had indeed been responsible for the death of her child.

If only!

"Then behind you will come the body. Following Abel's bier will be the hired mourners and flutes. After them the congregation. Everyone has come to honor your son, Eve. Be consoled. He was beloved."

Eve swallowed hard and allowed herself to be guided out into the late-afternoon sunlight.

Silence from the multitude.

A bird sang from the lilac bush.

She blinked in disbelief at the sky, the clouds drifting peacefully above the city walls. Was the soul of Abel hovering just above her head?

Her gaze flitted to the familiar shops and houses of the crowded lane. All unchanged! How could it be that the whole world was untouched, undiminished? Why did the earth not cry out at the loss of one so dear? How was it possible the ground did not quake beneath her footsteps?

A sea of familiar faces stared at her. Curiosity and sympathy mingled in equal doses.

Could it be? Could it really be happening?

The wicker pallet bearing Abel was borne from the house by six young men with whom he had shared bar mitzvah. A collective groan rose as the bier, rocking like a little ship, emerged.

Rabbi D'varim, an old man with a flowing white beard and a walk-ing staff, tore his tunic at the sight. He raised his chin and cried, "Look upon this grieving mother! You who say her grief is not your own. Is she not every mother since Eve who has ever buried a child? Look upon her with compassion and take up her sorrow as your own. Say to yourself, 'Behold, our son, Abel, is fallen. It is the will of the Lord. Who are we to question his judgment? Weep for our son!'"

Women tore their clothes and wept.

"*Baruch HaShem!* Blest be The Name! Blest be the God of our fathers. *Hear, O Israel: The Lord our God, the Lord is one.*"[8]

The congregation responded with a unified shout, "*Hear, O Israel: The Lord our God, the Lord is one!*"

The procession began. Friends and neighbors rushed in to replace the young pallbearers. Every few yards a new team of men grasped the wicker bier and lifted the corpse high. The undulating cry of mourning shattered the peace of the countryside. Flutes playing the dirge were nearly drowned out by the clamor.

Rabbi D'varim's praise of Eve's son was unheard.

All the while two words played over and over in Eve's mind: *if only!*

They passed the white stone hall of the synagogue, where she had married Absalom and dedicated her son to the Lord. Where his bar mitzvah had taken place.

If only!

They descended the Street of the Wool Merchants, where she had sold her loom to pay tuition for Abel's lessons.

If only!

Turning onto the main thoroughfare, they approached the arch of the city gate. Was it only one day earlier when she and Abel had walked out with such hope in their hearts?

Now curious watchmen peered down at her from the parapets. These same fellows had been on duty yesterday. They had wished the boy luck when he told them he was going out in search of a miracle to cure his illness.

The crowd shuffled through the gates.

The cortege's somber pace was broken at intervals for new hands to grasp the burden, for new voices to offer praise or lament. Covering the short distance to the rock-wall-enclosed cemetery east of town would take the better part of an hour, though it was no more than a ten-minute walk away.

Hazak! Be strong!

Too prolonged and too brief, both at once. For Eve, every step was a portent of long years alone. After she laid Abel in the ground . . . when the spade had gone round and round the circle of men, and the dust had been heaped over his face . . . the parting would be complete, final!

Faces and forms of old friends surged around her like a dream. Here, at the stone marker, only yesterday mother and son had paused to rest. His breathing had been labored. She had asked him if he wanted to return home. "*Hazak!* Be strong, Mother!" He would not return.

If only!

Raising her eyes to the crossroads where the highway led to Capernaum, she spotted the large crowd of travelers solemn and silent, waiting for the procession to pass.

Or perhaps they had come to join the mourners. Had someone carried the message of Abel's death to Shunem or to Endor? Had people come so far to pay their respects to the widow's son?

At her back she heard voices.

"*It's him!*"

"*Well, he's come along too late to do her any good!*"

"*Pointless. Salt in the wound, that's what it is.*"

"*Are you sure?*"

"*It's Yeshua and his talmidim all right. The tall one at the fore. I saw him a month ago. Yeshua.*"

"*Yeshua. Too late!*"

Yeshua? Now? Why has he come today? her heart challenged. *Why not yesterday, when it mattered?*

If only!

What could the miracle worker offer her now but empty platitudes and sympathy?

Yeshua's appearance with the mob of followers and eager supplicants only served to remind Eve that Abel might still be alive today if they hadn't gone in search of a miracle.

Yeshua, hands clasped before Him, seemed rooted on the crossroads.

No holy man would accept the defilement that came with the presence of death. Surely He would remain where He was, merely observing with lowered gaze Eve's passage . . . the embodiment of grief.

Rabbi D'varim called ahead to the travelers the prescribed formula. "Weep with her, all ye who are bitter of heart! Cry and—"

Yeshua stepped into the center of the road and blocked the procession. He strode past Rabbi D'varim and came toward Eve as though He had always known her.

When He lifted her chin from staring at the dusty path, she took in His sweat-stained robe and brown beard. Sad brown eyes flecked with gold regarded her.

Quietly, privately, as if for her ears alone, He said, "Shalom. Peace. Woman, *don't* cry."

A hush fell over the congregation. The sound of flutes was replaced by birds chirping in the orchard.

Eve's heart rebelled at His callousness. How could she not weep? Who was this to give such a command?

"You! You're too late. My boy and I . . . searching . . . for you . . . when he collapsed. *Va'etchanan*, I pleaded with Adonai. If only you had been here, Lord, my son wouldn't have died."

If only!

He frowned and nodded once, understanding. She heard a deep voice, unspoken yet resounding in her mind:

"Y'varekh'kha Adonai v'yishmerekha.
May Adonai bless you and keep you.
Ya'er Adonai panav eliekha vichunekka.
May Adonai make His face shine on you and show you His favor."[9]

Yeshua's eyes brimmed with compassion. With His right thumb He brushed a tear from her cheek. "Don't cry." His earnest gaze steadied her. *"Hazak!* Be strong!"

Leaving her, He approached the body. He stood too near death to remain undefiled. Gazing down into the ashen face as though He knew the boy, Yeshua touched the bier. Closing His eyes, He lifted His face toward heaven.

The bearers blinked dumbly at Him. Was this man seeking to take a turn carrying the corpse? Confused, they lowered the bier to the ground.

Yeshua opened His eyes, leaned close to Abel's face, and spoke quietly, as though waking him in the morning. "Young man? I say to you, get up!"

An instant of stunned silence passed.

"What did he say?"

Somewhere over the hill a cow bawled from the pasture. And then . . .

Abel's chest heaved as he inhaled deeply.

Imagination?

A woman screamed. Others saw it too!

The flutter of Abel's lashes moved the coins on his lids.

Hazak! Be strong!

And then in a barely audible whisper the boy began to recite the first words of the Amidah as he had every night and every morning in the months before his bar mitzvah: *"Adonai, open my lips, that my mouth may declare your praise."*[10]

Yeshua brushed the coins from the boy's eyes, touched his mouth, then straightened, towering over him. The pallbearers gasped, abandoned the bier, and scrambled to escape.

The world spun around Eve. Her knees buckled and she fell. "Abel?" Someone helped her stand.

The boy's eyes snapped open, and he stared up in wonder at Yeshua. "Blessed . . . blessed are you, Adonai, our God and our ancestors' God. King, Helper, Savior, and Shield! You are mighty forever, O Lord!"

Struggling against the shroud, Abel sat up and raised his hands to Yeshua, who untied his wrists.

The second blessing of the Amidah poured out of Abel's mouth:

"You are strong; you sustain the living in mercy and reanimate the dead in abundant compassion. You heal the sick and release those who are bound, and establish faithfulness to those who sleep in the dust. In the blink of an eye, you bring salvation. Blessed are you, Adonai, who gives life to the dead."

And then, without a sign of wheeze or hesitation, he prayed the third blessing of the Amidah as Yeshua helped him stand and gave him back to his mother:

"Your name is Yeshua, Salvation! Holy are you, and your name is revered; there is no god like you. Blessed are you, Adonai, the holy God."

It was winter. Gray and dark. Each day grew shorter, much to my regret. Cold rain drummed on the roof of the Capernaum synagogue where a handful of us—Yeshua's trusted followers—had been summoned in secret to hear the stories of two miracles.

Beyond the walled compound, torrents sated the cisterns of the Galil. Streams tumbling into the Sea of Galilee overflowed banks and irrigated the thirsty earth.

In Capernaum it was hoped that Yeshua, the Teacher, Healer, and Miracle Worker, would soon return from the territory of Caesarea Philippi. Speculation among the village rulers was that He might spend the winter in the fishing village. Over the weeks since Sukkot, a number of His Galilean talmidim had come home. Women and children from among Yeshua's followers had already returned, but Yeshua and His close inner circle had not yet appeared.

The villages of the Galil—Capernaum, Chorazin, and Bethsaida—profited economically during the times Yeshua lived and taught in the nearby fields and by the shores of the lake. Food enough to meet the needs of thousands, sales of shoes and clothing—all boosted the village economy. The inns were crowded to overflowing. Spare rooms in homes were rented. Miracles in Capernaum were altogether good for business. When Yeshua traveled, however, the crowds of *am ha aretz* thinned and the financial benefits dwindled.

There remained some, like me, who longed to see Yeshua's return not for monetary gain, but because He had loved us first. In tonight's gathering of forty at the Capernaum synagogue were men, women, and children who had experienced a life-transforming miracle at the hand of Yeshua.

Beside me, Peniel, was old Zadok, former Chief Shepherd of the flocks of Migdal Eder. Zadok had lost three sons thirty years before in Beth-lehem at the hand of the Butcher King. Tonight he nestled three adopted sons: Twelve-year-old Ha-or Tov had been blind. Six-year-old Emet, deaf and dumb. Ten-year-old Avel had nearly died of a broken heart. Yeshua had healed them all, then sent them to heal Zadok's wounded soul.

I spotted others who had lived without hope but were now restored to full health. Blind, deaf, lame, demon-possessed, dying of cancer or consumed by leprosy, oppressed by drink . . . too many stories for anyone to tell in a lifetime. Every life a story with a happy ending, as rewritten by Yeshua.

Tonight the two young witnesses at the center of the congregation brought good news far greater than anything anyone living on earth had ever heard before! The boy, who was just past bar mitzvah age, declared, "Heaven is as real as Capernaum. We have seen *olam haba*. Those righteous loved ones you thought were dead are alive. Yeshua told me after death comes life. His words are true!"[11]

I closed my eyes, shutting out the glow of the torchlight and the eager expressions, and I listened.

The heartbeat of hope pulsed within the room.

Thirteen-year-old Deborah, daughter of Ya'ir, the Capernaum cantor, sat beside Abel, fourteen-year-old son of Eve, the widow of Nain. Until tonight neither young person had met or spoken to the other, yet the details they shared were nearly identical. Both were adolescents. Both had suffered and *died* of terrible illness. Both had been prepared for burial. And, as many witnesses could attest, both Abel and Deborah, stone-cold dead, had returned to life at the word of Yeshua!

Over the last few months each had been interrogated separately by hostile religious authorities dispatched from Jerusalem. The investigators could not explain away what Yeshua had done. Even so, the Sanhedrin mocked and refuted what their eyes and ears told them was true.

Tonight in Capernaum there was a flood of friendly questions from those who had experienced the life-changing power of Yeshua. Where had Abel and Deborah gone the instant their souls had flown away?

Abel and Deborah recounted their journeys to *olam haba*.

The rabbi of Capernaum asked, "Children, please tell us—tell us old ones . . . say what you remember—were there others in *olam haba*? People you recognized?"

Abel frowned, then grinned, as his changing voice cracked. "Rabbi, Your Honor, there were many there who I knew must be from of old. Though I can't name them, they seemed as though I knew them from my Torah studies. My bar mitzvah. And some from my family. But the one I met first was my father. My father was there, waiting just on the other side, in the light. *Such light!* Golden. Shimmering! Waiting for me, I think, so I would not be afraid. Only he was very tall, young . . . without age . . . and strong. He called out my name in welcome. He embraced me. I clung to him and wept for joy for a very long time. I was so happy to see him, to be with him. Then I knew I was not finished here. I was needed here. My mother, you see . . ." Abel gestured toward his widowed mother, who sat beside the mother of Deborah. "It was so wonderful. I didn't want to come back. I would have stayed except for . . . Yeshua's voice."

The rabbi steepled his fingers. "Yeshua's voice? In *olam haba* you heard Yeshua speak to your soul? Though he is here on earth? You heard him?"

"Clearly."

"But this place—*olam haba*, the world to come—what was this place like? Where you saw your father?"

"A garden . . . such color!" Abel spread his arms wide as though color in heaven was a tangible thing to be embraced and not just experienced with the eyes.

Deborah bobbed her head in agreement. "Yes! I was in the same place. The garden. Flowers! Such fragrance! No thorns! Waterfalls so high I couldn't see the top. Rainbows. Hues so deep the air hummed with the music of color. I never knew color is music. Seven colors matched seven musical notes. But all with different shades and voices.

Reds and blues and greens, a thousand pitches of every color. I can't explain it. I try, but I can't. . . . It's so . . ."

"And the stream!" Abel placed his hand on the girl's arm. "Deborah! Could you hear the voices singing in the waters?"

"The song! Yes. Oh!" Deborah shook her head in wonder as she answered him. Suddenly the two were speaking to one another as though no one else was in the room. "Was there ever such music?"

He laughed. "I dream of it."

"Remember?" Deborah lowered her chin and quietly hummed the first notes.

Abel brightened in recognition of the music. Though he had never sung before, Abel began to hum with her, testing his voice.

Thunder rumbled outside, rattling the nerves of those who listened to the description of heaven. What the eyes of the two children had seen was more . . . more . . . than anyone imagined! And these beloved children who had been dead, prepared for burial, had returned to tell about a place they knew was real!

For the moment the two found connection and comfort in the song they had learned in Paradise. A few notes and Abel's strong tenor joined Deborah's sweet soprano in perfect unison of unrehearsed lyrics and harmony.

"Praise the Lord, O my soul;
All my inmost being, praise His holy name."[12]

Though each child had made the journey to *olam haba* at a different time, both recalled the identical tune.

Deborah, made brave by Abel's voice, sang louder:

"As high as the heavens are above the earth,
so great is His love for those who fear Him!"[13]

At that instant an echo resounded from above, turning faces to the rafters. I gasped, certain I was *not* the only one to hear. Distant music! Sweeter than earthly voices! What chorus was singing with them?

"But from everlasting to everlasting
the Lord's love is with those who fear Him,

and His righteousness with their children's children—
with those who keep His covenant!"[14]

Another clap of thunder shook the synagogue as though the portals of heaven had cracked open to let the joyful songs of both worlds unite.

Abel raised his eyes toward the ceiling and lifted his hand in greeting.

I followed his gaze. Who or what did the boy see? Was there a sparkle of light on a golden face? the rustle of wings on the air?

Lightning flashed a response.

The listeners linked arms and grinned nervously as yet another crash of thunder rolled across the Galil. It seemed a thousand voices joined the melody:

"The Lord has established His throne in heaven
and His kingdom rules over all.
Praise the Lord, you His angels,
you mighty ones who do His bidding,
who obey His word.
Praise the Lord, all His heavenly hosts,
you, His servants who do His will.
Praise the Lord, all His works,
everywhere in His dominion.
Praise the Lord, O my soul."[15]

They ended their song at the same instant. Words and music of the hymn reverberated in the room. The flames of candles flickered in the breath of unseen angels.

And then, silence.

The rush of wind and rain outside the synagogue sounded like applause from a great amphitheater.

Deborah and Abel blinked at one another in relief. *Yes! The testimony of two witnesses. A boy and a girl. The testimony of two!*

They laughed and huddled with heads close together. They seemed to me like old friends meeting unexpectedly on a lonely and distant shore. They rejoiced as they remembered the familiar sights and sounds of their much-loved home.

In this case heaven was home. This *present* world was the strange and distant shore to which they had returned.

Many listening that night had, like me, received a personal miracle at the word or touch of Yeshua. Across Eretz-Israel there had been countless wonders performed by Yeshua. How many had He healed and for the sake of safety instructed, "Tell no one"?

I knew well that every book ever written could not contain all the Teacher had done in secret for the sake of mercy during these years.[16]

But the stories of Abel and Deborah were unlike any others. Deborah, only daughter of the cantor of Capernaum, dead for hours. Abel, only son of the widow of Nain, carried toward the grave the previous spring. Yet here they were—laughing, talking, singing, surrounded by friends and family! Abel and Deborah were two witnesses to the eternal life Yeshua promised those who followed Him. On the other side of this life was *LIFE*! They had personally experienced the joy of heaven!

And then Yeshua had called them back to live again: two witnesses, as required in court by the laws of Torah. Witnesses to resurrection! Yeshua had restored these only ones to full health and placed them again in the arms of grieving parents!

"After death comes life," Yeshua often told us.

I pondered the meaning of the Master's teaching. *After death?* LIFE! Here was the proof!

At the end of the evening it was Deborah who embraced her friends and family with a smile and summed up what it all meant. "We all have so much to look forward to. Everything he told us is true. And we never, ever, have to be afraid again!"

Centurion Marcus Longinus ducked his helmet into the bitterly cold wind. The ride from Petra east of the Dead Sea to Jerusalem was desolate and challenging at the best of times. Now, facing the teeth of the winter storm and anxious to get back to Judea, the journey was particularly frustrating.

Only one thing warmed him: the thought of seeing Miryam again. She had been far to the north, in the Galil, but he had heard she recently returned to her brother's estate in Bethany. If true, she would be only two miles from where his orders now carried him.

Marcus had once been the senior Roman officer in Judea, ranking just below the political appointees. Hero of the battle of Idistaviso and a member of the equestrian order, Marcus still had powerful friends in Rome.

He also had powerful enemies—Governor Pilate among them. Marcus' being named "special emissary" to the neighboring kingdom of Nabatea was a mark of distinction. He also was aware of Pilate's real intent. From the desert lands Marcus could not forward to Rome any firsthand accounts of Pilate's political missteps.

The distance between Petra and Jerusalem kept Marcus safe from assassins . . . but also kept him far from Miryam.

Too far. His concern for her, growing for months, outweighed personal concerns. It was time to head home.

The wind whipped Marcus' russet curls when he turned his head to inspect the troop of cavalry. The forty riders were not regular legionary soldiers. Instead all were handpicked mercenaries. Marcus wanted men around him he could trust. Since Marcus had become known as a follower of Yeshua, Pilate was not the only threat for Marcus to regard.

Guard Sergeant Quintus, noting his commander's speculative glance, rode forward to inquire if all was in order. The iron-jawed, seemingly indestructible trooper had been watching Marcus' back and fighting at his side for over fifteen years.

Touching his fist to the polished brass symbol of his rank displayed on his helmet's cheek piece, Quintus remarked, "Fords of the Jordan in two hours if we push on. Sleep in the Jerusalem barracks tonight. Be the first time in months I didn't expect to wake up with a knife at my throat."

"The Nabateans don't love us," Marcus acknowledged, "but King Aretas is no fool. If he wants to hang on to his throne he'll not give the Empire an excuse to take it away . . . much as Herod Antipas would prefer that."

"Jews don't love us either," Quintus said roughly.

One does . . . or did, Marcus thought.

The guard sergeant's rasping voice continued, "For all that we guard *their* borders and *their* throats. Beggin' your pardon, sir, for speakin' so freely." Quintus had been speaking his mind and apologizing for it since before Idistaviso.

"As you were, Guard Sergeant," Marcus said, gesturing Quintus back into line with a wave of his dried-grapevine officer's crop.

"Sir!"

Despite Quintus' disapproval, Marcus had two pressing issues in mind: Miryam of Magdala and Yeshua of Nazareth. Both of them needed protecting from enemies at *their* backs.

If the river was not too swollen from all the recent rain, the troopers would sleep in the Antonia in Jerusalem tonight. Then he would be only two miles from Miryam's childhood home . . . and perhaps only two miles from her as well.

PART II

SEVEN THINGS DETESTABLE TO THE LORD

There are six things the Lord hates,

seven that are detestable to Him:

haughty eyes,

a lying tongue,

hands that shed innocent blood,

a heart that devises wicked schemes,

feet that are quick to rush into evil,

a false witness who pours out lies

and a man who stirs up dissension among brothers.

PROVERBS 6:16-19

pon first meeting him, everyone liked Ra'nabel ben Dives. Who could help but like him? He had celebrated his forty-fourth birthday just after Purim, but his boyish face gave him the appearance of someone ten years younger. He was above average height, but he slouched slightly when in social situations. This bad posture was assumed by all to be the result of an excess of humility or long hours hunched over a Torah scroll. He often mentioned how many hours he studied Torah and how hard he worked at his religious duties. Stooped shoulders seemed evidence of a humble and pious man . . . a small price to pay for such a desirable reputation.

Ben Dives' complexion was tan and healthy from long hours spent each afternoon walking in the garden of his large house in the fashionable western hills of Jerusalem. Although ben Dives' plain brown hair and plain brown beard were thin, by the help of a hairdresser he was able to disguise this physical flaw. Thick, healthy hair was secretly purchased twice a year from young women forced to sell their curls in order to buy food or pay Herodian taxes. The strands were woven into ben Dives' beard. No one realized his beard came from a poor woman's head, of course. It was virtually undetectable. Not even his own wife seemed aware. If she in fact knew, ben Dives was confident she held him in such awe she would not dare mention it. The result was that all who met ben Dives commented on the luxurious texture, length, and shine of his facial hair. He prided himself that even physical flaws could be managed if one was daring enough to seek an answer.

The man had inherited his exalted position in the community of Sadducees. As his father had spent his life seeking wisdom and acclaim, so Ra'nabel ben Dives now followed in his footsteps. He secretly hated the fact that his father had carved an easy path for him. At the very mention of his father's legacy ben Dives paled and reemphasized how he had achieved his own greatness as the right hand of High Priest Caiaphas.

Ben Dives earnestly believed that everyone must like him instantly if they had any brains at all. Was he not pious? Did he not have a sparkling wit? Did he not know how to pray the right prayer at the right moment?

In spite of the issue with his beard, he was attractive. He had wide-set eyes of a striking emerald hue and long, almost feminine eyelashes. He was proud of the color of his irises. They were the most beautiful irises his mother had ever seen, as she had often told him. He believed her. Though he looked no other man straight in the eyes, he had purchased a silver mirror in Rome and kept it in his lavatory, positioned so he could look himself in the eye. The Sadducee practiced smiling warmly. Did he recognize himself in the mirror? Which ben Dives did he see there?

Ah, well. No matter. Who could resist such a charming fellow?

Perhaps here and there in Jerusalem there were men who suspected all was not as it seemed. There were some who, after knowing him awhile, came to believe ben Dives' eyes displayed a trace of darkness. He never gazed directly into the face of anyone, even while speaking the most flattering, ingratiating words. Instead, the Sadducee focused on an ear or a forehead or past the left shoulder of his companion as he spoke. Or, while engaged in conversation with one, he frequently glanced at the expression of someone else. By this he ascertained how his words were being received by onlookers. *Do you like what I am saying?* his beautiful eyes seemed to ask. *Do you respect what I am saying? Do you believe that I am wonderful and friendly and wise?*

After longer acquaintance, most people noticed some incongruities in his character. While boasting hundreds of admirers, ben Dives had no true friends, certainly none who would question his motives. Asserting the proposition that he was both humble and talented remained extremely important to Ra'nabel ben Dives . . . more important than anything else.

The desire to keep his reputation unchallenged made him dangerous.

To prove his goodness, ben Dives frequently made promises to those over whom he held sway, while never intending to keep them. He made commitments that he forgot as soon as they were out of his mouth.

When later reminded of his pledges, he denied he had made them, cited misunderstanding on the other's part, or laid the blame elsewhere. Those who asked for accountability became his sworn enemies. How many lives had he destroyed? People learned it was unwise to remind ben Dives of promises he had broken.

There were some who, by accidental expression or sigh, expressed their doubts of ben Dives' humility, sincerity, or friendly disposition. With these few he openly displayed injured feelings. *How can you doubt me?* his downcast features inquired. *Surely not me?*

If self-pity did not work to raise the level of admiration in the eyes of those who had resisted his charms, then ben Dives moved on to other forms of coercion. Other methods.

It was paramount to ben Dives that he be liked, paramount that all speak well of him, paramount that men seek his advice and favor. He was, after all, private secretary to High Priest Caiaphas. Though not a member of the ruling council, ben Dives sat at the feet of the *cohen hagadol*, was privy to the high priest's secrets, and scribbled down every word that dripped from the lips of such an important man. The words of Caiaphas were, after all, the rudder directing the ship of Israel. The high priest's voice was that of religious common sense . . . and sensible business dealings too.

Yes. *Everyone* with any notion of self-preservation in Jerusalem liked Ra'nabel ben Dives. *Everyone* admired him. *Everyone* praised him. *Everyone* spoke highly of his intellect. *Everyone* sought his influence as a gate by which to enter fellowship with the mighty.

Everyone followed after Ra'nabel ben Dives step by step . . . *or else.*

With a familiarity born of years of service, Quintus tugged the folds of Marcus' uniform cape into position and squinted at the polish on the centurion's silver-handled ceremonial rod of office. Muttering to himself about having the hide off the trooper who had improperly oiled the leather fittings of the armor, the guard sergeant pronounced Marcus ready to meet the governor, grunted, and withdrew.

It was unusual for Pontius Pilate to hold any meetings in the Antonia. For some twenty-five years now Herod's Jerusalem palace on the other side of the city had been home to the Roman governors. Herod's baths, gardens, council rooms, and throne were the property of Roman officials. Even the Herodian pretense of Jewish rule over Jewish land was long forgotten. Pilate hated Judea and Judea's capital but when absolutely necessary occupied Herod's Jerusalem palace.

Today, having sent a courier ahead to announce his intention, Pilate and a picked squad of Praetorian soldiers traveled across the city. The four-towered bulk of the Antonia Fortress, located on the northwest corner of the Temple Mount, glowered down across the Temple courts. Built as barracks, armory, and stronghold, the structure served the Empire well as a reminder to the Jews of the power of Rome and the impotence of any god other than Caesar.

Today the officers' mess, oak-plank tables scraped clean and flag-stone floors scrubbed, served as the meeting place. Chosen because it was the only chamber in the Antonia large enough to be suitable, it was also desirable because it possessed two fireplaces. Both blazed with flames and black smoke, the result of the olive oil used to encourage the wet charcoal to burn brighter.

Preceded by a trio of black-uniformed guards and followed by another three, the clean-shaven, gray-haired Pilate mounted a raised platform in the center of the room. When the governor extended his manicured hand and beckoned, the centurion advanced and dropped to one knee before him.

"Rise, Centurion," Pilate invited. "We have come to honor you." The prefect seated himself while all the other witnesses remained standing. "You have done well in your mission to Nabatea. Letters from King Aretas have reached me in which he credits you with settling certain trade and border issues and keeping the peace."

While mouthing the appropriate modest responses, Marcus had opportunity to ponder what this visit was really all about. Even before the execution of his sponsor for treason, Pilate had walked a knife edge with the emperor. Bringing Roman standards into Jerusalem and thereby insulting Jewish religious sensibilities, conspiring with the high

priest to use sacred Temple funds for constructing an aqueduct, allow-
ing a riot to become the Passover massacre—all these were blots on
Pilate's record. Let any more complaints be filed in Rome about his rule
and his tenure would be over. The governor would go home in disgrace
to face censure . . . or worse.

"For your service I would like to restore you to the position of
Primus Pilus . . . 'First Javelin' and highest-ranking centurion of the
army in Judea."

Marcus' hope soared. Restored to his previous rank!

"I would like to, but I cannot," Pilate concluded. "The new head of
the Praetorian Guard, Naevius Macro, is dispatching his own selection
to be Primus Pilus. The new man will be arriving soon. But we have an
even more important task for you."

Marcus hoped none of the disappointment he felt showed on his
face. He would not give Pilate that satisfaction.

Gesturing for Marcus to approach nearer, the governor lowered his
voice. "These Jews," he said with a poorly concealed sneer, "are stiff-
necked and proud. Almost ungovernable. After tenaciously asserting
that there is only one god, they fight among themselves over religion
. . . incomprehensible to any civilized nation. But you, Centurion, seem
to have gained their trust. You even seem to have special insight into
their motivation."

Where was this leading?

Pilate continued, "Though the weather is terrible here, there will
still be pilgrims coming to Jerusalem for this Feast of Dedication.
There is poverty. . . . There is disease. There is perhaps fuel enough to
ignite a revolt. It has always been your duty to serve the Empire and,
if possible, to protect these hardheaded subjects from false leaders and
rabble-rousers. Isn't that so, Centurion?"

"Excellency, I—"

"You have some contacts with the Healer from Galilee. Don't
bother denying it. I'm not asking you to arrest him or even denounce
him. What I want you to do is to use your influence to keep him away
from Jerusalem. Let him preach to the country folk—let him go preach
to the Syrians if he wishes—but I'm convinced if he comes to Jerusalem,
there will be trouble. Just as you served me in Nabatea, I charge you
with this special task."

Raising his voice again, Pilate intoned for all to note, "You are hereby charged with keeping the peace in Jerusalem and given the rank of centurion in command of the Jerusalem garrison. This is of special importance since I am returning to Caesarea Maritima." From a fold of his purple-striped sleeve Pilate withdrew a small scroll: written orders. No doubt a copy of these orders resided in the archives of the palace . . . so that if anything went wrong, the blame could be squarely laid on Marcus' shoulders.

Roman soldiers did not refuse orders. Clasping his clenched fist to his chest, Marcus replied, "It shall be done, Excellency."

en Dives turned the pages of the journal he had acquired from the archives under the Temple Mount. Many of the records had been lost in the Great Fire in the time of King Herod. Most of what remained were merely census scrolls, tax receipts, judicial findings, and other bureaucratic debris.

But in a cupboard near where the geneology records had been before their disastrous loss, ben Dives found a treasure. Some Levite named Eliyahu, an otherwise unknown rabbi, had recorded events related to a previous claimant to the title of Messiah.

The journal recounted how prophecies about the promised descendant of David had been fulfilled thirty-three or so years previous, or around the time of the conflagration. According to Eliyahu, a whole sequence of miraculous events began when an angel appeared to an aged priest named Zachariah, promising that he and his equally ancient wife would have a son. This baby was said to be the forerunner of the Messiah, as spoken of by the prophet Malachi. King Herod, disliking any reference to someone other than himself as "king of the Jews," sought the parents but could not find them.

Then, the record continued, about a year and a few months after the first angelic announcement, Jerusalem was again disturbed by astounding news. A group of Levite shepherds, Beth-lehemites, were said to have also had angelic visitors. Rabbi Eliyahu claimed that he had been with the shepherds when the angels appeared. At their direction, he and the shepherds found an infant whom Eliyahu believed to be the promised Messiah . . . newly born in a lambing cave and lying in a manger.

Ben Dives raised his head, frowned, and bit his lower lip. Not an auspicious beginning for the Anointed One. Maybe the rabbi was crazy, or maybe he was trying to cover something up.

The Saduccee returned to his reading.

After the prescribed forty days, the child was presented in the Temple. This occurrence was said to be witnessed by many, including an ancient holy man called Simeon the Elder.

Once more ben Dives' brow furrowed. The father of the renowned Pharisee scholar, Reb Gamaliel, had been called Simeon the Elder. Could this Eliyahu have been writing about the same man?

Ben Dives rolled up the right-hand edge of the scroll and revealed a new page on the left. The lettering went from carefully spaced to uneven and jagged, as if the writer was in the grip of great emotion. Here and there on the parchment were discolored spots . . . tears?

Eliyahu wrote that King Herod, taking no chances with any baby's claim to his throne, ordered the slaughter of all the two-year-old and younger males in Beth-lehem. This command, carried out in a single night's slaughter, eliminated all such children, including Eliyahu's own son.

Ben Dives drew a deep breath. How much of this did Lord Antipas already know? Ben Dives had heard rumors of such a massacre, but the details were always confused: The raid had been against traitorous rebels and had not targeted children at all. Or the raid had been launched by Idumean bandits or Nabatean invaders, and lives had been lost even though Herod's men had tried to protect them.

Then the scroll added a startling, cryptic, and final note. In a firmer hand it stated: *But he escaped.*

The child, the messianic pretender, escaped that destruction? And today He would be . . . thirty-two. How old was Yeshua? It could be Him, ben Dives mused. It could be.

But Yeshua was widely known as being from the Galil, even called Yeshua the Nazarene—not that being from Nazareth was anything of which to be proud!

Ben Dives chuckled and it became a snort of derision.

Still . . .

This would bear closer examination. Not that ben Dives believed Yeshua's claims . . . not for a minute. But if He was the same as this fortunate surviving infant, might He not use that circumstance to advance His claim?

And ben Dives would be able to turn that news to his own advantage.

The snow fell harder now, obscuring the pinnacle of the Temple. Though the weather was markedly colder, the drifting flakes were a welcome relief to the priests and the worshippers. The damp, clinging mist with which Jerusalem had been cloaked for the preceding week had kept the oily, black smoke of the sacrifices trapped around the Holy Mountain. All its stone and gilt surfaces were grimy with soot and grease. Though the Levite attendants busied themselves from dawn till dusk with the cleaning, at the completion of one circuit of polishing it had to be done all over again.

It was still an hour until the evening sacrifices. The courts were empty, save for a handful of pilgrims. All the priests had retreated indoors.

El'azar of Bethany and Nakdimon of Jerusalem, friends and brother Pharisees, huddled from the frigid curtain of storm in the lee of the wall forming the north boundary of the Court of Women. The overhanging cornice of the Chamber of Lepers kept the drifting flakes from piling atop their shoulders, but icy drips still coursed around El'azar's thin neck and down his back.

"Could you have chosen a colder place than this?" El'azar demanded of his larger, fur-wrapped friend.

Nakdimon seemed not to feel the cold. At least not compared to his apparent sense of mission. "No spies come out in weather like this, though no one would question our right to pious worship," he explained. Then he added, "Bethany may be only two miles from here, but it must be in another century if you don't yet see the need for caution."

The accumulating snowflakes covered the parapets and the courtyards, restoring at least the appearance of pristine perfection despite what really lay underneath. Still, the snow was no aid to the poor of Jerusalem. Huddled under the viaduct bridging the wealthy quarter of the city with the Temple Mount, they struggled to keep warm. Keeping both warm and fed was almost impossible. Cold, soggy weather kept pilgrims away from Jerusalem. No pilgrims meant no alms. What aid was distributed by the Temple authorities would go for either meager scraps of firewood or meager scraps of food; it would not extend to both.

Nakdimon instructed, "Lord Caiaphas is no longer content with the network of creatures who already do his bidding. In exchange for bread and blankets he recruits additional spies from among the beggars of Yerushalayim. The more pathetic the better, you see, since the poor and crippled can easily get near the Master without question."

Both men were disciples of Yeshua of Nazareth, but Nakdimon only secretly so. El'azar, on the other hand, had welcomed Yeshua and His talmidim into his estate and openly assisted with the group's material needs.

"Surely it isn't as bad as all that," El'azar protested. "Lord Caiaphas must know by now that the Master has no plan to lead an army. The people would have made him king long ago if he had agreed."

"But the Romans don't know that! Herod Antipas doesn't know that!" Nakdimon snorted. "I heard fat, greasy Antipas thinks Yeshua is Yochanan the Baptizer come back from the dead! Anyway, Caiaphas will sell information where and when it most benefits Caiaphas! Or if a killing would be regarded favorably . . ."

Nakdimon's words trailed off into the sighing of the breeze around Nicanor Gate and the incessant dribble of snowmelt from the eaves of the Chamber of the Lepers. A noise like the crack of an icicle turned out to be the opening of a door at the side entry to the high priest's chamber. Nakdimon hurriedly pressed El'azar farther into the angle of the walls. The abrupt shove bruised El'azar's hip on the trumpet-shaped mouth of an alms box. His protest was cut off as Nakdimon shushed him.

"Listen," the larger man muttered. "You're about to see the other reason for meeting here."

By a trick of architecture, sounds originating within the arch that composed Nicanor Gate carried into the alcove sheltering the two Pharisees, though the two men could not even be seen from the archway. On quiet, uncrowded days like the present inclement afternoon, the echo was perfectly transmitted.

Two voices, one pompous and stentorian, the other higher-pitched and obsequious, sounded as though they came from just around the corner from Nakdimon and El'azar.

"There are always ways and means. Ways and means may always be found," the more baritone-timbred speaker declared.

"Caiaphas," Nakdimon hissed.

El'azar nodded.

"Exactly, my lord," the tenor agreed. "If the man himself cannot be located, then perhaps he has been warned already."

"A wise thought, Ra'nabel ben Dives," Nakdimon growled.

"Ways and means," ben Dives repeated as though savoring the wisdom of the high priest's words. "Even if this false Messiah has gone to ground, some of his followers have not."

El'azar and Nakdimon both stiffened.

"We cannot arrest men of influence," Caiaphas protested. "There would be an inquiry by Governor Pilate. We don't want that."

"I was thinking of some of the *am ha aretz*, Lord Caiaphas. People of no consequence. Beggars whom this charlatan claims to have healed, or even members of his family. Either they can be induced to supply his whereabouts or . . . they say this Yeshua is so kindhearted. Perhaps when he hears of their . . . distress . . . he will step forward."

"See to it, ben Dives. With discretion, of course."

"Exactly, my lord."

The voices, accompanied by the scrape of snow beneath their feet, moved off toward the Court of Priests and out of earshot.

"I'll strangle ben Dives with my own hands," Nakdimon vowed in a hoarse whisper. "See if I don't."

CHAPTER 6

Nakdimon stretched his broad hands toward the brazier that warmed the library of his uncle Gamaliel's spacious home. Leader of the minority party of Pharisees on the Sanhedrin, Gamaliel bar Simeon was the first to come to Nakdimon's mind after the encounter with High Priest Caiaphas and Ra'nabel ben Dives.

Gamaliel was a full head shorter than his nephew, and his formerly jet-black beard was now grizzled, but the eyes of the fifty-year-old scholar were as lively as ever and his wits as quick. *Much too quick for me to follow sometimes*, Nakdimon thought. He watched his uncle pull a shawl tighter around his shoulders, though the room was already warmer than necessary.

Gamaliel and El'azar studied the open lambskin scroll of the prophet Haggai.

"Here it is. The prophesied date of Messiah's birth." Gamaliel read aloud:

> *"From this day onward, from the twenty-fourth day of the ninth month, give careful thought to the day when the foundation of the Lord's Temple was laid. Give careful thought: Is the harvested grain*

any longer in the barn? As to the grapevine, the fig tree, the pomegranate, and the olive tree—they have not yet borne fruit. From this day on I will bless you."[17]

"The text asks us to consider the significance of a day and date. The twenty-fourth day in the month of Kislev. That is soon," El'azar observed, sniffing and absentmindedly wiping his nose on the sleeve of his robe.

"You know the meaning of the date Haggai gives."

"It is the day before the Feast of Dedication. The day before Hanukkah begins. The Festival of Light."

Gamaliel confirmed this conclusion with a judicious bob of his head. "The date Israel's Redeemer will come. And the promised blessing of the covenant will begin."

"*Will* come?" El'azar inquired. "But isn't Haggai's prophecy already fulfilled? With the defeat of Greek rulers in Yerushalayim? Haggai predicted the Maccabee revolt and their victory over the foreign rulers three hundred years before it happened. The Maccabees liberated the Temple grounds and purified the Temple. That is *why* we celebrate the Feast of Dedication."

Gamaliel smiled and shook his head. "Only one reason. '*Consider carefully,*' the Lord says. Five times in Haggai the Lord says, '*Give careful thought.*' Dig deeper into the meaning of the words and find yet another layer of truth, El'azar; truth that is all about our Redeemer, the Messiah of Israel."

Gamaliel picked up a brass bucket and dumped another handful of charcoal onto the flickering embers. The new fuel caught at once, and a tracery of flame danced over the heap.

El'azar inhaled deeply and let his breath out cautiously as he considered the words. "We have all spent too many days tending our vines, our fig trees, our pomegranates, our olive trees and not enough studying Scripture. If this speaks of the Messiah, what does it mean? Tell me plainly."

Nakdimon thought he knew the meaning, but he did not answer in deference to the learned elder Gamaliel. Still, he leaned forward eagerly.

Gamaliel traced the line of letters with a silver-tipped ivory wand. "Stand in the Temple and look around you. What symbols adorn the stone? The fig tree represents the nation of Israel in prophecy. The vine, the pomegranate, and the olive tree—each of these is a symbol of the coming Messiah. When Haggai says these have not yet borne fruit, this means that the true King of Israel is not yet born. And then Haggai gives the date of his birth. The date when the fruit of Avraham's covenant will be born. Messiah will be Prophet, Priest, and King. Haggai says he will also be a descendant of Zerubbabel, himself a descendant of David." Gamaliel turned to Nakdimon and spread his hands. "Will you not speak to our young friend?"

Nakdimon cleared his throat, pleased that his uncle called on him. "You're too young to know, El'azar. You weren't born then, and I was too young to recall these things for myself, but we've heard of them. Thirty years ago angels spoke in the Temple to an old priest named Zachariah. The father of the Baptizer. Shortly afterward the signs in the heavens declared a King had been born in Israel. Angels showed themselves to Temple shepherds on the same night the prophet Haggai promised. The echoes of their shouts are still in the memory of the people. No baby is ever born already ruling as a king. First the baby must be a prince. But those who saw the signs knew that the one born in Beth-lehem in the time of the Feast of Dedication was, according to the prophecies of Haggai and Micah, the true King of the Jews. Wise men, who had studied the weeks of years spoken of by Dani'el, came from distant lands to worship this new King. My grandfather—Reb Gamaliel's father, Simeon the Elder—actually met the promised infant when he was brought to the Temple for his dedication."

El'azar's eyes glowed at the vision of this event that had occurred near where he and Nakdimon had just stood and not half a mile from where they now sat.

From an inner room came the noises of a table being laid for supper.

Nakdimon continued, "Old Herod feared this prophecy above all others and ordered the children of the City of David murdered."

"Yes, I've heard the story," El'azar remarked. He ran his fingers through his brown, curly hair.

Gamaliel finished, "Each year at this time, the people recall the prophecy of Haggai. They wonder if the Son of David, grown to manhood, will come to the Temple."

Nakdimon added, "Herod Antipas, the son of the old Butcher King, now sits on his father's throne. He fears the same prophecy. He killed the Baptizer, succeeding where his father failed. Antipas fears that maybe the butchery of that long-ago night in Beth-lehem did *not* kill the promised King Messiah. And he is right, eh?"

El'azar concurred. "Yes. It is Yeshua. I've heard the story myself from the lips of old Zadok the Shepherd, who saw the angels. He whose own baby boys were murdered. The Feast of Dedication comes soon again. The shepherds of the Temple flocks in Beth-lehem say this is when the angels told them to seek a baby in the lambing cave."

Gamaliel pondered the statement. "And was that baby Yeshua? High Priest Caiaphas and his minion ben Dives dread that Yeshua *is* the child the shepherds found. They fear he escaped the slaughter and that he may come to the Temple on that date."

El'azar counted the remaining days. "The twenty-fourth day of Kislev."

Nakdimon stared hard at the book of Haggai. "As Haggai predicted. The Feast of Dedication." He stretched bullish shoulders as if preparing to grasp a staff and do battle.

"What will the people do if Yeshua comes?" El'azar wondered aloud. "Will they crown him now?"

Gamaliel closed the scroll. "The leaders of Caiaphas' party have joined with the Herodians. *They* will not crown Yeshua. They will kill him and all who are allied with him. The *am ha aretz*. His talmidim. His family. Those he has healed. His mother."

Nakdimon added, "It's sure Adonai let us overhear their evil thoughts. They've laid a trap for Yeshua if he shows himself here in Yerushalayim during the Festival of Dedication."

El'azar frowned and said quietly, "Then he shouldn't come here. Must not come."

"Do you know where he is?" Gamaliel leaned across the table. "Your family is very close to him, they say. Your sisters, Miryam and Marta. Yeshua has stayed in your home. Taught in the synagogue of Bethany, they tell me."

El'azar stared hard at the scrolls. "He was in Caesarea Philippi for Sukkot . . . last we knew."

"And now?"

"Home in the Galil, I think. That's the rumor."

Nakdimon and Gamaliel exchanged looks of consternation. "What should we do?" Nakdimon asked. "The Galil. Still in the jurisdiction of Herod Antipas."

Gamaliel rubbed a hand over his brow and muttered, "What a time we live in. If he is who we believe, can it be?"

"We should warn him." El'azar's brow wrinkled with worry.

Gamaliel sighed and sat down heavily. "Warn? Yes. By all means. We should send a delegation . . . or a messenger into the Galil. And they'll bring the saddest tidings in the history of Israel's rebellion against the Lord's Anointed. 'So, Yeshua,' they'll say. 'Don't come to Yerushalayim. Don't reveal yourself to your people now, though we know who you are already. The rulers of Israel are sold out to the Romans. They will kill you. Plunge a dagger into the heart of your blessed mother. Do not come down to the Festival of Lights this year . . . although you alone carry the light of God within you.'"

Nakdimon stood slowly. "I'll travel north. Find him. Warn him of danger."

Gamaliel leveled his gaze on Nakdimon and then El'azar. "I'm not well enough to travel now. The weather is . . . inclement."

El'azar reached toward the warm brazier. "I'll go with Nakdimon."

"Who can we trust?" Nakdimon asked Gamaliel.

"No one," the elder replied. "No one in this city. You'll have to leave without being seen. The chief priest and his contingent have hired assassins. We know that. You'll have to leave Yerushalayim quietly. Travel as poor men."

"Six days to Capernaum," El'azar remarked. "On foot. Let's hope he's still there when we arrive."

Gamaliel continued reading from the scroll.

"Again the word of the Lord came to Haggai on the twenty-fourth day of the month saying, 'Speak to Zerubbabel governor of Judea saying, "I will shake the heavens and the earth. I will overthrow the throne of kingdoms and I will destroy the strength of the kingdoms of ungodly nations.""[18]

"But that's enough prophecy to digest for the moment. Let's go in to supper."

The smell of rain was on the air.

Across the Sea of Galilee to the east, whitecaps defined the churning waters and the approaching wind. A bank of storm clouds advanced over the mountains of Syria toward the Galil.

El'azar tugged the hood of his warm wool cloak closer about his shock of brown curls and considered the feeble, dark, amber bead of sun hanging low in the west. "Still three hours' walk to Capernaum. And only an hour of daylight."

"Shabbat. We won't make it." Nakdimon adjusted his pack and growled as they trudged northward. "There'll be a storm tonight, sure. Or sooner," he added in a tone of resignation. The two men were in the hills beyond Tiberius, trudging over stones on a little-used shepherds' path. There was easier walking near the lakeshore, but by unspoken consent the travelers avoided the trade routes near the home of Tetrarch Herod Antipas: too many guards, too many questions.

"Just six days' walk from Bethany in summer. But the days are so short now," El'azar explained.

The Pharisee snorted. "Even Romans are indoors, warming their backsides beside their fires." Nakdimon flashed El'azar a smile, conveying that only bigger fools than Romans were on the road on such a day.

El'azar winced. "Cold. And . . . yes, I admit it, Nakdimon. Yes. You were right about the horses."

Nakdimon shook his bearlike head and raised enormous hairy hands in a gesture of mock surrender. "Ah, well, El'azar. No. No. This proves *you* were right. It's the disguise, you see. Who would think to find a member of the Sanhedrin trekking along a road in the Galil in the dead of winter, eh? The Romans and Herodians have taken no notice. Of course, we haven't seen any. But all the same, we're two poor, mindless idiots walking to the Galil. Horses would have drawn attention. Of course, we would have been at the house in Capernaum three days ago, and we've met no one else on the road but lepers, beggars, and bandits. . . ."

"I thought we'd make it to Capernaum before Shabbat. Warn Yeshua not to come back to Judea, to stay away from Yerushalayim and the Feast of Dedication."

"And if he's already on his way?"

"Well then . . ."

The wind erupted from the face of the water, drowning out El'azar's reply. Trees bent in the force of it. A fat raindrop splashed on El'azar's cheek as he squinted up into the glowering sky.

"There!" Nakdimon pointed with his walking staff. A stone sheepfold with a fallen-roofed shelter stood in a deserted canyon. "We'll camp there!"

The two men sprinted for the enclosure as the rain drummed hard on their heads.

Ra'nabel ben Dives' smile was at its ingratiating best. Seated in Gamaliel's study, the high priest's personal scribe was surrounded by leading members of the Sanhedrin. Members of Caiaphas' own party of Sadducees agreed with everything he said while the opposition Pharisees regarded him with suspicion.

So far Gamaliel remained aloof and noncommittal. Ben Dives knew Gamaliel disliked and distrusted him, but holding this gathering here was part of the scribe's plan. If he could mold a consensus out of this group of enemies, then his future was assured.

"We are met," ben Dives suggested as latecomers found seats on benches around the walls, "to consider the claims of the man known as Yeshua of Nazareth . . . whom some are calling the Messiah."

This statement, uttered blandly without comment, drew the immediate responses ben Dives expected. The Sadducees scoffed and laughed. Most of the Pharisees expressed outrage; a handful, including Gamaliel, maintained guarded expressions.

"He breaks Sabbath," one Pharisee growled, "then has the impudence to take us to task for a lack of compassion."

"He eats with sinners—prostitutes and tax collectors—and seems to relish their company," another reported grimly.

There was a collective drawing up of robe hems as if just the mention of such unclean wretches might soil clothing.

"His closest disciples are fishermen and the like. No scholar can possibly take them seriously," offered a Temple official.

"Let's not quibble over surface matters," ben Dives suggested, much to the annoyance of a roomful of self-righteous men. "If he is . . . pardon me . . . when the true Messiah does appear, he will display certain signs, agreed? If Yeshua does not produce such, then his claim can be dismissed. At that point he is either a lunatic, a charlatan, or a rebel. And in every one of those instances, what he speaks is blasphemy."

A murmur of consent swept the room.

"So, what miracles are attributed to this man from the Galil?" Ben Dives had the list already in mind but wanted this self-important group to believe they and not he directed the conversation.

"He has healed cripples," one Pharisee mentioned.

Ben Dives did not need his prepared response, as someone else offered it for him: "Fakes! We all know beggars who earn their living by pretense! Some of them are convincing, but they're still frauds!"

"Do any of you have firsthand knowledge of an actual healed cripple?" ben Dives inquired.

None did.

"What about the reported miracle that he fed over twenty thousand people on a handful of fish and bread?" the scribe next asked.

One of the Pharisees, who appeared to have never missed a meal in his life, intoned, "Nonsense! He merely shamed the people in the crowd into sharing! No one wanted to eat in front of thousands who had nothing, so he embarrassed them into giving to their neighbors!"

"Very like a Pharisee," a Sadducee suggested.

Before a sectarian brawl could erupt, ben Dives quickly said, "But what about the blind beggar—the one blind from birth—whom many of you in this room questioned in person?"

"Another faker!" someone shouted.

"But he and his parents were well-known," Gamaliel countered softly.

"But he, a beggar, challenged the authority of the Sanhedrin," ben Dives commented. "And where is he now? When Lord Caiaphas wished to inquire more closely into the matter, the youth had disappeared."

"Sensible," Gamaliel muttered, to the amusement of his neighbors.

Ben Dives bit his lip, then said, "Anything else?"

"I heard he calmed a storm," a minor Temple official reported in a nervous, squeaking voice.

General laughter rattled the chamber. The speaker shrank back, as if trying to hide behind the wall hangings.

"What about raising the dead? A girl in Capernaum, a young man from Nain?" ben Dives suggested in an offhand way.

This time the scribe allowed the angry babble to fill the room and made no effort to intervene until it naturally subsided. "So you believe the reports to be untrue?" he summarized at last.

"Of course they're untrue!" a prominent Sadducee exclaimed. "No one has raised the dead since the days of the prophets."

"And you have some doubts about even them," Gamaliel observed dryly. "But can we dismiss these cases so blithely? One was the daughter of a synagogue official."

"Who might have been merely . . . asleep," ben Dives noted.

Approving laughter.

Gamaliel continued, undeterred. "And the son of the woman in Nain was well-known . . . and on his way to his tomb."

"Another fake!" someone shouted.

"Merely unconscious," another yelled. "Such cases are not unknown and much more believable than anyone raising the dead."

"And even if true, he works evil magic," an elderly Pharisee contributed, his voice and entire body trembling with outrage.

"But we have arrived at the heart of the matter, have we not?" ben Dives suggested. "If Yeshua can indeed raise the dead to life, then his claims must be given serious consideration."

"Never happen," the senior Sadducee concluded. "The fact is, no one can raise the dead! Dead is dead! There is no more basic fact than that!"

PART III

SEVEN CHARACTERISTICS OF WISDOM

But the wisdom that comes from heaven is first of all
pure;
then peace-loving,
considerate,
submissive,
full of mercy and good fruit,
impartial
and sincere.

JAMES 3:17

It was a short ride from Jerusalem to Bethany but today the distance seemed long. Because of the additional duties required of the newly appointed garrison commander of Jerusalem, Marcus' visit to Bethany had been delayed. With each passing day his nervousness at finally seeing Miryam again had increased.

Pavor, senses stirred by the cold air, wanted to gallop. Tossing his sleek, black head and pricking his ears, he seemed to share his master's impatience.

How many months had it been since Marcus had seen Miryam? And yet every day on patrol he had thought of her. Warning Miryam's brother to stay clear of Jerusalem during the Festival of Dedication afforded Marcus the excuse he needed to go to her home. Asking them to warn Yeshua to stay away was an urgent reason to go to Bethany.

Marcus nudged Pavor into a slow lope up the road skirting the Mount of Olives. Leaving behind his uniform and donning civilian clothes, the centurion could have been a Gentile merchant on his way to discuss the purchase of fine-grade olive oil from El'azar of Bethany.

The road to Bethany was deserted. Patches of dirty snow covered the shaded parts of hillsides. The red-tiled roof of the estate was like a warm island set amid a sea of leafless gray branches.

The spring and summer of their love was gone. Yet Marcus could recall the days and nights he and Miryam had spent together as if those times had only just happened.

Did Miryam ever hear the poetry of Propertius in her dreams?

Your house is blest—if only you have a true friend.
I will be true: then hasten, girl, to my bed.

Marcus had been true to her. He would not love another. Longing for her washed over him as he dismounted and knocked on the massive gate of the compound. *Here is where she lives day to day. This gate where she comes and goes. The sky where she looks up each day to pray . . .*

Pavor stamped impatiently. Marcus knocked again. The laughter of children rose from behind the walls.

A small, square view-port in the pedestrian gate snapped open. The wrinkled, homely face of Miryam's servant, Tavita, scowled out at Marcus.

"Tavita?" Marcus greeted the old woman. She had long been his friend and supporter.

Her dour expression melted into pleasure. She cried, "Why bless me! Bless me! It's Centurion Marcus Longinus! And the black horse with him! Pavor! Two old friends on such a windy, cold day!" She struggled with the bolt and threw open the door. Behind her a dozen children played tag in the courtyard.

Miryam, beside the fountain, gazed at him with passive pleasantness. The features registering approval at his arrival told him he was welcomed as an old friend—only a friend.

Tavita embraced him and pulled him into the courtyard, crying out his name like a mother reunited with a long-lost son. "Here you are then! Back from the bandit wars and distant expeditions!"

"Tavita! Old girl! You haven't changed."

"Oh? Not changed? I've grown fatter since you were here last!" The short-statured serving woman was as round as an apple in both form and features.

"It suits you, Tavita." Marcus tried not to stare at Miryam. She had grown more serene and still more beautiful since his last visit.

Tavita winked and crooked a finger at the old gatekeeper. "Come take the gentleman's horse." She squeezed Marcus' arm. "Grain for Pavor and I'll go fetch you a meal. Hot spiced wine on such a cold day, eh?" The old woman scuttled past Miryam and into the house.

Miryam smiled and came toward Marcus with her hands extended. "Marcus. So many months. You didn't send word."

He bowed slightly in greeting. "There was little word to send. Border raids and bandits. Politics and politicians. Items of small interest to a lady. I'm back now. Still a soldier. Here to winter in Jerusalem."

"When did you return?"

"A few days ago," he temporized. Marcus scanned the parapets as though searching for something. "I've come to speak to El'azar."

"He's gone. Come and sit. Warm yourself by the fire."

"Gone?" The happy shrieks of children nearly drowned out his voice.

"An errand. Business." Her deep brown eyes held him, warmed him.

Would it always be so?

"I've come to tell him . . ." Marcus could not help drinking in her beauty: thick, dark hair braided but lying across her right shoulder. Soft, smooth skin. "Will you . . . give him word for me?"

"He'll be gone for some time, I fear."

"Ah." He tried to conceal his happiness that he could speak with Miryam in the absence of her brother. "Well then, I can tell *you* why I've come."

"It's a cold, rainy day to ride."

"I didn't ride for pleasure." Marcus stared at his muddy leggings below the short green tunic, wondering how much of that statement was the absolute truth.

"Then what you have to tell my brother must be important." Miryam led the way into the interior warmth of the house. A servant brought warm water for Marcus to wash. He held his tongue until they were again alone.

"Miryam, where is the Teacher?"

"Not in Judea."

"Do you know where he is?"

"Not here."

So in spite of everything they had been to each other she could not trust a centurion in the pay of Rome with such information. Her cautious, coy behavior wounded him. "Miryam. I wish you would . . . you must . . . must . . ."

She silenced him with a frown. Placing a finger to her lips she inclined her head toward the doorway leading to the next room.

"We have two dozen children staying here now," Miryam said, cheerfully changing the subject. "Remember Beth Chesed in Magdala? Just like that. God sends them to us and somehow we always have room. My brother. My sister, Marta. All of us working together."

He nodded, perceiving there was someone in the house whom she did not trust. Her reticence was not about him after all. A wave of relief swept over him and his lines of dialogue sounded stilted even in his own ears. "It's good to see your work for the poor."

"Good of you to come, Marcus. We've not forgotten all you did for us in the Galil."

He blinked at her dully, wondering if she meant she had not forgotten how he loved her. "Yes."

"My brother, El'azar, will be happy to discuss the purchase of olive oil. . . . Where are you staying now?"

"The Antonia. On duty . . . I'll send Quintus to discuss the transaction with your steward. Provisions for so many. Rome pays well."

Again she silenced him with a hand on his forearm. The sound of footsteps retreated down the corridor.

Leaning forward she whispered, "A serving woman. We took her in only two months ago. That she is a gossip we soon realized, but lately she seems to listen *too* intently. So many souls are bought and sold. So many in the pay of Herod Antipas."

"If you know where the Rabbi is . . ."

"El'azar and Nakdimon have gone to warn him."

"None of you must come to Jerusalem during the Festival of Dedication."

"We're afraid he will come."

"The Herodians *hope* he'll come to the Temple. They're laying a trap for him if he does. It's dangerous, Miryam."

"We knew even before you came. Your arrival is confirmation."

He pressed his lips together as the serving woman passed the door and glanced furtively in. Marcus said cheerfully, "When your brother returns, tell him there's no need to sell his wine and oil anywhere but Jerusalem."

"I'll tell him." Miryam stood abruptly. "But you're sure you can't stay for lunch?"

"Another storm's coming. I can't stay."

The two continued empty chatter about the weather and the snow as Miryam walked him to the gate.

Marcus mounted Pavor, who spun and danced, eager to be gone. Miryam thanked Marcus with a steady gaze. There was nothing more to be safely said except farewell.

Sun broke through the clouds as Nakdimon and El'azar approached the fishing village of Capernaum. Waves dashed against the stone break-water. Seabirds, driven inland by the gale, soared and shrieked above the water. The streets seemed deserted.

Nakdimon considered how changed he was since his first journey to the Galil to meet Yeshua so many months ago. He had come to the Galil as a skeptic, intent on silencing Yeshua. When, after some weeks, he had returned to Jerusalem to offer his report to the Sanhedrin, he had carried with him the confirmation that Yeshua preached the good news of salvation, healed the sick, and yes . . . Yeshua raised the dead.

Rumors of Deborah, the twelve-year-old daughter of a synagogue official in Capernaum, being raised from the dead had already spread throughout Eretz-Israel like a wildfire. They had reached Jerusalem long before Nakdimon's return.

Caiaphas, the high priest, and the majority party Sadducees of the ruling council dismissed the stories as the wild rantings of an uneducated populace.

Then Nakdimon, a respected member of the Pharisee sect on the council, appeared in the Chamber of Hewn Stone to give eyewitness account of the miracle.

The Sadducees did not believe his testimony.

"Raised from the dead? Returned from death?"

"Trickery."

"Illusion."

"The girl was not dead!"

"She was sleeping. He said it himself!"

"Asleep is not dead."

The skepticism of Nakdimon's colleagues turned to fury at his insistence that he had witnessed the miracle with his own eyes. "So, Nakdimon ben Gurion! Are you one of his simpleminded talmidim also?"

The meeting of the Sanhedrin had dissolved into a shouting match. In the end, only his uncle Gamaliel and Yosef of Arimathea trusted Nakdimon's word.

Today, as Nakdimon and El'azar strode toward the village, Nakdimon marveled at the change Yeshua had brought into the lives of so many.

El'azar was also a different man. Witnessing Deborah's death and return to life had changed the young landowner's life forever. He had come to the Galil with Nakdimon the first time as an arrogant, opinionated, bitter young man. Together the friends had moved from suspicion and ambiguity to the belief that Yeshua was at the very least a great prophet . . . and perhaps even more than a prophet.

Who was Yeshua? By what authority did He speak? Where did His mysterious power come from?

Over the centuries, how many men had come to the people of Israel, claiming to be the long-awaited Messiah? Some, like the clan of the Maccabees, had raised armies to fight against tyrants. Many had fallen in battle and their wars of liberation had ultimately failed. Not one of them had caused a lasting transformation or turned the hearts of men back to the Lord.

Famous teachers had also existed in Israel. Men of profound intellect had pondered and exposited the mysteries of Torah. Gamaliel, Nakdimon's revered uncle, was considered one of the wisest scholars in Jerusalem.

But Yeshua was unlike anyone Nakdimon had ever met. Though He had not been educated in the Yeshiva schools of Jerusalem, His teachings reflected wisdom beyond the wisest sages in Israel's history.

Though the Sanhedrin had the authority to judge and condemn men, Yeshua had the far greater authority to heal men's souls and bodies. He called them back to God from the far exile of sin and proclaimed mercy and forgiveness in the name of His Father.

Yet the unrighteous now sat in judgment of Him.

The universe was upside-down!

All hope that Yeshua could soon enter Jerusalem as king had vanished. Now the best Yeshua could hope for was to survive long enough for the world to be turned right again.

Yeshua's survival depended on staying far away from Jerusalem.

Capernaum seemed almost deserted when Nakdimon and El'azar arrived just after noon. The wind off the lake was ice-cold, and violent waves battered the stone breakwater. A bigger storm was brewing in the north. Thick clouds concealed the peaks of Mount Hermon forty miles away.

Nakdimon and El'azar paused at the well where a grizzled old drover watered three scrawny goats to ask, "Yeshua? The Teacher? The Prophet of the Almighty?"

The old man swayed a bit and his breath smelled of ale. He cocked one eye and stared upward at the gray sky. "Which way does the wind blow? That is the question. Fishing season is finished. Where else would Yeshua be this time of year? Eh? Eh? It's bitter cold and all the crowds have gone home. Like ducks flying south for the winter. Yeshua and a few of his talmidim . . . his mother too . . . are staying as guests at the home of Ya'ir the Cantor. The very same house where Yeshua called back the soul of Ya'ir's young daughter from *olam haba*. I was not invited to the girl's wake, but I came to the celebration feast. A pretty thing she is. Her father has betrothed her to the son of a vinedresser. And the girl is fully alive or the wedding would be off." The old man shook his head. "Aye. She came back to life at Yeshua's bidding. Although why any soul would want to return to a world ruled by Romans and Herod Antipas I cannot imagine."

Nakdimon scowled and glanced furtively over his shoulder. "Unless you wish to leave this world soon, you'll do well to remember that the Galil and all the land is full of men who would hear your words and call them treason."

At the realization he might have spoken to a Herodian spy, the old man spread his arms wide in protest. "We are alone in the street, sirs. As for myself, sirs, I am drunk. There is little else to do in Capernaum but fish and drink and beget children. My wife is dead, and fishing season is at an end. I did not mean to say what you think I said. I was alive when old Herod lived and have survived this long. Am I a fool? Perhaps I am, but I am happy to go on living, drunk or sober, in this world, no matter who rules it. The Galil is as far from Yerushalayim as heaven is far from hell. Therefore, may the King awaken in Yerushalayim and leave us here in the paradise of the Galil to dream our dreams of liberation."

"And may your dreams be happy," El'azar assured him, placing a coin in his palm. "We know the house of Ya'ir. We know the family. I am kin to Ya'ir. My sisters and I were here in the Galil when the girl died, and we know the one who commanded her to rise up. We know Yerushalayim and those who rule her too."

"Ah, well then, Your Honors! You know everything firsthand and know full well I am a fool, for a man cannot be too careful what he says. Or who he says it to."

"Antipas takes pleasure in hanging old fools in trees," Nakdimon warned.

"And young ones too." The old man bowed slightly. "I am too old to offend the Almighty with a lying tongue. And, like his father before him, we hear Herod Antipas is eager to attach Yeshua of Nazareth to a tree as a scarecrow to frighten away the vultures of rebellion. Or perhaps Antipas dreams of lifting up Yeshua's head on a pike over Dung Gate, eh? So. The great battle is coming. We are praying it will come soon. If Yeshua can raise a child from death, he will make a fine king to lead an army into battle, eh? Who would be afraid to die for one who could raise you back to life? I ask you. Meanwhile, it is winter. No one wishes to fight the Romans in winter. Everyone who followed Yeshua in the warm summer months has gone home. Everyone knows and it is no secret. Yeshua is staying at the house of your kinsman, Ya'ir the Cantor."

It was in the Capernaum home of Ya'ir the Cantor that Nakdimon and El'azar found us.

While the two men from Judea to the south had toiled through the rain to bring us their warning, the band of Yeshua's talmidim, of which I was a member, had been returning from Chorazin to the north. Yeshua had been teaching us there, but privately, away from the crowds.

Yeshua seemed neither discouraged nor disconcerted by the message of danger. He thanked Nakdimon and El'azar warmly and inquired about their families. He said He was aware of the threat posed by the hatred of Herod Antipas. He also added that they must have no fear on His behalf since His time was not yet come.

I noticed El'azar and Nakdimon exchange a glance at these words, but neither asked Yeshua to explain further.

I was glad they did not because when we were near Caesarea Philippi, Yeshua spoke openly of His death. It caused great grief and furor among us, and none of us wanted to hear more. The consensus was this: If we ignore that subject, it will go away.

In any case there was soon a diversion.

While Yeshua conversed quietly with the two Judeans about matters in Jerusalem and Bethany, I sat beside Alexander and his son, Hero. Eagerly I recorded as many details of their experience as I could get them to recall and share.

Hero's story is recounted elsewhere,* but briefly, it is this: Alexander was an apostate Jew, a musician and flute maker by trade. His wife died, leaving him alone to care for their one child, Hero.

Hero was oppressed by demonic forces. The child was driven to throw himself into fire and into water, more than once almost dying as a result.

His father despaired of his son's life. In fact, Alexander was advised by some to poison the boy and end the agony.

Two things intervened to change the outcome of this near tragedy. Alexander met and fell in love with a true daughter of Zion, Zahav, daughter of Rabbi Eliyahu, Zadok's brother-in-law. Not only was this romance a godsend for both Alexander and Zahav, they joined forces to appeal to Yeshua for help.

While the disciples were powerless to deliver Hero from the grasp of the Evil One, Yeshua restored the child to perfect health and joy. It was the details of this miracle of which I had only witnessed part that I recorded in Ya'ir's home.

Little knots of conversation went on pleasantly around the room until, quite casually, Yeshua addressed a question to John. "What were you talking about on the road today?"[19]

John's broad face flushed guiltily. His head drooped as if he had been caught in a lie, and he did not answer immediately. Those in the group nearest John—Shim'on Peter; his brother, Andrew; and also Judas Iscariot—likewise fell silent. Most hung their heads—all except Judas, who glared around angrily. He glared at me, as if accusing me of having carried a tale to Yeshua.

Now the road from Chorazin had been tedious. In the course of that hike we had all discussed many things: the day's teaching, where Yeshua meant to go next, whether He would go to Jerusalem soon, and even the news we received of someone not of our band who performed healings in the Name of Yeshua.

So while many exchanged puzzled glances at Yeshua's question, that hostility from Judas actually confirmed for me which conversation Yeshua meant.

* See *Third Watch* in the A. D. Chronicles series.

I had overheard an argument that day. Shim'on Peter vigorously asserted his opinion over some trivial matter regarding alms for beggars. Judas, who had the keeping of the money pouch, bristled at what he saw as a criticism and an invasion of his personal duty.

Judas said that no brainless fisherman from the Galil could be expected to count past ten. Then he added that controlling the money was proof Yeshua trusted him more than the others. And he added this: "When Yeshua comes into his Kingdom, I expect to be more than just his steward. I'll be the treasurer of the Kingdom."

Far from settling the argument, Judas' assertion sparked a huge debate about who would be greatest in the Kingdom. Peter bristled as if he wanted to strike Judas. Andrew—kind, gentle Andrew—tried to calm matters by reminding Judas that he and his brother, Peter, had been among the very first of Yeshua's followers and therefore had a certain higher place in the reckoning.

Instead of settling matters, Andrew's words had the opposite effect. Ya'acov and John, the Zebedee brothers, took exception to what Andrew suggested. After all, John said, he and his brother were always consulted on important matters and Yeshua always sought their advice.

The way he said it implied that Shim'on Peter's advice was often wrong.

I don't know what offices each of them had in mind—treasurer, seneschal, captain of the guard—but each believed and managed to say that he was the greatest in the Kingdom. The uproar increased as each man managed to imply that the sooner the others acknowledged his superiority, the better it would be.

This discussion had only subsided when we reached Ya'ir the Cantor's house in Capernaum.

Now Yeshua deliberately raised the issue again, proving He never, ever missed anything.

He called the Twelve to gather closely around Him; the rest of us ranged in a larger circle to listen. This is what He said: "If any one of you wants to be the first, he must be the very last, and the servant of all."[20]

Then He did something that startled us all.

With a wave of His hands, Yeshua motioned for Judas and John to step apart. The lane thus formed pointed directly at the boy, Hero.

With a big grin and a crook of His finger, Yeshua summoned Hero to come and stand exactly next to Him, which the beaming child did with a sprint. Master and child studied each other for a moment; then Yeshua turned Hero around to face the group.

With His chin resting on Hero's shoulder and the boy wrapped in a tight embrace, Yeshua said, "Whoever welcomes one of these little children in my name welcomes me; and whoever welcomes me does not welcome me but the one who sent me."[21]

The faces in that room were a study in consternation. Big, bluff men, puffed up with their own importance, were told that first place in the new Kingdom belonged to . . . a child?

And I knew what other thoughts raced through their heads: *We saw this very child convulsing on the ground, wetting himself, barely alive in the grip of evil . . . and now he's held up to us as the foremost example of who will have the highest position in Yeshua's Kingdom?*

John seemingly could not bear the implications and, still trying to recover from his embarrassment in front of the talmidim, blurted out, "Teacher! We saw a man driving out demons in your name and we told him to stop, because he was not one of us."

"Don't stop him," Yeshua replied with a hint of exasperation. "No one who does a miracle in my name can in the next moment say anything bad about me, for whoever is not against us is for us. I tell you the truth, anyone who gives you a cup of water in my name because you belong to Christ will certainly not lose his reward."[22]

Then, not willing to let John change the subject, Yeshua returned to His theme: "And if anyone causes one of these little ones who believe in me to sin, it would be better for him to be thrown into the sea with a large millstone tied around his neck." And He added, "See that you do not look down on one of these little ones. For I tell you that their angels in heaven always see the face of my Father in Heaven."[23]

Turning back toward Yeshua, Hero threw his arms around Yeshua's neck and gave Him kisses on both cheeks. The boy scampered back to his father then, and Yeshua resumed His teaching.

I stood on a broken stone fence with a leather-wrapped manuscript under my arm and watched as farewells were made. Inside the package were all the notes I had recorded about the miraculous birth of Yeshua.

The manuscript, with other precious things, would travel south and east with Zadok the Shepherd.

Old Zadok swung Emet, his smallest boy, onto his shoulder as if he were carrying a lamb in from the field. Zadok's other two sons skipped around the big man as they prepared to lead the pack animals. A small brown sparrow fluttered from tree to thornbush and then onto the outstretched finger of little Emet.

The warning from Nakdimon and El'azar was clear: Even here in the Galil, in the dead of winter, no one was safe from the combined forces of Herod Antipas, High Priest Caiaphas, and the hostile Pharisees. The two messengers had left before daybreak for their return to Jerusalem.

Yeshua clearly had taken the warning to heart, but not for Himself. There was Yeshua's mother to think of. She knew the whole story of Yeshua's miraculous birth. Surely Herod Antipas wanted to silence her as his father, the Butcher King, had tried to murder baby Yeshua thirty-odd years ago. Memories of those long-ago visiting Magi, flaming stars, and angelic appearances aroused old hatreds anew in the marble palaces in Jerusalem and Tiberias.

Moreover, there were now several dozen others whose miraculous healings by Yeshua put them at risk. How much better would it be for the Herodians and the Temple authorities if a boy healed of deafness had his new ears destroyed by boiling oil? Or if a once-mute child who proclaimed the One who healed him should have his tongue cut out? Or if one born blind had his eyes put out by a red-hot iron?

I shivered at the stunning, almost incomprehensible thought: It was a dangerous time to be healed by Yeshua. A crippled beggar, whose life had not been worth two pennies before experiencing Yeshua's touch, might find it cost him that life now.

No wonder Yeshua warned so many to tell no one!

"Well, then—" Zadok embraced Yeshua—"y' watch yourself with the wolves of Yerushalayim. Be careful. Don't show yourself."

Yeshua did not reply to the warning for caution. He addressed the dozens who were to accompany Zadok to the place beside the Jordan River where Yochanan the Baptizer had preached. "Set up camp. I'll see you soon."

A breeze drifted down from the hills. A lazy fistful of wind flicked dust between the two groups as if we already saw each other across miles of separation.

Zadok caught my eye and lifted a hand in farewell. The old shepherd called out to me, "Mind y' keep outta sight too, lad. Caiaphas considers those fine new eyes of yours a threat." Touching gnarled fingers to the black patch covering his own missing left eye, Zadok ducked his chin as one speaking from experience. "Y' know there're dangerous men where you come from. They won't like t' see you again."

Yeshua clapped Zadok on the back as if to say, *Peniel and the others will be safe with me.*

Yeshua embraced His mother again and committed her to the care of Zadok. Zadok and a handful of Yeshua's followers would head south to make winter camp in Perea, beyond the reach of Herod Antipas. Though the tetrarch was nominally ruler of the east bank of the central Jordan Valley as well as the Galil, swaths of Perea were rough country.

Even better, such primitive living did not attract many comfort-loving Pharisees or Herodian spies. Yeshua would join them there. But first Yeshua and another group of us were headed back across the Galil, then on to Judea and Jerusalem.

Mary placed her hand on Yeshua's cheek. "You'll join us soon, Son?" she asked. Beneath her question it seemed to me I heard another, unvoiced query: *Is it time? Will it happen now?*

"After Kislev, Mother, expect me," Yeshua reassured her.

Mary's courage seemed to falter for a moment. "You won't come now? Your birthday?"

"The Festival of Dedication, Mother," He said in gentle teasing. He kissed her forehead. "My Father's house. You know I must be about his business."[24]

"Yes. The Festival of Lights." Mary raised her head and peered past Him, over the tops of leafless trees and into the sky, where some memory of an angel's words must have been written in the clouds.

Rabbi Eliyahu, who would turn back now toward his home in Caesarea Philippi, hugged Zadok and ruffled the hair of Zadok's three adopted sons—Avel, Emet, and Ha-or Tov. "You boys be good, eh?"

Zadok sniffed and enfolded his brother-in-law, Eliyahu, with a great squeeze. "We're gettin' t' be old men, eh? Eh? But y' are a grandfather and I am a father again t' these three boys. It gives me hope we may live t' see one another again."

"I do not doubt it, Zadok. Zadok! I do not doubt we will live to see one another again. Even if we die first." Eliyahu's gray beard trembled.

Zadok caught sight of me staring as I strove to build a perfect recollection. "Here, Peniel! Since you got your eyes, you stare at everyone."

I grinned and glanced down. "You know me. I love a good story."

Zadok bellowed, "Are you sure you won't come with us then, boy? T'other side of the Jordan? Out of the reach of the Herodian demons. They'd like t' take your eyes back, I'll wager."

I shook my head. "The better story is in Yerushalayim with Yeshua this year."

Shim'on Peter replied, "Yerushalayim won't recognize you anyway. You've grown a foot taller since you begged at Nicanor Gate."

"Aye!" Zadok roared. "And there's some meat on y' now, boy. And a fine red beard too in the last year."

Peter slapped a donkey on the rump. "If he had been a fish I'd have thrown him back when first I saw him. But Yeshua saw some worth there, eh?"

Yeshua laughed. The cloud of gloom at parting dissipated. "We have something in common, don't we, Peniel? I love a good story too."

I drew myself up and leapt from the fence. "That's us, Lord!" I felt like I could crow as I extended the manuscript to Zadok. "A very good story indeed."

Zadok touched the patch covering his eye, then took the package. "There'll be a happy ending come for all of us by and by."

Yeshua made the baracha over men, women, children, and beasts of burden. No use in delaying further. By nightfall they would all be out of the Galil and safe . . . for the moment.

It was on the journey from the Galil to the Feast of Dedication at Jerusalem that I came to comprehend why the brothers John and Ya'acov were sometimes called Sons of Thunder. I had met their father, Old Zebedee, and thunder did not seem to be a large part of his personality. Old and bent from years of hauling in heavy nets, and given to complaining as is every fisherman's right, he was gruff but not threatening.

John was a burly man, a wrestler in appearance, but he had an easy smile and a pleasant manner that concealed the force of his will. Ya'acov was a thinner, quieter version of his brother with a headstrong streak and a tenacity of purpose.

In other words, neither man could easily be turned aside from a course of action once it was settled in their Galilean brains. Both had well-controlled tempers, but tempers nevertheless.

Still: Sons of Thunder?

Perhaps it was the nearness of Shim'on Peter that prevented me from seeing it sooner. Peter was loud and blustery. He did not take criticism gracefully either, but it was the Zebedee brothers who had the title.

Just outside the Samaritan village of Ginae, I came to understand why.

Ginae is on the border of the Galil and Samaria.

There is no love lost between Jews and Samaritans. Jews regard Samaritans as apostate because they do not go up to the Temple to worship and because they honor only the Books of Moses and not the rest of the Tanakh. Many Jews also speak of them as half-breeds, because of their intermarriage with Gentiles.

The Samaritans return this regard with interest.

Still, it is Rome that builds and patrols the trade routes. A Samaritan innkeeper might curse under his breath but he would accept Jewish silver just the same, unless he felt himself insulted.

So it was that while the main body of talmidim rested under olive trees beside the highway, Yeshua sent couriers ahead to Ginae to arrange lodging for the night. For this task he selected another pair of brothers, Thaddeus and Little James. These two, practically voiceless when compared with Shim'on Peter or some of the others, were cousins to Yeshua's foster father, Yosef. Also, their mother was close friends with Yeshua's mother.

Sprawled beside a tree trunk I watched with interest as its shadow moved and grew longer, spindly fingers pointing back toward the northeast. I had studied this motion for about an hour when Thad and James returned. They shuffled their feet as they walked and were clearly embarrassed about something.

The two approached Yeshua, who waited patiently for them to speak. James nudged his brother. Then Thad, who was the elder, finally said, "I . . . I'm sorry, Master. We failed. Everything was fine until I . . . I mentioned that our leader is a Jewish prophet and that we were going to Yerushalayim . . . to the Temple . . . for the festival."

"Then the innkeeper insulted us," James added. "Threw our money back in our faces."

"You said what?" Shim'on Peter spouted. "To a Samaritan? Don't you have any sense?"

This from a man who scarcely ever thinks before speaking!

Silencing Peter with a look, Yeshua told Thad not to worry, that God would provide for their needs anyway.

It was then John demonstrated that his nickname was accurate. His face turning redder by the second, John swelled as though he might explode with indignation.

"Master!" he said forcefully, while his brother nodded vigorous approval. "How dare they treat you that way? Shall we call down fire from heaven and destroy them?"[25]

Not to be outdone, Ya'acov added, "Like the prophet Elijah did on Mount Carmel?"

"No," John corrected. "More like the way Sodom and Gomorrah were leveled. Shall we? Now?"

This time the Master's rebuke was not merely a disapproving frown. "Stop!" He said with astonishing vehemence. "You don't know what you're saying!"

John and Ya'acov were so surprised at His response that they each stepped back a pace.

The Master went to them and, putting an arm around each of their necks, drew them to Him. He whispered something to them that I could not hear. Taking time to meet each man's eyes, Yeshua waited to receive nods of acknowledgment before releasing them. Then, lifting His voice again so all of us could hear, the Master said, "There is another village beyond Ginae. We'll press on and stay there tonight instead."

As we fell in along the road I found myself walking next to Levi Mattityahu. To him I mentioned I regretted not being able to hear what passed privately between the Master and the Zebedees.

"Can't you guess?" Levi questioned without any hint of banter or teasing. "I'm certain he told them to be careful, because if they had spoken their thoughts as a command instead of as a question, Ginae would already be a heap of ashes smoldering on the plain."

𓏢

I paused outside the doorway of the Jerusalem potter's shop, frozen with apprehension. Even though I had been anticipating this moment, planning for it, I had also been dreading it.

Closing my eyes I drank in the sounds and smells. My father was working: the steady *thump . . . thump . . . thump* of the potter's wheel with each revolution told me so. The air was redolent with damp clay. On the few bright days of my youth I connected the aroma with freshly plowed earth after a rain. Darker moments produced gloomier associations: a newly made grave when one of my beggar companions was interred in the Potter's Field . . . so named because a broken bit of jar or lamp used as a headstone was the only remembrance of a life.

Peering in, I had not yet spoken, had not revealed my presence. Balanced against the desperate longing for my papa to *see* me was the overwhelming urge to flee. To escape the crushing pain of rejection.

Papa stopped the wheel to inspect the amphora he was creating. Likewise I studied him. My fingers tingled at the *remembrance* of a familiar, and dearly loved, figure and form.

Papa—Yahtzar ben Adam—had corded muscles that began in his neck, traversed his shoulders, and corkscrewed down his arms like braided ropes. My papa's tunic was pulled up tight and knotted at one side of his head, leaving his limbs mostly bare. Hands and forearms were gray with mud to the elbows, spawning the illusion that the clay was creating the man instead of the other way around. His beard, grizzled and spattered, was trimmed short and his hair was tucked up under a bowl-shaped cap that covered his ears.

The light behind me left me silhouetted against the doorway. Inhaling deeply, I stepped into the shop.

My father turned at the movement.

I found I could not speak. Dread and emotion choked me.

"Yes?" Papa inquired. "Is there something I can help you with?"

No hint of recognition was in the well-remembered, well-loved voice!

Glancing down at myself, I realized what my father saw. In place of a scrawny, ragged, blind beggar, the young man who now stood framed in the entry was taller, broader, stronger. I had a beard, of sorts. My hair was neatly trimmed and I was acceptably, if modestly, dressed as one of the *am ha aretz*.

And I had a working pair of eyes.

At our last encounter my father had not wanted to look into my eyes; he had forced himself to not see the pain and the longing there!

"You've come to purchase a menorah?" Papa gestured toward the shelf holding dozens of clay candlesticks of various sizes. "A lamp for everyone. Rich or poor."

I gazed at the tallest menorah. How many times in my blindness had I blundered against a shelf in the workshop and heard the shattering of crockery accompanied by the enraged screams of Mama? Now I could see everything. Everything. Such a small workshop. So many clay pots and cheap oil lamps for Mama to sell to the pilgrims in the Temple courtyard. Was she there now? in the house?

I cleared my throat, unable to step closer and so reveal my identity. "Sir. You make fine lamps for the Feast of Dedication."

"Business is not so good. I can't be two places at once. Working here. Selling in the Temple."

"Your wife. Your daughters. Last time I was in Yerushalayim they sold your wares in the Court of the Gentiles."

"Then it has been some months since you were here last." Papa wiped the wet clay from his fingers and scrutinized me with curiosity. "My wife resides in the bosom of Father Avraham. I do not envy him, but Avraham was known for his patience with shrewish women."

I gasped. "You mean . . . your wife? She is . . ."

"Dead. Aye. Six months ago. In a rage at a clumsy customer and with her mouth filled with curses, she dropped to the ground like a stone. Like a stone!" He tossed a shard of pottery to the floor, where it landed with a crack that made me wince. "In her tracks she fell down . . . never spoke another word and died three days later. And my daughters are wed and gone from my house. They have married potters in the guild, as befits the daughters of a potter."

I'm sure my voice trembled. "Sir, you had a son also. Did you not? The blind boy who begged at Nicanor?"

"The only one worth anything. And it was two sons I had. Both gone now." Papa sighed and stared down at his empty hands. "My oldest son is also flown away to *olam haba* . . . many years ago he died. My younger son—Peniel, he is called. 'Face of God' his name means. A good boy he was. . . ."

"But you speak of your younger son as if he is also dead."

"May as well be. You are right in the details. He was blind from birth. A beggar at Nicanor Gate in the Temple. Then one day: a miracle! Yeshua of Nazareth came, spit in the dirt, and made clay like a potter. He put it on the blind eyes of my boy and commanded him to wash in the Pool of Siloam. So Peniel did. And when the clay on the blind eyes of the potter's son was washed away, there were eyes where *nothing* had been before.

"I tell you, Yeshua is the True Potter sent from heaven, for he alone ever made eyes for a boy blind from birth. And all Yerushalayim knew it. Peniel, his new eyes shining, gave testimony before the Council of what Yeshua had done. And his mother and I just pretending nothing important had happened. 'He's of age,' we said. . . . 'Ask him yourself!' So Peniel is thrown out for . . . for being *healed* by the great Rabbi Yeshua. I was too afraid to speak up. Because of my cowardice, my son was sent away by the synagogue authorities. Ah, that I could see his face now and ask his forgiveness!"

I covered my eyes with my hand. Tears brimmed, spilling down my cheeks and onto my beard. At last I stepped into the light. "Papa? Don't you know me?"

Papa's face paled. His jaw dropped. Rising slowly, he turned his head suspiciously to the side as though examining a clay pot just off the wheel. He studied me through one eye. His expression registered but could not reconcile recognition and disbelief at the transformation from ragged beggar to full-grown man. "Peniel? Son? Is it you?"

"Yes, Papa. I'm Peniel. You know me. Came to find you. To tell you . . . no, to *show* you the rest of the story. Papa! Yeshua has returned to Yerushalayim for the Feast of Dedication. Or rather, I have returned with Yeshua. I wanted to—"

"Oh, my son!" Papa replied with a ragged sob. He reached out and grasped me, pulling me tight in an embrace. "My son! My son! Oh, Peniel! My son! You've come home!"

PART IV

PURIFIED SEVEN TIMES

"Because of the oppression of the weak
and the groaning of the needy,
I will now arise," says the LORD.
"I will protect them from those who malign them."
And the words of the LORD are flawless,
like silver refined in a furnace of clay,
purified seven times.

PSALM 12:5-6

Charcoal braziers smoked fitfully in every corner of the old Hasmonean Palace. Windows and doorways were shrouded with thickly brocaded fabric. Even though Tetrarch Antipas had summoned High Priest Caiaphas to the private audience chamber and not to the great hall, it still seemed impossible to keep even the smallest of the drafty rooms warm. Caiaphas, with Ra'nabel ben Dives standing attentively behind his left shoulder, was already seated when Antipas swept in, unaccompanied.

Antipas scowled around the room with barely disguised distaste. It was well-known that he felt entitled to the newer, more expansive, and beautifully furnished palace built by his father, but that edifice was reserved for the Roman governor, Pilate. In fact, Antipas would much prefer to be wintering on Cyprus, or perhaps even in Rome, but not this year. As much as the tetrarch despised Jerusalem in winter, many things demanded his attention here.

"What progress on the matter of the Galilean charlatan?" Antipas inquired abruptly.

"Majesty?" Caiaphas returned with a tone and expression of innocent ignorance.

"Come, Priest!" Antipas spat. "Don't bandy words with me! I know you are threatened by his popularity. I know you have tried to trap him with his own teaching . . . and failed miserably."

Caiaphas' bushy eyebrows arched above his long, pointed nose, and he steepled his fingers. "But it is said Yeshua calls on the *am ha aretz* to repent and seek the way of HaShem." The high priest spread his hands and shrugged slightly. "There is nothing subversive in such a message . . . a message much the same as his cousin, the Baptizer, preached."

Antipas paled, but whether from fear or rage, ben Dives could not say.

It was a dangerous game Caiaphas played. Ben Dives knew it—and encouraged it. The high priest held his office directly by the sufferance of Rome. Antipas had no authority to dismiss him.

Antipas likewise drew his authority from Caesar, and only at Caesar's whim remained tetrarch.

In the sense that both were subservient to the emperor, it was a stalemate.

Antagonizing the tetrarch was not safe, but Herod Antipas controlled a substantial part of the Temple tax collected in Galilee and Perea. Ben Dives believed a greater share could be diverted directly into the high priest's coffers with a little effort at persuasion.

"Perhaps you should send for Yeshua and hear him for yourself?" Caiaphas dropped the question suggested by ben Dives into the conversation as casually as one might toss a blade of grass into a pool of water.

Antipas blinked rapidly and stared upward. His reaction confirmed what ben Dives had heard rumored: Antipas had already tried such an approach. Yeshua had avoided the summons and the trap that went with it.

Ben Dives saw Antipas bite back a harsh reply. An ingratiating smile spread across the tetrarch's bejowled and grizzled features. His sallow cheeks and rheumy eyes did not present an appealing picture, despite the smile. "We must not quarrel, you and I," Antipas said. "How can we aid the Lord Pilate in governing properly if we cannot correctly assess the moods and thoughts of our people? And who is better placed to know their thoughts than their spiritual mentor? their high priest? the spiritual heir to Moses? The *am ha aretz* are like children . . . no, sheep. That's it. They need a spiritual shepherd to keep them safe from the wolves of false teaching. Isn't that your calling?"

The two men were fencing, seeking weaknesses that could be exploited to advantage. The ultimate threat was an accusatory report to Pilate. The same threat applied to both men. "I am always open to the concerns of the people," Caiaphas acknowledged pompously.

In the end the two leaders, ambitious and scheming, agreed to cooperate, at least as far as Yeshua of Nazareth was concerned. They would plan and scheme separately but meet again to share their ideas.

The passage of High Priest Caiaphas through crowds of Temple worshippers resembled the progress of a heavily laden ship under full sail. With a phalanx of scribes and Temple guards to clear the way, Caiaphas' approach generated respectful greetings like a galley's bow pushed aside waves. Hemmed in behind by a double row of marching guards, Caiaphas was thus able to carry on a private conversation with his constant companion, ben Dives, even while crossing the Temple courts.

"Antipas is afraid," the high priest noted. "He thought that Governor Pilate had made enough mistakes that Rome would order his recall and promote Antipas. But killing Yochanan was an error. There's no other reason Antipas would seek my help now. He wants to make sure I don't side with the Pharisees who want Antipas ousted. He wants me on his side against Pilate."

Ben Dives made murmurs of concurrence, then added, "Lord Antipas also hopes that if any further mistakes are made, there will be someone besides himself around to blame."

Caiaphas glanced over his shoulder and down his pointed nose at the secretary. "Meaning me?"

"Exactly, my lord. But neither can you let Lord Antipas succeed alone and derive all the benefits."

"Antipas is a clumsy fool. Use a bludgeon where a gag is needed. Murder Yeshua, and Antipas will spark the very rebellion he wants to prevent."

"Bludgeon and gag," ben Dives repeated. "That's very apt, my lord. So your plan is not to kill the Nazarene but rather to discredit him with the people. Trap him with questions that either put him in the wrong with Rome—and subject to arrest—or in the wrong with the people, who will then drop him like hot oil spilling from a lamp."

Caiaphas pushed a lock of hair back up under his white linen turban. "Naturally," he intoned. "Exactly my plan."

"Brilliant, my lord," ben Dives praised. "A gag, not a bludgeon. I'll write that down."

It was at that moment a Temple attendant, one of the Levites appointed to oversee almsgiving who was also one of Caiaphas' spies, came dashing toward them. His sandals slapped the pavement in his haste. "He's here! He's come!" he announced breathlessly. "Yeshua of Nazareth. He's come suddenly to the Temple!"

"Now's your opportunity, ben Dives," Caiaphas instructed. "See that you make the most of it!"

It was the twenty-fourth day of the ninth month. What had begun with Yeshua's quiet teaching among the columns of King Solomon's Portico was interrupted by hostility.

All in the crowd around Yeshua fell silent, shocked by the thinly veiled sarcasm in the voice of ben Dives. "Rabbi? How long are you going to keep us in suspense? If you're the Messiah, tell us plainly." Puffs of breath in the cold air punctuated his words like steam above a cauldron.

I felt sick. I saw the hostility—the hatred—in the eyes of all the great men who surrounded the Master like jackals around a wounded animal circling for the kill. Instinctively I stepped closer to my father and saw Papa's fists clench.

All of Yeshua's talmidim, those brave, strong men of the Galil, were silent, listening, afraid to speak—afraid of what Yeshua might say. Perhaps they were afraid of what He would not say in reply to such a challenge.

From my place near the center of the crescent-shaped mob, I saw El'azar of Bethany on one point, Nakdimon ben Gurion on the other. El'azar frowned; Nakdimon glared. Neither seemed close enough to intervene if things turned ugly . . . and they already had. Thomas, standing beyond my father, put a hand on the hilt of his sword in readiness.

Then Yeshua's lips curved in a slight smile as though He greeted only friends. "I have already told you."

There was a snort from the outer edge of the pack. One of Gamaliel's talmidim openly heckled, "Tell us again, Rabbi! Who are you? This time in plain language!"

Yeshua did not falter. He fixed His gaze on ben Dives and then past him to where the bulk of High Priest Caiaphas stood framed in the doorway of a dressing chamber. "The proof is what I do in the name of my Father."

There was a ripple, then a roar from the scribes and Pharisees. "Your *father*!"

At the hatred and scorn poured into the word, I jumped as if stung. I moved toward Yeshua, wanting to be a shield for the man who had given me eyes . . . and sonship. Without any request being spoken, Papa appeared to know what was wanted. The grip of his powerful hands shoved men aside as if he were tearing chunks from uncooperative clay. A passage opened for me, as long as I kept close behind my father.

"Do you mean the Holy One, blessed be he forever, is YOUR father?" a Levite challenged Yeshua. "You claim to be the Son and Heir? You claim that what you do is from the Holy One?"

Elbowing with unaccustomed discourtesy, I forced my way through the crowd. Glowering rebukes were infused with hatred as I was recognized and the word spread.

"The man born blind . . . it's him, I tell you!"

"Your *father*?" one of the Pharisees bellowed at the Teacher. "You are the Son of the Almighty? Blessed be he, and cursed is your blasphemy of HaShem today!"

Now I stood directly beside Yeshua. Papa loomed just behind us, a sturdy pillar of barely controlled righteous anger. The awareness of my papa's fury strangely warmed me.

How could they accuse Yeshua of blasphemy when clearly the miracles were proof of His goodness? Didn't Yeshua Himself teach that good fruit didn't come from bad trees? I raised my fingers to my eyes, remembering my darkness. I thought of the shadowed quiet of the Holy Place, where prayers were recited day after day. I considered how in the interior of that sacred building men spoke in hushed whispers as they breathed air thick with the incense of half a thousand years. And yet! Had none of the holiness of the place entered their souls? How could those who lived and breathed the worship of the Almighty be so insensitive to the fragrance of Messiah?

The religious leaders shouted and shook their fists and pressed in nearer to challenge Yeshua yet again. Some of the brandished knuckles were directed toward me.

"*Fraud! Blasphemer!*"

Cocked eyebrow and uptilted nose conveyed the interest of the high priest, who as yet remained offstage.

"Who do you think you are?" shouted Heled, one of the members of Caiaphas' family and thus a member of the ruling council.

I recall blinking rapidly. The man spoke clearly, but to my ears the words were merely an echo. A chill coursed through me as a low-pitched, inhuman grunting uttered the same objection a beat ahead of the human tongue. *Who? Who? Who do you think . . . you are? If you are? If you really are the Son . . . the Son of God . . . who do you . . . ?*

Unperturbed, Yeshua leveled a gaze that seemed to pierce through the young man's insolence. The man backed up a step. Suddenly the clamor quieted, waiting for Yeshua's answer.

I recognized the bleat of sheep in the pens where a thousand lambs were waiting to be sacrificed.

Yeshua raised His fingers slightly as if to draw in the clamor and hold it in His palm. "You don't believe me because you're not part of my flock." Then embracing with His eyes all those who had risked everything to follow Him, He continued, "My sheep know my voice. I know them and they follow me. I give them eternal life, and they will never perish."

For the sheep of Yeshua's flock, there was no more need to die because of sin.

The stirring of evil began again. I sensed it more than I heard it. A shadow hovered for a moment above ben Dives before merging with his body. Then the eyes of Ra'nabel ben Dives hardened with something beyond human darkness.

This time the not-human protest I heard was higher pitched, whining: *Life? You give them . . . ?* It came just fractionally before ben Dives repeated the phrase. It was as if someone was putting words into the minds and mouths of Yeshua's opponents. *Life? You . . . ?*

Yeshua did not pause or equivocate, making clear they should understand the authority with which He spoke. "No one will snatch my sheep away from me. My Father has given them to me and he is more powerful than anyone else. So no one can take them from me."

The hair on the back of my neck rose. Yeshua was speaking directly to the unseen shadow-thing contorting ben Dives' face.

"Your father?" ben Dives demanded. "More powerful? Who is your father?"

Yeshua said distinctly in a tone reserved for speaking of Elohim Adonai, the Lord God: "The Father and I are One."[26]

A high, keening shriek erupted from a wealthy woman who stood beside her Pharisee husband. A hundred human voices seemed to join with ten thousand thousand other wails of horror and fury.

Yeshua had said it plainly. He had told them all in the Temple. Today. Now. That the prophecy of Haggai had come true! Blessings were here for the nation of Israel! Forgiveness and Life were being offered today for everyone, just as the prophet had foretold!

The supernatural din increased. Men and women who had been gathered at the feet of the Master now ran for cover behind the thick marble columns of Solomon's colonnade! On the steps beside Yeshua two women remained seated. I noted the pinched, angry features of Marta, red spots glowing above each cheekbone. Next to her, her sister Miryam's face was sad and drawn as if with pain.

Did Miryam also hear the demonic mockery?

I crouched and covered my ears at the clamor. Clattering noises and exclamations of exertion increased the commotion as leaders of Israel rushed to pick up stones to kill Yeshua then and there.

The other voices exulted, adding urgency to the atmosphere. *Do it!* they urged. *Silence him now!*

Yeshua, unafraid, confident, faced them as they encircled Him. Arms were raised to cast the first stone.

"At my Father's direction I've done many things to help the people." With seeming unconcern at the tumult, Yeshua extended His hand till it rested lightly on my shoulder. "For which of these do you stone me?"

His words rocked Yeshua's foes back on their heels. For a moment even the spirit voices were mute, unable to think of a reply.

Then the babble began again. Ben Dives was first to recover his wits: "Not for any good work!"

Another Pharisee: "For blasphemy! Blasphemy!"

A scribe could not resist his natural inclination to repeat and reinterpret: "Because you, a mere man, have made yourself equal to HaShem!"

Stone him! the whispering voices urged.

By way of response Yeshua quoted Psalm 82: "It is written in Torah that God said to certain leaders of the people, 'I say, you are gods.' And you know the Scripture cannot be altered. So if these people, when as judges they exercised the power of life and death, acted as if they had God's authority, why do you call it blasphemy when the Holy One who was sent into the world by the Father says, 'I am the Son of God?'"

The hissing murmurs began again. *Stone him! Stone him!* They whooshed in my head like the susurration of tree limbs in a high wind. *Ssstone him! Sssstone him!*

I saw ben Dives pry a fist-sized rock loose from a sheep pen. El'azar and Nakdimon, as if waking from twin nightmares of being bound, started toward Yeshua's aid.

Yeshua appeared to pay the accelerating threat no mind, though He did have to raise His voice to be heard above the tumult. "DON'T believe me UNLESS I carry out my Father's work."

Ssstone him! Stone him!

"But IF I do HIS work, believe in what I have done, even if you don't believe in me. THEN you will realize that the Father is in me . . . and I am in the Father."[27]

Heled, the high priest's cousin, swept his arm forward and leveled an accusing finger at Yeshua. "Blasphemy! Seize him! He must be tried!"

Ben Dives countered: "No trial! His own words condemn him! Stone him!"

Many fists waved in the air, brandishing stones. I knew the first flight of a chunk of granite would unleash a barrage. Thrusting myself upright, I wished I were taller, larger—not so I could fight, because I'd never learned how, but so I could stand between Yeshua and the attackers. As it was, I could perhaps shelter the crouching women.

I saw El'azar grab the wrist of an enemy and twist it downward until the rock clattered free. On the other edge of the mob, Nakdimon thrust himself between two ranting scribes. As he flung them aside on the cramped steps, six others also fell in a heap.

I heard cries of fear and the clash of swords. Where was that coming from? Beside me Thomas still clutched the hilt of his weapon. He had not drawn it yet.

It was in the air! The voices of incitement were being put to flight. The whispers grew shrill—angry, but also frightened. Blows were being struck! Wounds given! Terror inflicted!

"Soldiers!" someone shouted. "Soldiers coming!"

The mob, so recently focused on assaulting Yeshua, turned like goats toward a marauding hyena. A centurion at the head of a double file of red-tunicked Roman legionaries advanced toward the clamor. "Break this up! Now! Disperse!"

The crowd scattered. Some exited through the Eastern Gate toward the Mount of Olives; others moved south toward the anonymity of the crowd in the courtyard beyond. In the confusion and panic, fistfights broke out.

I sighed with relief and helped Miryam to her feet. Marcus Longinus at the head of his men was the one furious Roman I was actually pleased to see. I was certain Yeshua would be pleased to see Marcus as well.

Turning in place, I scanned the crowd for the Master. Yeshua was no longer present. In the uproar He had slipped away.

But echoing from the tops of the olive grove in the garden of Gethsemane below the Temple Mount, I heard the noises of a vanquished army of accusatory voices in headlong retreat.

A single rock, arching high into the air after being flung at random by a retreating coward, struck me a glancing blow on the temple. I staggered sideways, putting a hand on a marble column to keep myself from falling.

Arms, powerfully muscled, scooped me up. I was drawn close to a barrel chest and a beard that smelled of clay. My papa carried me, as Zadok had carried his sons, out of the melee and out of danger.

High Priest Caiaphas smashed his fist into his palm. "Absurd!" he spouted. "This Yeshua appears openly at the Temple. We hear him utter blasphemy. And yet we cannot arrest him? We cannot even stone him and make it appear like the actions of an outraged mob?"

Ben Dives spread his hands in a sympathetic gesture, inclining his head to one side as he did so. "He is a masterful speaker, sir. Even the Temple guards fell under his spell. But we would have had him, were it not for that interfering centurion."

"And now where's the Galilean gone?" Caiaphas interrogated. "We hear he teaches openly in this village or that town. Some Pharisees locate him and get close enough to ask him questions. But when I send men after him, they come back with excuses about how they were afraid of the crowds!"

Ben Dives' eyes grew hooded. While the high priest continued to rant about how hemmed in he was by incompetents, his secretary was hatching a new plot.

"What if . . . ," ben Dives pondered aloud, "what if we knew ahead of time that Yeshua would return to Yerushalayim, and exactly where he'd be? And what if we knew there'd be no clamoring *am ha aretz* to rescue him and no Romans to intervene?"

Caiaphas paused in his tirade to sneer. "And what if the so-called prophet gave himself up to be crucified? What if he just died suddenly?"

Though bowing his neck obsequiously, ben Dives still raised a cautioning hand. "No doubt this is a worthless idea. You have probably already considered it and discarded it as unworkable."

Flattery worked its magic on Caiaphas as it always did. "In regard to what?"

"Is that merchant galley still in harbor at Caesarea?"

"The one in quarantine?" The high priest shuddered. "Every day more slaves die chained to their oars. More bodies are burned on the docks. It's said they picked up the disease in Syracusa. On the voyage here more than half were sick. They'll all die, I expect."

"Pity Yeshua isn't in Caesarea," ben Dives mused. "The way he heals beggars and lepers and sinners of all kinds . . . galley slaves might appeal to him."

Caiaphas snorted. "Pity, but he isn't anywhere near Caesarea, is he?"

"But suppose some of the beggars of Yerushalayim were taken sick with such a dread disease. If Yeshua heard of it, would he not return to help?"

The high priest's chair squeaked when he leaned back in it. In that posture he regarded ben Dives down an even greater length of nose. "Are you insane? Deliberately bring plague into the Holy City?"

"Suppose I knew a way to keep it confined in a small group. And suppose this group would especially appeal to Yeshua's . . . duty."

"Go on," Caiaphas offered grudgingly. "You have my attention."

CHAPTER 11

The weight of disappointment was crushing. My heart hurt more than the knot on my head. Yeshua, the One Greater than Solomon, had been run out of the Temple as though He were a leper. *What will Papa think?* I wondered.

My father slept peacefully beside me in the stable. He had not said a word about what had happened. I closed my eyes but could not shut out the image of Yeshua teaching Truth to the people in Solomon's Portico. How desperately I hoped Papa would see Yeshua and know He was the Messiah they had all longed for.

Yeshua, like Solomon, the son and heir of David's throne, had entered the Temple to rededicate it to true righteousness.

Yeshua, like Solomon, was filled with wisdom and able to reveal Truth to Israel and Jerusalem.

Yeshua, like Solomon, was the only one wise enough and compassionate enough to judge the hearts of men.

Yet the result had not been the reestablishment of David's throne and Solomon's kingdom. Instead, Yeshua was driven out. Yeshua, feared and hated by those in leadership who hid their deception and hypocrisy behind the outer trappings of religion.

Ben Dives' face burned like a light in my brain. What Ra'nabel ben Dives could not completely control he dedicated himself to utterly destroy.

It appeared to all as though Yeshua had been defeated. What would Papa think now in the face of such undeniable victory by the religious leaders?

A tear escaped as I squeezed my eyes tight, trying to forget the hatred on the faces of Yeshua's accusers. I felt like a small child again, alone and afraid in the darkness. But there was no one to comfort me. None could explain why Yeshua had run away. Why had Yeshua, the only one worthy to rule in Solomon's place, allowed evil, ambitious men to drive Him out?

I knew the voices and personalities of those who ruled the Temple and measured their success by each day's cash contributions. How often as I sat on the steps of Nicanor Gate and begged had I heard them mock and laugh at vanquished political enemies?

It did not matter to such men what the facts and prophecies of Torah proclaimed about Messiah. No matter that Yeshua healed the sick and gave sight to the blind. No matter that He was Wisdom personified and taught the truth about the One True God. Tonight the twisted, bitter hearts of religious rulers gloated together at the resounding defeat of Yeshua's influence in the place where the heart of Jewish worship beat. Any claim Yeshua might have made to the throne of David had been stillborn.

I prayed, *Oh, Adonai! How can it be that the One who is Truth could be driven from the place Solomon built to honor your Name? Is your eternal Truth so weak against the power of human pride? Who will understand Truth unless you reveal it by strength and power and might?*

Yeshua's talmidim had been right as they passed through the unbelieving villages of Samaria. Why didn't Yeshua call down fire from heaven and destroy those who rejected and mocked true righteousness?

I turned my face into my cloak and wept quietly. My grief was disguised beneath the drumming of rain upon the roof. At last, exhausted, I slept.

The winds stirred dead branches in the orchard beyond the compound. The patter of rain dripping from the eaves increased to a steady stream splashing noisily on the pavestones in the courtyard.

Lightning flashed, penetrating my lids. A deep rumble of thunder followed from a far-distant place.

I inhaled the rain-washed air. The night was cold. I shifted on my side, careful to lie back where my body had warmed the straw. Light shone against the limestone wall of the stable. Someone was up and moving toward me. The air crackled with the energy of the storm.

Peniel? A woman with a foreign accent called my name. No doubt one of El'azar's servants. *You are . . . Peniel?*

I groaned and pulled my blanket over my head.

Peniel ben Yahtzar? She held a lamp close enough for the light to seep through the woven fabric. *Follow me, quickly.*

I peeked out, unable to make out her features behind the light. "What? What? Where? I don't know you."

You are Peniel. The man who sees.

"That's me." And I knew she was a dream. "*Ulu Ush-pi-zin,*" I whispered. "Welcome, Exalted Wanderer. You are welcome, although no one here is happy after what happened today. You are welcome to share our disappointment."

The King requires witnesses. She smiled down at me. Her skin glowed golden. Eyes were bright blue and dazzling. The scent of lavender suffused the atmosphere.

"No beautiful woman ever speaks to me. When I was blind I smelled beautiful sights as a rich woman passed by and dropped a coin in my bowl. But I only imagined they were beautiful from the sound of their voices or the clink of their money. But you are beautiful. And what I mean is . . . I am sure you're a dream. Am I meant to go somewhere with you?"

She did not contradict me. *The King needs witnesses—honest men to write down the words of the story so many will comprehend. You must follow me now . . . into the court.*

"Which king? Who? Yeshua?"

A son of David—a wise man—he who was first to sit upon his father's throne. He who pointed the way to Messiah. You will know him at once when you see him. The story must be witnessed, the testimony of Truth revealed for many, and judgment sealed for those who reject Truth and will not believe.

The faint tinkle of bells increased.

"What is your name?" I asked.

Chesed, she replied. *Mercy.*

I sat up and stretched out my hand to her. "Chesed. You know me—I'm Peniel. And I love a good story."

She touched my finger, and suddenly we were in the bedchamber of a palace. Moonlight streamed through a window. The floors were marble, columns and beams covered in gold, but the roof was open to the starry sky.

A young king, handsome, with thick, black hair, lay sleeping on his bed.

From the open sky a resonant voice, too rich to be the voice of a mere man, whispered to the sleeping king, **Request! What should I give to you?**

I drew my breath in sharply, knowing what I was witnessing. I cried, "It's Solomon! The young king! I am dreaming of Solomon's dream!" My words did not penetrate the scene being played out before me but seemed muffled and distant, as though spoken underwater.

Young Solomon did not open his eyes when he gave a drowsy reply. "You have shown to your servant David, my father, great mercy and loving-kindness, according as he walked before you in faithfulness, righteousness, and uprightness of heart with you. And you have kept for him this great kindness and steadfast love. You have given him this day a son to sit upon his throne. Now, HaShem, my God, you have made your servant king *Alef Tav* instead of my father, and I am but a lad in wisdom and experience. I know not how to go out or how to enter! So, give me a discerning heart to govern. Teach me to know the truth!"[28]

I dropped to my knees, startled that the king had spoken a word I had never heard read aloud in the Haftarah before. I looked around, aware that we were in the antechamber of a great hall.

Chesed said to me, *Yes, Peniel. Solomon asked for the wisdom to discern the Truth. What is truth, men ask today? Is there truth anywhere in all of Israel? Truth is written* Alef Mem Tav—Alef *the beginning and* Tav *the end, a sign, a portent.* Alef *is also the first letter of the word* Truth. Mem *is the middle letter of the word* Truth. Tav, *the last letter of the word* Truth.

She passed her veil over my face, then removed it. We entered a judgment hall and stood beside a great lapis pillar with the word *EMeT*—"Truth"—inscribed upon it.

The wind howled outside. Two young women stood pleading a case before King Solomon. A tiny infant in a basket lay sleeping at the feet of the king.

The first young woman cried, "And we were alone in the house. She lay upon her son as she slept and he died. Then, as I slept, she put her dead son at my breast and took my baby as her own!"

The other argued: "Not so, great king. She is trying to steal my baby. He is mine! Her child is dead!"[29] At this the second woman began to sob bitterly.

I knew the story well enough, but as I watched the event play out before my eyes, I could not judge which woman was the true mother of the infant. Both were weeping, both calling out for heaven to judge rightly. How could Solomon tell the difference?

As if Chesed heard my unspoken question, she addressed me. *Hear and understand the meanings of Truth, Peniel. Truth, spelled EMeT,* Alef Mem Tav . . . *these are letters in the beginning and the middle and the end of the alphabet. The root of Truth is spelled* Alef Mem. *What is the meaning of these letters?*

I answered, "The word is *EM,* 'Mother.'"

Well spoken. Now look upon true wisdom. . . . See how Solomon seeks and finds Truth.

Before my eyes the great king stood up and drew a giant sword from its jewel-encrusted sheath. I knew this was the sword of old Goliath, the giant killed by Solomon's father.

With the tip of the sword Solomon thrust back the blanket covering the child. He flung away the covering as the infant began to awaken. A feeble cry like that of a kitten emanated from the basket.

The first woman fell to her knees, hands outstretched. Every fiber in her body seemed to cry out, *Be careful!*

The second woman, hands on hips, looked on, scowling at the first.

Then Solomon spoke: "Cut the living child in two and give half to one and half to the other."

The first woman begged, "Please! Oh, please, my lord! Give her the living baby. Don't kill him!"

Her adversary argued, "Neither you nor I shall have him. Cut him in two!"

When Solomon smiled, I knew he had discovered the Truth through the compassion of the mother. He sheathed the sword and returned to his throne. He spoke. "Truth, *EMeT.* Give the baby to the first woman. *EM*—she truly is mother of the baby. Amen."[30]

The vision faded. As I watched, the first woman gathered her infant son into her arms and washed his face with her tears. The second angrily stalked from the presence of the king.

Chesed spoke quietly as we walked back among the sleeping

comrades. *Only one of the women was the baby's true mother. Judgment without Truth required the death of the baby. Yet Solomon revealed the undeniable Truth. The key to EMeT was uncovered in the compassionate heart of EM. Because of love, the mother sacrificed her own rights so her beloved baby would not die.*

I asked, "Everything means something. How did Solomon know both women wouldn't agree to divide the baby?" I turned to Chesed, who smiled at me and led me back to my bed.

HaShem's Truth and HaShem's Mercy and HaShem's Love are One.

"And what can such a story mean today?"

The sword of HaShem's judgment is raised. Israel is the baby before the throne of the Almighty. Satan cries that the nation is his, and he demands death and division as justice. Chesed stepped away from me. *Yeshua is EMeT, and He pleads mercy and life for every child of the covenant. His heart, warmed with compassion, does not insist upon His rights."*

The words echoed in the room as I lay down. Thunder like an approaching army rumbled in the distance. I fell into a deep sleep.

12

Behind the high walls and massive acacia-wood gates the interior of El'azar's large house hummed with activity. Marta muttered as she swept past me, "Dozens of mouths to feed. And so many beds! I should have been an innkeeper." Marta clamped her thin lips shut, as if consciously preventing herself from continuing to gripe.

A bubbling pot of stew simmering over a charcoal fire added a comforting aroma to the room. *So much to arrange so the fugitives can sleep comfortably through the dark night.* It was Hanukkah, after all, and platters were already heaped with food and ready for the celebration.

The atmosphere, however, was somber. Two miles from Jerusalem was not far enough for safety. The stark reality that the Herodians and Temple authorities could join forces and send a contingent in search of Yeshua was on everyone's mind. Had any of the Temple authorities noticed the identities of Nakdimon and El'azar in the midst of the confusion? Or had the eyes of Yeshua's enemies been blinded for a moment as Yeshua escaped?

Beyond the success of the Maccabee warriors and the miracle of the oil, I also remembered other Hanukkah stories. Drawn from the historical accounts of the Maccabees, the less cheerful parts concerned the heroic martyrdom of those who resisted giving up their sacred beliefs.

How very like the events of Maccabean times my world appeared. Then as now, foreign rulers pressed in. Then as now, the foreign rulers were aided by turncoat Jews who valued their wealth and position. Caiaphas and his cadre would rather destroy true worship than challenge their overlord's authority.

Might it also be true, now as then, that martyrdom was required?

I knew nothing was impossible for Yeshua. I was still uncertain how we had managed to slip away from the Temple grounds. One minute Yeshua was about to be stoned to death, and the next minute the Roman centurion Marcus Longinus was at our backs, quelling the disturbance as we hurried along the dark road toward the home of Yeshua's friends in Bethany. The unseen clash of heavenly swords rang in my memory.

But still, we had walked the same path King David walked as he was driven from Jerusalem by his rebellious son Absalom. Like David, Yeshua walked the road silently, weeping for the people of Eretz-Israel.

I knew something far beyond mere human tragedy had happened this night. On the very day the prophet Haggai had promised Messiah would come to the Temple and bring blessings to His people, the Messiah had been driven out by the leaders of Israel.

Tonight's Hanukkah reading, recited by El'azar in a distracted tone, was from the prophet Isaias:

"Woe to those who call evil good and good evil, who put darkness for light and light for darkness, who put bitter for sweet and sweet for bitter! Woe to those who are wise in their own eyes and clever in their own sight! As tongues of fire lick up straw and as dry grass sinks down in the flames, so their roots will decay and their flowers blow away like dust; for they have rejected the law of the Lord Almighty and spurned the word of the Holy One of Israel."[31]

Yeshua Himself had not spoken since we left the Holy Mountain, except to make a blessing over the food. Tonight He let everyone else discuss His life: how they would save Him, and where He should go to escape the Herodians and the Sanhedrin and the Pharisees.

Marta, pushing back a wiry lock of gray hair with visible irritation, took charge of the household tasks. She ordered Miryam and the servants about, as eighteen men discussed a plan for spiriting the Master away safely.

I studied the concerned faces of those around Him.

El'azar leaned close to the fire, nudging embers with a charred stick. "There is no safety for you, Yeshua, in the territory of Judea. Herod Antipas is worse than his father. Remember what his father failed to do when you were an infant? Now Herod Antipas will strive to accomplish what his father did not. Though the high priest hates Antipas, they agree on one thing: They hate and fear you even more. Your murder is on the agenda of the Sanhedrin and the Herodian high council."

"Kill him?" Peter bristled. "They'll kill me first."

"And me," Thomas concurred. His voice showed tightly controlled emotion. I saw the cords in Thomas' neck draw taut like bowstrings.

The other disciples added their pledge to protect Yeshua to the last drop of their blood. My father joined in the vow.

Nakdimon, dark eyes betraying his anger, agreed. "Another country. Like King David, eh? David went to another land while Saul wanted to kill him. That's it . . . somewhere else until Yeshua can raise an army and return."

Yeshua let them talk. I noticed how the Master savored a date stuffed with walnuts and gazed sadly into the flames as His followers talked over His head and around Him. Were there ever eyes so *filled* with sorrow? Today at the Festival of Light, He who was the Light of the World had been rejected.

"Master," El'azar queried, "what do you think?"

Yeshua did not reply. Everyone was silent for a long time, waiting for His answer. The crackle of the fire and the faint drumming of rain on the roof were the only sounds.

Peter cleared his throat loudly. When he stood abruptly, he shuffled his feet before speaking. Silence seemed to make him uncomfortable. Staring into the rafters, his sunburned face clenched and unclenched like his fists before he spoke. "So. Such a day. We're not welcome in Yerushalayim, unless we want to attend our own funerals. Eh? Not welcome! Yerushalayim? Lord, you could go to . . . Alexandria. A million Jews there, I hear. So said Zadok's brother. A nice temple too. Alexandria. A good place, eh? What will we do, Lord? You know what the Herodians did to your cousin the Baptizer." Peter drew his finger slowly across his throat.

At this Yeshua raised the gaze of His gold-flecked brown eyes and instantly silenced Peter.

The big fisherman sat abruptly, then shifted uneasily on his cushion before he dared speak again. "Well, you know what I mean. We should leave. Yes? Don't you think? Go. Should we? Get out of here?"

El'azar rested his cheek on his hand. He agreed with Peter. "Lord? Alexandria? Not a bad idea. You have friends there, eh?"

I thought of how good it would be to step off a ship in Alexandria with Yeshua. Yes, Peter had come up with a good plan. I, who knew the story of Yeshua's childhood escape to Egypt, had heard every detail from Zadok and from Yeshua's mother.

Peter said quietly, "You escaped to Egypt as a child. When Herod the Butcher King, father of the present King Antipas, killed the babies of Beth-lehem."

El'azar seemed satisfied. "Your life is worth more than the world, Lord. More precious than anyone or anything. We depend on your life. The cost of passage to Alexandria is small. A few years' teaching there. We'll help you get to Joppa and then you'll sail in a ship to Alexandria and set up a Yeshiva where you can train many more disciples and return when your people are prepared to receive you in Yerushalayim as king."

When all present had agreed that Alexandria was a proper, safe distance away, Yeshua spoke: "We're going to Perea."

Peter blustered, "Not far enough! Not nearly—"

Yeshua silenced him with a look. "Across the Jordan. About one day's journey from here. Have you forgotten? It's where I sent the rest of the group when we left the Galil. I need to teach in the villages there. The time grows short."

And that settled our plans.

My father first had to return to his shop in Jerusalem. When he gave me a farewell embrace, he whispered, "The big fisherman is right. Perea's not far enough. But above all else, don't let Yeshua return anywhere near Yerushalayim. Not for any reason!"

PART V

SEVEN THINGS THE LORD WILL DO FOR ISRAEL

I will gather you from all the countries. . . .

I will bring you back into your own land,

I will sprinkle clean water on you, and you will be clean;

I will cleanse you from all your impurities. . . .

I will give you a new heart and put a new spirit in you;

I will remove from you your heart of stone and give you a heart of flesh.

I will put My Spirit in you and move you to follow My decrees.

EZEKIEL 36:24-27

iryam and El'azar stood for a long time on the balcony above the gatehouse to watch as Yeshua and His little band strode eastward toward the river. Stars faded. The eastern sky ripened with the approach of morning.

Miryam remarked, "The children will be sorry they didn't get to say good-bye."

El'azar nodded. "It's best they're not aware. If anyone should come looking and ask which way he's gone."

"How long until he can return in triumph to Yerushalayim? How long do you think, El'azar? All the people want him to take the throne, as it is written." In the willow thicket in the canyon at the back of the house a night bird trilled an emphatic coda to his evening performance.

El'azar cleared his throat, sending a plume of steam spiraling lazily into the chilly air. "They say the stone gods in Caesar's house are golden. Marble cloaks set with ruby buttons and carved feet shod with lapis shoes." He shaded his eyes against the glare of the rising sun. "And Yeshua comes to earth from heaven dressed in flesh like our own. The sages tell us Messiah, by his word, created the sun. Yet Yeshua wears a cloak of homespun wool to keep himself warm. And he gives away his cloak to one who has none. This is a different idea of Messiah than any of us imagined."

"There is no idol Rome could erect that would not crumble by one word from Yeshua's mouth." Miryam lost sight of the Master's form as dawn broke over the mountains of Moab.

"Yet Yeshua waits for men to tear down the idols. Though he could make all things new with a word, he is waiting for us to do something first."

The creak of barn doors announced the arrival of a new workday. El'azar's farmhands would be ploughing the damp earth, readying it for planting barley and flax.

"The people listen to him like they listened to Yochanan. They are turning their hearts back to God."

"And that's why Caiaphas and the council hate him so." El'azar turned away and leaned against the parapet. "See there, Miryam." He pointed westward to the distant spires of Jerusalem as the sunlight seemed to set the golden roofs on fire. "The Temple authorities think God prefers incense from Arabia and formal prayers dripping from the lips of men without mercy. If they knew Yeshua, they would see that The Eternal enjoys the scent of apples roasting over a fire while old friends talk of the wonder of the stars that came into existence at his command."

As if perched atop one of the Temple parapets, the wandering star known as Shabbatai, The Lord of the Sabbath, gleamed briefly before fading from view.

"Pity them." Miryam shook her head and laid a hand on her brother's sleeve.

"Pity? Them?"

"They think today is all there is to live for."

"They'll kill him if they can." Clasping his hands together, El'azar blew into cupped palms to warm them.

"You know the Truth. They can't do anything unless he permits it."

"Yeshua brings heaven's Truth to Israel. Truth that, when revealed, condemns liars and phonies," El'azar mused. "Darkness hates light because it reveals lies for what they are."

"He is the Truth."

"Truth is different than I imagined it to be. No armies or clashing swords. Not even an excess of words. He asks us so many questions about ourselves. What do we think? He waits for us to answer. We reply with old clichés. He nods once when we get it right and says to us, 'It's so simple. I am the way, the truth and the life,' he says."[32]

"But along with the old sayings, the true things, he adds this: Even if we die, if we believe in him, we will live.[33] Do *you* believe him, El'azar?" Miryam turned her deep brown eyes full on her brother's face.

"I believe it, when I see it myself. The daughter of Ya'ir raised from death in Capernaum. The son of the widow in Nain. Lepers healed. Blind. Deaf. Can I doubt it when I hear you tell of what he did—healing so many in the Galil?"

Miryam leaned against the wall and remembered the condemnation she had faced in Jerusalem. "And in my own life. He raised me from a kind of living death. Called me from the grave of my sin."

El'azar studied his sister for a long moment as though he had forgotten what Yeshua had done for her. "You are someone else now."

"It is written that he fills the house of the barren woman with children." Miryam smiled as the groans and chatter of waking children sounded from the courtyard. "That's the point, isn't it? Yeshua takes the mess we make of our lives and makes us new and alive again. Fills our lives with his great love and heals us with his mercy and forgiveness. And then he tells us to give away the best of what we have. These little ones are the life he gave me."

El'azar embraced her. "Yes. Yes. I believe him. Gold and rubies and lapis shoes are nothing compared to the face of God that smiles in our home."

A flock of river warblers alighted from the willows onto the banks of the irrigation ditches, noisily beginning their day's efforts. The recent frigid weather had kept them huddled together, but today would be warmer and drier, and they seemed eager to go about finding the insects and worms uncovered by the ploughing.

"It's breakfast," Miryam said, descending the steps. "Marta will be expecting us."

⚓

I learned surprising lessons about God's covenant as I watched Yeshua interact with people. Perhaps the most startling of all was that those who appeared to be the most outwardly holy were often the most corrupt inside.

It is written in Torah, in the scroll of Deuteronomy:

The Lord will circumcise your hearts, and the hearts of your descendants, to love the Lord your God with all your heart, and with all your soul, that you may live.[34]

The Roman centurion Marcus Longinus seemed by every outward sign to be the opposite of what the Pharisees and Sadducees considered a righteous man. Yet his heart was circumcised by the Lord. The covenant of mercy was within him. He was, I thought, more acceptable to God than those who knew all the correct prayers, yet had forgotten compassion.

I stood on the parapet above El'azar's gate and imagined the talmidim listening to Yeshua teach before they slept. Turning my face toward Jerusalem, I grieved at the spiritual darkness that seemed to have settled there. Yet even as I pondered this, secret friends of Yeshua gathered information.

Marcus and Quintus, his guard sergeant, stepped from the narrow passageway leading from Pilate's mansion to the Antonia Fortress. The streets of Jerusalem were ominously dark.

"No Sparrows out tonight?" Quintus grumbled. "Too cold for the link boys to be out with their torches? Lazy creatures. Or is it only this station beside the Roman governor's palace they've deserted? No light for the Roman legionaries, eh?"

"Come." Marcus pulled the fur hood of his civilian cloak over his head and settled his palm on the hilt of his sword. He stepped out into the narrow street. "Watch my back."

Limping along behind, Quintus replied somberly, "Aye."

Marcus made his way through the inky blackness from Pilate's mansion by memory. The street was entirely devoid of the usual brazier fires and gatherings of orphan boys who lit the streets of the city.

Was their absence some sign of imminent revolt? Had Jerusalem's

Sparrows been warned to stay off the streets tonight? Marcus rounded the corner near the viaduct. A light beamed ahead. A single torch.

"Steady, sir," Quintus warned. "The entrance to the Sparrows' quarry is there."

Marcus felt the hair on the back of his neck prickle as his body prepared for an assault. He stopped and drew his sword. Quintus did the same. Then Marcus shouted, "Sparrow! A light here!"

There was a moment of hesitation before the torchlight dipped and bobbed as one ragged boy about ten or eleven years old hobbled toward them. "Aye! A light! Sparrow here, sir. Where shall I lead you?"

"Sparrows always travel in twos. Where's your partner?" Marcus queried as the gaunt child peered up at him.

"Sick," the boy answered, thrusting out his hand palm up for payment. "A penny, Your Honor."

Quintus objected. "A penny? But there's only one of you. Only one torch."

"The fee is set, sir. A penny for Sparrows' link torch through the city. All the Sparrows may die this winter, but the Sanhedrin sets the fee for a link and that cannot be changed . . . though I may be the only Sparrow left."

Marcus placed the coin in the boy's grimy hand. "We've walked all this way in the dark from the governor's palace."

"Pilate's house, eh? I could tell you was a foreigner. Where to?"

"Antonia."

"Huh." The boy grunted disapproval and turned on his heel, thrusting the torch forward. "Come on, then." In the flickering torchlight, the lane glinted with the hollow eyes of the homeless staring out from doorways.

Marcus did not sheath his sword. "Your partner?"

"Aye. Sick. Hungry. Business ain't been enough to keep our bellies full since the Festival of Dedication ended. Always bad this time of year."

"Where are all the other link boys?"

"Sick mostly," the boy answered curtly. "None but a handful able to carry a link. Sparrow who don't work, don't eat. That's the rule. All sick. Worst I've seen. Ever. No hope. Hardly any boy inside the quarry who ain't sick. I won't go back to the quarry to sleep. They'll start dying soon. Hunger and cold take the little ones first. And do you think anyone cares?"

"But the charities. The poor boxes in your Temple," Marcus began.

The Sparrow replied with a bitter laugh. "It's plain you ain't from here." He waved his torch toward the lights of a great mansion on the western hill opposite. "The rich men? Made their money from the pilgrims. All the important men'll be leaving Yerushalayim soon. The rich ones who count the coins in the Temple poor boxes. Aye. They take their children away. They're afraid we carry more than torches. Every year when the torches go dark and us Sparrows begin to die they bar their gates and close their shutters tight. Some Sparrows thought the Messiah would come to the quarry this year. Hoped he'd feed us free bread. Aye. Some said he fed people in the North, but I never saw him. And if he did feed people in the North, nothing changed here. Our bellies? Empty again. The littlest Sparrows won't see spring."

The boy led Marcus and Quintus to the gate of the Antonia. Marcus pressed a shekel into his hand and left him gawking at the treasure. One shekel would make very little difference to the hundreds of homeless boys who lived in the quarry. Since hope had been driven from the courts of the Temple along with Yeshua, it seemed that nothing in Jerusalem had changed after all.

Marcus spurred Pavor to a gallop up the slope of the Mount of Olives on the road to Bethany. Early afternoon sun was low along its winter track and warm on his back. Despite the sun's reassuring touch, Marcus' thoughts were gloomy and troubled. Every winter brought sickness and death to the poorest quarters of Jerusalem. But this year, being especially cold and damp, presented the prospect of much greater threat than usual.

This morning Herod Antipas and his court had packed up and headed to Caesarea Maritima on the seacoast. High Priest Caiaphas and others wealthy enough to have villas on the shore also pulled up stakes and moved their entire households to Joppa until the danger was past.

This left the religious oversight of the Temple to a handful of elders and common priests, none of whom would defile themselves by going among the dead and dying. Instead, like the merchants and shopkeepers, they shut and locked their gates, transacting business only through messengers and servants until the plague passed.

Civil rule of the city fell under the absolute authority of Governor Pilate and the Roman legion. Though Pilate had given the order for slaves of the wealthy to attend to the evacuation of the sick, few heeded the command. Pilate would not risk the health of his officers or soldiers for such an ignoble task.

And so the orphan flock of Jerusalem Sparrows was left to care for one another. One death so far. . . . many more expected.

The red-tiled roof of Miryam's family estate towered above the gray, leafless branches of the dormant orchard. A short two miles from the desolation of Jerusalem, Bethany and the great house of El'azar loomed like an island of peace and safety in a sea of trouble.

Marcus prayed Yeshua was still there. He was the best, perhaps the only, hope for those who had no money for food, clothing, or shelter, let alone physicians and medicine. Unless Yeshua could be brought back in secret to end the plague, how many beggars would die?

arcus leapt from the back of his mount and slammed his fist
hard against the massive gate as I carried wood for the fire.
The happy laughter of children escaped from within. Marcus
pounded again.

"Coming! Coming! So impatient! You'd think the world was coming to an end!" Old Tavita pulled open the peephole and squinted out
at Marcus. "Well, Adonai bless you, Centurion! Back sooner than we
supposed but not sooner than we wished."

"Tavita, I've come seeking the Rabbi."

She fumbled with the bolt and opened the gate for him. "Yeshua?
Oh, sir, he's long gone, I'm afraid."

"There's sickness in Jerusalem."

The old woman's face puckered with consternation at the news. She
involuntarily stepped back as though the disease might pursue Marcus
into the courtyard of the estate. "Begun first in the household of Herod,
we can hope!"

Pavor followed Marcus like a dog as he entered. I caught up the
reins to lead him to the stable. "No. The cave of Sparrows."

The old woman clucked her tongue. "Ah. Poor things. Poor, poor things . . . and none to aid them, I suppose."

Marcus shook his head curtly and looked past her as El'azar and Miryam emerged from the house. I saw plainly that Marcus' heart surged with longing at the sight of Miryam beside her brother. She smiled at him, but not with the smile of a lover.

"Shalom, Marcus!" El'azar greeted him like an old friend. "Giving up the comforts of the Antonia? What brings you our way?"

Tavita replied, "Centurion comes to your gate with sad news. Plague among the Sparrow lads. Dyin' like flies, they are, and none to help."

Marcus saluted and bowed at the neck. "Shalom, El'azar. Miryam. Peniel. Aye. What Tavita says is mostly true. Breathing troubles. Fever. Those who might help have gates locked and double-barred. I hoped Yeshua was still here. Otherwise there's none left to aid the lads."

"He's gone, Marcus," Miryam replied. "Last week. Over Jordan. Perea. He's safe there."

Marcus nodded. I comprehended he had hoped Yeshua would be near enough to help, but he would not call Him back. "Herod Antipas has fled the city. Caiaphas as well. They fear for their households."

Tavita waved her arm and scowled. "Cowards, they are. All of 'em! Better care for their dogs than for the wee small boys who live in that cavern. Well, no use us goin' hungry. I'll see to lunch. Cowards, every one of them."

El'azar watched her as she retreated, muttering, into the house. "As well they should be. Such plagues come when the Lord is angry against Israel."

I disagreed. "It isn't the corrupt houses of Herod Antipas or Caiaphas that suffer, but the Sparrows. The boys, the lights of Yerushalayim."

Miryam added, "This is no judgment from God, El'azar. It is the winter sickness that comes every year to cold and hungry children. It comes because wealthy men do nothing. This evil isn't judgment. Judgment against the innocent ones who die? No! It's evidence in God's judgment against the wealthy men who might save one poor child with a crust of bread. And yet the rich hoard their treasure and run away to eat a feast in safety and warmth. Then they falsely praise God, as if he is pleased because the plague does not take them."

El'azar touched his hand to his brow in acknowledgment of his sister's wisdom. "Yeshua's gone. What should we do?"

Marcus shook his head. "Dangerous times. We mustn't fetch Yeshua back. Lord Caiaphas and the tetrarch have doubtless left plenty of spies behind for just such a chance. This illness will just have to run its course, as it does every year in every great city of the world among the poor and hungry. I've seen it in Rome. Thousands of children dead. The streets emptied of beggars in one season. No strength to fight the illness. Starving and cold. They'll perish in Jerusalem too. And the poor will bury their dead for a half penny a head offered by Pilate and the government."

El'azar stared at Marcus' muddy shoes for a long moment. His head snapped up. "Miryam is right. Bread and broth. Warm blankets. Small things to help strengthen those who aren't yet ill. It's not beyond hope. Not if we save even one."

I also caught El'azar's vision. "We'll go too. Marta and I." I was certain I, who had lived among beggars most of my life, would not become ill.

"You, Peniel, yes." El'azar held up his hand. "But Miryam and Marta and Tavita must stay. A houseful of healthy children right here. Ours to protect. This is for me to attend. Supplies enough from the souks. Everything can be bought in Yerushalayim. Blankets. Clean clothes. Medicine and food. For now, Marcus, can you wait?" To Miryam: "See to my clothes. I may be gone awhile. When we leave, lock the gates and allow no one to enter. And none of our people must go outside. No one until you hear the plague is past. For the sake of the children here—the ones the Lord has given us to care for—lock the gate. Do as I say."

A Roman centurion and a Jewish landowner. Could there ever be two such unlikely allies? Yet Marcus and El'azar were united in purpose. That night I began to fully comprehend that Yeshua had come to confirm a new covenant with us.

It is written in the scroll of the prophet Ezekiel:

A new heart also I will give you, and a new spirit will I put within you; and I will take away your stony heart out of your flesh, and I will give you a heart of flesh. And I will put My Spirit within you and cause you to walk in My statutes, and you shall keep My judgments and do them. Moreover I will make a covenant of peace with them; it shall be an everlasting covenant with them.[35]

Though unlikely allies, Marcus of Rome and El'azar of Bethany had both been transformed by Yeshua. Hearts of stone had been cut away and replaced with hearts of compassion.

A child's body was being carried out even as Marcus and El'azar and I arrived at the entry to the abandoned quarry. Wrapped in rags, dirty, bare feet and a thatch of fair hair protruded from opposite ends of the shroud. The pitifully small frame of a dead Jerusalem Sparrow began his last journey across the Holy City. Two foreign-born slaves, impressed into the work, seemed disgusted and fearful at their task as they hurried out with the corpse.

Ducking his head because of the low overhanging rock, Marcus stopped in the entry to the caverns. This was the source of cut stone now reassembled on the Temple Mount. The honeycomb of passageways and chambers was home to the orphaned or abandoned boys who were Jerusalem's torchbearers.

The air near the gaping mouth of the cavern was frigid. Once inside, the chill stabilized at an endurable level. Corners where emaciated children huddled were heated by small fires of gleaned—or stolen—charcoal.

But which turning led to the collection of sick and dying boys? Someone unfamiliar with the expansive quarries could easily become disoriented and lost . . . or die by plunging over an unexpected precipice.

Fortunately the wall of the tunnel changed from inky black to gray to pale yellow with the approaching footsteps of someone carrying a torch. Orange flames emerged first, followed by the hand of another servant wearing the insignia of the captain of the Temple guards.

Marcus stopped the man. "So your master is here, then, is he?" It was the duty of the Temple authorities to oversee the torches provided to the Sparrows and to maintain order within their ranks.

The man's face was pale, even green, in the flickering light. "No." He choked, sounding as if he was about to vomit. "Sent me to bring . . . report."

"And that report?"

Thrusting the firebrand into El'azar's hand, the servant retorted, "See for yourselves. Just let me go!" The man then rushed out into the open air and did not return.

I regarded Marcus. "Can it have gotten so bad so soon?"

The passage curved to the left. After a hundred paces, a chorus of coughing and wheezing greeted us. Two steps inside the chamber and the rasping noises resembled the gabble of a great flock of croaking shorebirds.

To this were added thin cries for water . . . and for Mother.

Three Gentile gravediggers tasked with disposing of dead bodies stood gaping at the mess. Where to begin?

In the space between two pillars of rock left in bygone ages to support the roof, sick and dying boys mingled together.

A lad of about eleven lay with his body curled protectively around a friend. His companion was already blue and stiff.

Thrusting his torch forward, Marcus made a rapid circuit of the chamber. Eighteen children seemingly past caring. Sixty-six more barely alive.

"Where are the other boys?" El'azar demanded of a gravedigger.

"Fled. Afraid to stay here."

"And why are you just standing about?" Marcus snapped. "All of you! Give me your cloaks!" Then, "You! Go fetch stretchers. And you! You go with him . . . bring blankets! And baskets of charcoal for fires."

Even without his uniform there was no mistaking Marcus' air of command. "Clean water!"

El'azar commanded the workers to separate the living from the dead.

Marcus commented, "My mother nursed me through one such winter in Rome when I was a boy. I have known such illness. Later I saw such a plague strike my legion one hard winter on the Rhine. Many died, but I was never sick."

El'azar stripped off his own cloak. With it he wrapped a child as the servants took away the body of his friend.

Sputtering hoarsely, the boy's eyes glittered with fever. "Please, sir," he begged. "My brother's worse'n me. Help him first!"

"We'll have to move them. Can't stay here. Livestock in Israel get better care." El'azar ran a hand over his brow in a gesture of frustration.

"Neither Temple nor palace will be open to them," I observed quietly. "What do we do?"

"Stay and see to the fires, the blankets, and the water," El'azar said. "I'll arrange . . . something. Maybe rent a house . . . buy one, if necessary. I'll be back within the hour!"

Three and a half hours had elapsed by the time Marcus and I arrived at the makeshift hospital with a Greek doctor in tow. El'azar had already completed a huge task. The olive oil storage building El'azar rented for the dormitory was outside the north wall of Jerusalem. A pile of broken clay amphorae occupied one corner. A pervasive oily feel to walls and floor was all that remained after the year's oil press had been sold and shipped. The wealthy merchant had left Judea for the warmth of a winter in Cyprus, but his agent was pleased to see the empty quarters produce any income at all. In fact, he was so pleased at the rental that he was prepared to accept half his original, ridiculously high, asking price. He was even more pleased when El'azar accepted the quoted fee without quibble and paid a month's rent in cash.

As the agent departed, chuckling and jingling the leather money pouch, El'azar likewise breathed a contented sigh. The agent had not even inquired as to the use El'azar intended for the structure.

Within an hour charcoal braziers heated the space. Low pallets of rope strung on wooden frames formed three long rows running the length of the building. No more servants of the wealthy and powerful could be induced to carry sick children; neither bribes nor threats moved them. So El'azar located a relay of six sturdy beggars who willingly toted the boys for a denarius. Eleven trips apiece and all the coughing, sputtering Sparrows were lodged and blanketed.

Pots of lentil stew simmered over the coals. El'azar enlisted the beggars in helping the children sip broth and water. All responded gratefully, except for three who were unconscious and could not be roused.

El'azar awarded the beggars an extra denarius each as a bonus, instructing them to return the next day for more duties. Then at last he had time to survey his work with a sense of accomplishment. Already the soup and warmth were having a positive effect. If cold and privation caused plague, then this one was stopped in its tracks.

The man from Bethany clearly had greater success in his efforts than Marcus, whose only task was locating a physician. He finally returned with a Greek doctor named Sosthenes, who demanded silver before even entering the ward.

El'azar paid it promptly.

Without a word Sosthenes began his examinations. Oil lamp in hand, he peered into eyes and mouths and listened to the complaints of the sufferers. While this continued, Marcus and El'azar stood apart in whispered consultation. "First four names I got all refused to come," Marcus reported. "One said a plague among the beggars would do the city good. Two others just closed the door on me. The fourth would have locked me out, but I barged in regardless. All I got out of him was pious refusal and the name of this Greek." Marcus jerked his head toward Sosthenes, now muttering to himself halfway down the first row of cots. "And then I had to ride to Emmaus for him."

El'azar acted angry. "Jewish children should not have to wait on the kindness of Gentiles," he remarked. "But physicians are all charlatans anyway. See how much better the boys are already?"

I was not convinced. While all were no doubt better off fed than starving, the hall echoed with the constant racket of barking coughs. Several Sparrows had trouble swallowing; some were pale and trembling despite the warmth.

Sosthenes returned to us without even completing the first row of patients. He was shaking his head and stroking his short gray beard. His face was drawn and worry lines surrounded his mouth and eyes. "Get some pots of water boiling with oil of lemon," he instructed. "That will help some with their breathing. We'll also need oil of camphor and lots of sweet wine. Two or three drops of camphor in each mug. Give it slowly! Two times a day at least; three would be better. Finally tincture of phytolacca to paint their throats."

The doctor grasped El'azar's wrist and tugged him toward a patient who was sitting up. In my view the child did not appear unhealthy, except for a slight flush.

"Boy," Sosthenes demanded, "how do you feel?"

"My throat hurts," the Sparrow croaked. "I ache, and my nose doesn't work right."

The physician flung his right hand aloft. "See that? First stage."

"Common to every cold winter and lack of proper clothing and food," El'azar countered. "A simple breathing ailment."

Sosthenes' eyes narrowed. "You think so, eh? See here."

The doctor led El'azar and me to a boy two pallets farther down the row. This child was prostrate. His breath came in rapid gasps. Sosthenes placed El'azar's hand on the child's chest. "Feel that wheeze? See the blood and pus where he wiped his nose on his sleeve? And in his mouth. There! See those white spots on his tonsils? Stage two."

This time El'azar uttered no objection when the Greek delivered us to another patient with even more difficulty breathing. The child's face was pallid and his skin was clammy to the touch. This time the view inside the Sparrow's mouth showed not a white film but a furry, gray-green mass extending up and down the back of the throat.

El'azar jumped back in horror at the shocking sight.

Sosthenes stood erect. "Stage three, and proof. *Dipthera*, we call it. 'Leather-hide' . . . from that membrane you see there. Hippocrates described this four hundred years ago. The Syrians call it the 'strangling sickness.' Don't know if you Jews have a word for it. Now, can you get all the medicine I specified?"

El'azar nodded mutely.

Marcus spoke up on his friend's behalf. "Everything you say will be carried out."

"Good! Now, most important. No one must come or go from here. I saw an entire Egyptian village wiped out by this. A family all well one day; all dead in ten! It spreads like a fire in dry brush. Only those who have already survived a bout of *Dipthera* should be allowed to serve the patients."

I nodded. "Had it as a child."

Marcus confirmed that he too had survived the illness.

Physician and soldier turned toward El'azar, who had a stricken expression. "The beggars. The ones who carried the boys here. I sent them away."

"How many? Where? They must return here at once . . . by force, if necessary!"

"Give me their names," Marcus said to El'azar. "I'll get a squad of troopers and round them up."

"What . . . what will happen to these boys?" El'azar said, with a quaver in his voice.

Sosthenes' shoulders slumped slightly. "If you do everything I say, we may be able to save . . . half of them."

Stepping outside into the street, it was Marcus who spotted the two Temple guards standing in the shadows of an alleyway opposite.

"They're watching for Yeshua," El'azar surmised.

A moment later, the soldier Quintus rode up and saluted Marcus. "Centurion, I was sent to fetch you back to the Antonia. Here is an order from Governor Pilate."

Marcus unrolled a scroll sealed with Pilate's seal. He studied the writing then said, "I am ordered not to meddle in this. I . . . may not assist you."

We dared not go to fetch Yeshua back from Perea. It was clear to us the Temple rulers watched and waited, expecting the Master's return to Jerusalem.

"Surely he'll come," they whispered. "He cares for the poor. He loves the children. He won't let them die."

And the Temple guards kept watch . . . waiting. . . .

But we did not send word to Yeshua. Had He not anointed us to pray in His name? to ask of our Father and expect God to answer?

And so we prayed in Yeshua's name and worked among the Sparrows as if Yeshua were there with us.

Like stewards representing a king, we spoke the name of Yeshua and the demons trembled.

And as those who would be great in the Kingdom must be the servants of all, as Yeshua taught us, there was much work for us to do.

I could see Master El'azar was exhausted. The arrival of another dawn did not renew his energy. When we surveyed the ranks of sick Sparrows, we almost despaired. There were now close to a hundred boys and beggars in the infirmary. Some had come voluntarily, because of the reported food and shelter. Others arrived at spear point, rounded up and escorted by Temple guards.

In any case, the chamber was packed with sufferers in every stage of illness. By the doctor's order El'azar had tried to organize our charges so the still healthy-appearing were kept apart from the more seriously ill. The massive influx of additional patients spelled an end to that effort. There was barely room for us to walk between pallets, and the later arrivals had only blankets between them and the stone floor.

It was not that there was any shortage of supplies. I was sent to purchase grain, wine, oil, and firewood in abundance. Even the medicinal compounds ordered by Sosthenes were in plentiful supply. Financial contributions, it seemed, were easy to make. Money was as much a salve to the religious conscience as it was an aid to the suffering.

None of the Temple officials came in person. Only four menial-task matrons from the women's prison appeared in response to El'azar's plea for assistance. Those wealthy enough to have servants wanted no risk that the plague would come home with their servants, so they sent no servants.

And the four that had been dispatched were almost worse than no help, El'azar confided to me. I was daily sent to Bethany for supplies. Always I was grateful my duties did not keep me in the hall day and night. I saw plainly the toll that the task was taking on El'azar.

With twenty patients each to care for, every day was a constant circuit of spooning broth, swabbing throats, attending to sanitary needs, stoking the fires, and starting all over again. It seemed whenever El'azar asked one of the crones to work faster, she had an excuse even before his criticism was complete. If he requested one to stand in for him while he prepared medication, they acted so aggrieved and put-upon that he finally quit trying.

Nor did night bring relief. El'azar's moments of sleep were interrupted by the Sparrows' fits of coughing and choking and calls for water. The grizzled-haired matrons never heard the pleas; perhaps their own snoring drowned out all disturbances.

El'azar struggled to keep his anxiety in check, as well as his temper. On one hand, the treatment was working. But though no more of the Sparrows had died, many more were clearly in the grip of the disease. El'azar sensed the situation balanced on a knife's edge. He was exhausted. The three remaining assistants claimed to need rest as well, though how that could be true, El'azar could not fathom. The fourth had run away the day before, leaving the already crushing shared labor to be further increased.

El'azar needed help, and it was needed immediately. He and I could not keep up with the task. This chamber of hope could still become a charnel house.

Sitting with his back to the entry doors—to keep another servant from fleeing and because there was no other free space—El'azar felt the cold draft that was greater than the trickle of pale light filtering through the cracks. Nevertheless, he seized the moment to pen a note for me to carry to his sisters.

Need help at once, it said.

I hastened to Bethany with El'azar's plea tucked into my tunic. The weather had turned foul again. Drizzle soaked through my coat and dampened my spirits as well. If only we could ride to Yeshua and ask Him to return . . . for even one hour! Then all would be well.

Our own strength was failing. How many times had I seen Yeshua speak but a single word and effect an immediate recovery? El'azar and I had prayed in the name of Yeshua, yet our patients had not been healed fully. Though the advance of the disease had been halted, the boys continued to lie weak upon their beds. We labored on, feeding, washing, nursing them day and night. But they did not progress.

The spies of High Priest Caiaphas lurked outside, waiting to spring the trap if Yeshua appeared.

The situation seemed hopeless to me as I hurried to Bethany and pounded on the gate of the estate.

Old Tavita drew me into the warmth of the fire. I explained what was happening as I gulped a bowl of hot stew.

It was Miryam who made the decision. "Everything that happened now is meant to prove that God keeps his covenant with us. Yeshua has promised that if we have faith, we can do what he is able to do! Yeshua has promised us this! He would not have left the work for us to do if it was impossible. Come, Tavita! You'll go with me. Marta, you must stay to care for the children here."

"Aye," Tavita agreed. "Yeshua must not return to Yerushalayim. They expect him to come, but we'll go instead."

And so it was decided that easily. Though we could not know it at the time, we were on a path of grief that would lead us to the greatest joy we could ever know.

PART VI

THE SEVEN GIFTS

We have different gifts, according to the grace given us.

If a man's gift is prophesying, let him use it in proportion to his faith.

If it is serving, let him serve;

if it is teaching, let him teach;

if it is encouraging, let him encourage;

if it is contributing to the needs of others, let him give generously;

if it is leadership, let him govern diligently;

if it is showing mercy, let him do it cheerfully.

ROMANS 12:6-8

Two guards from the Temple police stood outside the warehouse, keeping watch in shifts in case Yeshua appeared.

"It's good we came," Miryam remarked solemnly to Tavita. The distinctive barking coughs echoed in the warehouse and left no doubt that the diagnosis of diphtheria was correct. "I count 109 boys. Peniel says the youngest is four. Oldest eleven."

Daylight seeped in from high barred windows. A dozen charcoal braziers warmed the space. Those children lying nearest the fires fared better than those on the outer perimeter.

"Aye. Little ones. Pity." The old woman tottered after Miryam and me through the rows of pallets. "If Yeshua were here . . ."

"El'azar is right. We can't send for him. Since Yeshua has gone, we'll manage. We have the strength to do what must be done."

Tavita paused for breath on the pretext of checking the lantern. She inclined her head to the far end of the room. There stood the three ragged female servants from the debtor's prison who had been conscripted to assist El'azar. The three crones were idle in spite of groans for attention from the sea of children. Two of the women stretched filthy hands to the warmth of a fire and cast furtive glances toward us. The third, tattered gray strands of hair half covering her face, whittled a toothpick from a goose quill.

Tavita scowled. "Filthy creatures. I see the quality of aid the masters of Yerushalayim have sent your good brother. They've managed to spare the crones who empty the chamber pots of the prisoners."

Miryam nodded her reply, then picked her way purposefully toward the trio. Alarm and resentment were plain in the expressions of the servants as she approached. They did not budge. Hands grasped for warmth. The knife flickered over the quill.

Miryam introduced herself curtly. "Shalom. I am Miryam of Bethany, sister to Master El'azar."

The one crone tested the tip of the quill, her head barely inclined in acknowledgment. "Aye, mistress. I am Rapha. Your brother. Master El'azar? He's sleeping now?"

"After a week without sleep." Tavita's eyes narrowed, defending El'azar.

"Soon enough they'll all sleep. Hopeless cases, these are, though your brother, kindhearted gentleman as he is, doesn't admit it." The second hag examined her broken nails.

The three cowered closer to the coals. "There'll soon be a hundred corpses laid out neat as can be in this room. We've been on burial detail before. Preparin' bodies of them as dies in prison. We know what to do when the time comes."

Rapha seemed satisfied with the sharpness of the quill. "No one to help but us three who were conscripted by the doctor because we have survived this plague."

A chorus of coughs echoed all around.

Miryam leveled a steely gaze at the uncaring face. "There is much to do. Past time to feed the boys."

Rapha sniffed. "They won't eat. Your brother tells us, 'Make them drink the broth.' But they set their teeth when anyone but your brother tries to make them drink. So we drink it."

"You've left it all to Master El'azar and Peniel?" Tavita clenched her fists.

"It's a cold day," remarked the third crone. "Very cold indeed."

Rapha pocketed the quill and turned her backside to the brazier. She whined, "My lords of the Sanhedrin sent your brother bad charcoal.

We spend all our day keeping up the fires. Cooking broth and such. Your brother tends to the boys, feeding them as will eat and emptying the chamber pots."

Tavita narrowed her eyes again.

Miryam grimaced. "El'azar says you're from the women's prison."

"What of it?"

Miryam raised her chin and lowered her voice to a menacing whisper. "So El'azar has been dealing with you . . . as well as the illness. Rapha is your name? Well, Rapha, let me tell you how it is. One word from me, and the guards outside this gate will carry you away. Back to prison. And I will guarantee you accommodations in the darkest, blackest hole if you don't obey every order. Understand? Tavita is the general. I am her captain. You remain here by her will alone."

Fearful nods and sudden deference replaced defiance in the expressions of the three.

Tavita's lip curled with authority as she issued the first command. "First, we rearrange the patients. Ten boys to each brazier. Heads toward the warmth at the center. Feet out like the spokes of a wheel."

The trio did not move. Their moment of hesitation was too long.

"You!" Miryam glared at the woman with the quill. "You will obey every order given by Tavita or back to prison with you! And you two. Get up. Begin there! Move the pallets in close to the fires or in an hour you will be shivering in the blackest hole of the prison."

El'azar slurred the names as he gave the nighttime instructions for medicines. He was fatigued to the point of near collapse and he knew it. I saw in the compassion on Miryam's face that she recognized it also. "Go back to sleep, Brother," she urged. "Tavita and Peniel and I will finish up the chores."

For once El'azar allowed his little sister to give him orders. Nodding wearily, he rolled himself into a blanket and curled up in his accustomed place near the gates. A major disaster had been averted; no more deaths had occurred, and several of the first to be taken ill were on the mend and now able to help their brother Sparrows.

As El'azar drifted off toward sleep, I overheard Miryam whispering to one of her charges, "Now, you're Lamech, right, child? Of course

I remember your name! Such a brave, strong boy. Here, now, open wide. This will sting a bit, but it's because you're getting well."

From across the room Tavita's shrill piping echoed. "But you must drink all of it! This tonic doesn't just help you get well; it makes your muscles grow too. You don't want to be the only scrawny Sparrow, do you? That's it, lamb! Nasty stuff, but you've drained it all. Well done!"

The Master often said to His followers, "You are the light of the world. You are the salt of the earth."[36]

Light to illuminate the dark corners of despair. Salt to remove the bitter taste of hopelessness and substitute the savor of joy.

At last I understood what the Master meant.

⚘

El'azar awoke to a miracle of organization. For the first time in a week we could see individual children instead of one undulating swamp of misery. The barking of croup was stilled. The air was warm and smelled of soap and ointment and simmering chicken broth.

Clean beds were made up for the ailing boys within five hours of Miryam's and Tavita's arrival. Spotless linen and blankets were laid on fresh straw. Jerusalem's Sparrows, bathed and dressed in soft cotton shifts, were fed soup and now lay in groups like spokes in a wheel, ten boys to each hub. Hot water for washing simmered over fires at the center of each circle.

The prison hags were set to work burning filthy clothes and boiling usable linens in the walled area behind the hospital.

El'azar observed Miryam with a new respect. She coaxed broth down the swollen throat of a four-year-old who lay limp as a rag in her arms. The swelling in his neck seemed less pronounced. This little one had not been expected to live, yet he gazed serenely up into Miryam's face.

"Dan? You can do this for me, eh? Just a swallow. I know, I know, but I promise you'll feel better tomorrow . . . yes. Yes. That's it, love. One more now. I'll stay near you. Yes. I promise." She cradled him and hummed with pleasure and approval at his efforts to drink the broth. Then she rocked him until he dozed off.

How did she know the child's name? El'azar and I had labored for a week and had not learned the names of any of the boys. I ran a hand over my aching head.

Nearby Tavita smoothed back the hair of an eleven-year-old boy, kissing his brow. The boy raised a trembling hand in gratitude, then let it fall back. Tavita said something to him and he smiled. Then she noticed El'azar. With a confident nod she shuffled toward him. Hand on her back, she appeared pained but pleased.

"A wonder," El'azar remarked. "Peniel and I've been treading water for a week while all around me . . . it seemed so hopeless."

The old woman raised exultant eyes toward the ceiling in thanks, then clasped El'azar's arm. "Praise be to Adonai! Master El'azar, while you slept we have washed 'em and anointed 'em and prayed for 'em. For every child. There is a mighty power in Yeshua's name! Poor wee things. Not one has had a mother's care, some for many a year. Miryam and me, we prayed and claimed health and life for them in the name of Yeshua of Nazareth. See for yourself . . . the light in their eyes! Miryam and me, we have prayed as he told us and, I am certain now, the heavenly Father heard our prayer. 'B'Shem, Yeshua,' we cried and life returned to their faces. Fevers fled, though still they are weak and must be fed and nursed.

"Didn't Yeshua teach us that the Eternal Father sees from heaven when even one sparrow falls![37] Are these boys not more important? Aye! Here it is! We have prayed and already see the tide turning. He who knows all things has heard. Oh, Master El'azar, here's proof! The very name of Yeshua means salvation! He holds every child in the palm of his hand."

φ

"It's nothing," High Priest Caiaphas had said. "Recover? They'll all die. Prayers or no prayers. What has Yeshua of Nazareth to do with sick link boys in Yerushalayim? The imposter is somewhere else. And if a handful survive? Yeshua cannot take credit for the charity human hands have given."

But after two weeks without another death, it became clear something wonderful had happened in the olive oil warehouse. Not one more Sparrow's soul had flown away! The children grew stronger every day.

Even with the repudiation of miracles by the high priest, the *am ha aretz* were stirred by the story of so many ragged boys surviving such a great and terrible plague. How had this been accomplished if it was not a miracle wrought by the disciples of the great Rabbi Himself?

The three prison hags, muttering complaints of overwork against El'azar, Miryam, Tavita, and me, were returned to their former haunt. Suddenly new faces of volunteers appeared at the gates of the olive oil warehouse. Two weeks and a day had passed when ben Dives himself, not wishing to be outshone by a farmer from Bethany, paraded through the streets of Jerusalem with a train of donkeys laden with supplies. Trumpets announced his arrival. There followed a retinue of servants wearing the livery of Jerusalem's wealthiest merchants. These were sent to assist in two twelve-hour shifts. The epidemic feared by the authorities of Jerusalem had been halted. They declared hard work had accomplished the feat. It was no true miracle, they said.

"My medicine," declared the Greek physician as he strode through the hospital and peered down the gullets of those children he had expected to be long gone.

In the souks of the city, the wonder was discussed and credit for the good deed advertised and put to use peddling merchandise.

"My charcoal," boasted the charcoal contractor to all who passed his booth.

"My blankets." The wool merchant held up the cheap fabric, much thinner than that which El'azar had purchased to cover the sick Sparrows.

"My barley." The grain merchant let the grain thinned with sand sift through his fingers. He went on to extol the miraculous advantages of barley grown near the seacoast.

"My bread," declared the baker, waving a thick, crusted loaf of tough, gritty bread. He guaranteed the healthful benefit of his product.

"Our righteousness," proclaimed the religious leaders of the nation. "Our prayers! Our ritual! Our strict observance of the Law! Not any doing of that charlatan Yeshua!"

⚓

At the diffident tap on his office door, High Priest Caiaphas glanced up from a sheaf of papers. An irritated expression was planted on his flushed features, and he flicked his palm upward with annoyance.

"What now, ben Dives? One interruption after another! My accounting of the korban is due tomorrow. How can I work with all these interruptions?"

Korban monies were those set aside to purchase sacrifices in the Temple. Any other application was considered sacrilegious. Even when Governor Pilate, with Caiaphas' approval, used the funds to build an aqueduct, there had been a riot in which many had died. That event, however, had not stopped Caiaphas from skimming from the treasury for his own aggrandizement, but he was now much more creative in the ways he accounted for the funds.

"Your pardon, lord, but I have something of interest in a special matter you charged me with."

"All right," Caiaphas grudgingly allowed. "Make it brief!"

Following ben Dives into the chamber was the largest of the prison matrons, recently discharged from assisting with the sick Sparrows. At the sight of her pinched features, oily, knotted hair, and soiled shift, Caiaphas' nose wrinkled with disgust.

Anticipating another protest from his master, ben Dives hurriedly explained, "In regard to the charlatan of Nazareth. At my order this woman was working with El'azar of Bethany, a known associate of Yeshua."

Caiaphas pushed his chair backward so abruptly the legs screeched across the marble floor. "In the plague ward? Are you mad? Get her out of here at once!"

"Bless you, sir," the hag crooned through the gap in her front teeth. "Not plague. The strangling sickness. There's a power of difference between—"

At a backhand cuff from ben Dives the woman shut up instantly. "Only speak when I ask a question, wretch," he ordered. Then to reassure Caiaphas, he added, "This woman lives amid all the diseases of the prison, my lord. She can go anywhere freely, it seems."

Caiaphas folded his hands together and ducked his chin into them. He acted calm but seemed to be holding his breath. "Go on," he demanded curtly.

"Woman, did you hear the name Yeshua of Nazareth mentioned while at the infirmary?" ben Dives interrogated.

The prison matron ducked her head out of reach of ben Dives' fist before replying. "Aye. That I did. More than once."

"By whom?"

"By that wicked woman, El'azar's sister, the one called Miryam. And by her servant . . . spiteful, bossy, arrogant old crone. Why she once—" At the mere flick of ben Dives' finger the hag's commentary stopped. "Tavita, her name is. And later, by Lord El'azar hisself."

"And what was said? How did his name come into it?"

Caiaphas leaned forward despite his obvious reluctance to be in the same room with the matron. "Plotting treason? Called him Messiah, did they? Mentioned his hiding place?"

"Oh no, your worship! Much worse than them things. Witchcraft, it was! They conjured with his name, they did!"

Caiaphas did not seem properly impressed, so ben Dives urged the woman to elaborate. "Were you surprised at the way the illness progressed?"

"Surprised? Amazed, one should say! I've seed many a pestilence in my time. I know this stranglin' sickness well too. Mostly all the young ones and old ones die of it. All! No fewer than half always die. Ten days . . . two weeks . . . most of 'em gone. But this time, not one more death. Not one. It ain't natural, I tell you."

Caiaphas was puzzled. "Not a single death? How do you account for that?"

"Ain't I been tellin' you?" the crone responded with asperity. "They was doin' magic! 'In the name of . . . ,' you know," she said, dropping her tone dramatically. "Conjurin', they was. And since then, no more sick ones come in. And all of 'em gettin' well. Not a single dead one with his throat all blown up and tongue a-stickin' out all black and swollen." She sounded disappointed.

"And you'll swear to this?" Caiaphas demanded. "Are there other witnesses?"

The hag got a sly gleam in her eye. "As many as you needs, your worship. Only let me do the arrangin', if you take my meanin'."

"Not a word of this to anyone!" Caiaphas commanded sternly. Then to ben Dives, "Give her silver and send her away. But know where to find her."

"It shall be done, lord," ben Dives agreed, bowing.

"And ben Dives," Caiaphas added, "I want you to take personal charge of the infirmary. Send El'azar and his people home. And warn them I don't want anyone spreading nonsense around Yerushalayim that the name of that country preacher has any power. See to it."

The journey from the house of the high priest to the warehouse hospital was a short walk. The supplies might have been easily transported on a single cart and unloaded without notice by two servants. But efficiency would have ruined the effect of the high priest's generosity for the recovering paupers.

Ra'nabel ben Dives, ever mindful of the public image of Caiaphas, issued the order for provisions to be loaded onto the backs of ten donkeys. An advance of three trumpeters announced ben Dives' approach at the head of the train. Forty liveried servants, including the head of Caiaphas' household staff, followed after.

"Make way for Ra'nabel ben Dives, chief secretary of *cohen hagadol* Lord Caiaphas! Stand aside, all citizens of Yerushalayim, for the gifts of charity offered for the welfare of those ailing orphan link boys, dependent on the charity of Lord Caiaphas!"

Ben Dives, prayer shawl covering his head, hands raised in salutation of the One True God of Israel, prayed loudly as he walked. The route taken to the warehouse was circuitous rather than direct. Thus the common people of the city were able to witness and comprehend the generosity of the House of Caiaphas.

The contents of supplies on the pack animals were read loudly for all to hear. The public was, in this way, impressed and even awed by the righteousness, deeds, and generosity of their high priest.

The stone steps of the warehouse were swept clean and scrubbed, a marked contrast to the sewage that coursed down the center of the street. A trumpet flourish announced ben Dives' arrival. The head servant pounded impatiently on the double wooden doors. Within moments El'azar and his sister Miryam appeared.

El'azar appeared pleased at the enormity of the gift from Caiaphas. His expression faded as ben Dives, smiling, climbed the steps and bowed ever so slightly.

Ben Dives' voice echoed through the streets, turning the heads of the curious. "Shalom! Greetings from Lord Caiaphas, *cohen hagadol* of all the people of Israel, to Master El'azar of Bethany!"

"Shalom," El'azar replied quietly as though ben Dives were a tradesman and not among the most important men in Jerusalem.

Ben Dives made certain his side of the conversation was loud enough to be heard at a distance. "Lord Caiaphas has heard the plight of these destitute children, ill and dying here, in need of charity and sustenance."

"All help is welcome. The danger is past, all praise be to our Eternal Lord. The boys are recovering. Daily gaining strength."

"Lord Caiaphas and the Sanhedrin understand the risk of death to these destitute beggars. The danger of contagion is great. It thanks the house of El'azar for its good service." He turned slightly, gesturing to the cadre of helpers. "So, El'azar, we have come. Your services are no longer required. You and your sister and your slave are . . . commended. You are to return to Bethany."

El'azar's brow furrowed. "We're doing well here. We . . . pardon me." El'azar coughed into his hand, then continued, "We welcome your assistance but . . ."

Ben Dives' smile hardened. He lowered his voice. "Hear me, El'azar, for I speak with the voice of Caiaphas. You are commanded to return to your own home and your own place. It has been reported that an incantation of magic has been used in the treatment of the boys. The link boys are all beggars under the care of the Sanhedrin and the Temple authorities. You are relieved of this . . . task."

"But, sir," Miryam began to protest, "the boys are getting on well. The danger is past. May we not—"

Ben Dives' lip curled with disdain, silencing her. His eyes glinted with cold fury. "You, madam. It seems you have led your esteemed brother astray about the Nazarene. A dangerous deception. In his mercy, Lord Caiaphas allows you to remain free . . . in spite of the fact that you are an open supporter of Yeshua. But now you indoctrinate these innocent boys with your blasphemy. It is reported you practiced some witchcraft over them, calling upon the name of Yeshua, whom we all know is a servant of the Evil One. You and your brother are to gather your things and return to your home . . . by tomorrow."

Miryam dispatched me to Bethany with a note for her sister to which El'azar added a brief postscript of his own. I was to deliver the message and then return at once to help with the abrupt departure.

Clouds closed over the sky. It was a gloomy, sodden day. The overnight drizzle soaked the road from Jerusalem. The children on the Bethany estate remained indoors today. The aroma of baking bread drifted through the rooms of the expansive mansion. In her classroom Marta taught five small girls their alef-bet.

I hailed the house from outside the walls. My voice croaked as I shouted up at the gate of the Bethany estate.

"Word from Lord El'azar and Lady Miryam. A message for their sister, Marta of Bethany!"

I was admitted into the courtyard by the old gatekeeper. The servant escorted me to Marta, who dismissed her five-year-old students.

"A message from your brother! Aye! He's sent word!"

Marta opened the note and scanned the contents.

Communication itself was no surprise. Many days El'azar and Miryam sent urgent requests for provisions from Jerusalem to their sister in Bethany. News had been both hopeful and grim as the fight to save the lives of the Sparrows continued. The boys were recovering, thanks to warmth, good food, and proper care. The doctor believed a major epidemic had been averted by the timely intervention of El'azar and Miryam.

Each morning, as Marta supervised the packing of supplies, there was a smile of satisfaction on her face. She considered that after the initial contributions no one else in all Judea had bothered to help the worthless link boys of the Holy City. Apart from the first pangs of conscience, the Sanhedrin had taken a "wait and see" attitude. Why expend funds on beggars who were going to die anyway?

The additional burden was a perverse source of pride for Marta. I had heard Marta pray, "Blessed are you, O Adonai, who remembers the deeds of the righteous. Only our house, eh? Yes? Only the family of El'azar. Surely the Almighty will reward us and our brother and sister for taking on such a task. I've counted the sum of our contribution, and it is considerable! El'azar has spared no expense on the urchins. Far beyond the required tithe. So now people will see how God favors the righteous in dark times."

Today the letter was in Miryam's handwriting.

Dearest Marta,

Not a single lamb has been lost since the first day. The doctor declares that the survival of the children is a miracle. He wonders aloud and tells all he meets that before this day he has never heard of so many ill who have survived diphtheria. Many of the wealthy are sending more servants to help with the care of those who recuperate. Our brother is hailed among the rulers of Yerushalayim as a truly righteous man. But now others seek their own glory, so we are dismissed! We're coming home tomorrow.

And there was an ominous postscript to the good news, written in a shaky hand.

Doris, the plump cook, appeared in the doorway and peered out at me. "School finished early? What news today? El'azar wants a flock of chickens and Miryam calls for another milk goat? They're eating better than we are."

Marta read the words slowly, deciphering what they meant. "El'azar and Miryam are coming home tomorrow. El'azar says we should prepare the empty vintner's cottage, behind the grain barn. He will . . . he'll be staying there, she says. Miryam will remain there with him. He'll be staying there . . . for a time."

"What?" Doris placed her fists on ample hips and scowled. Then she scowled at the letter in Miryam's hand. "El'azar? In that shack? Why?"

Marta replied, "My dear girl, ten days and nights El'azar has lived among contagion breath from the mouth of hell. Before this time it has carried away the young and strong as easily as the elderly and feeble. We've a houseful of babes and mothers here to protect. El'azar's taken ill. Or he expects to."

Doris lifted her chin and tossed her head. "Master El'azar? Ill? Never. Why would he who has been declared righteous by the Jewish religious leaders be stricken of God after . . . after such a righteous action? God would not permit such injustice."

Marta sighed and folded the letter, slipping it into her pocket. She caught my eye. "Please, Peniel. If you would supervise. See to it the cottage is clean. Two beds. Set the fire. Plenty of provisions. Warm. Mistress Miryam and Tavita and you will care for El'azar in shifts."

"Lady Miryam, working like a slave?" Doris protested.

"My sister survived the illness as a child. A light case, they said."

The gatekeeper concurred. "And Tavita also!" He nodded. "When the diphtheria swept through Yerushalayim thirty-two years ago. Yom Kippur. Thousands of pilgrims died that year. Strangled two of my own dear brothers. Tavita's case was called a light case." The old man clapped his hands in dismay. "Light, eh? Light, you say! There is no light case. Eh? Only those who lives and those who dies of it."

He peered at Marta through rheumy eyes. "And when your poor wee sister was sick. Remember, mistress? Remember how you wept outside the door for your little sister! Poor wee Miryam! As if this family could ever forget that nightmare. Wee Miryam home from Yerushalayim at Tabernacles. Barking like a dog. Nose bloody. Throat blue, then gray, and then black. Little chest heaving. A miracle Miryam survived that! The ears of the Almighty took a beating from your father's prayers, I can tell you! None could go near Miryam but Tavita herself. Tavita had survived the great plague in the time of the Butcher King. So she alone could nurse Miryam. In exchange for Miryam's life, Tavita bargained away every transgression she ever enjoyed! Turned the house upside down for weeks."

Marta's face softened at the memory. "They wouldn't let me near. . . ." She nodded, remembering and recounting to me Miryam's pitiful cries. Throat and lungs near bursting. Marta's sister had been only eight years old. Tavita had hovered over Miryam like a mother bird. Up at night to cool her fever. Coaxing broth down her throat by day. How close Miryam had come to dying! Night after night

Marta had fallen asleep in the next room with Miryam's coughing and Tavita's prayers seeping through the walls. Marta had wondered if her sister would ever awaken.

The old man continued, wheezing out memories and conclusions. "Remember what El'azar wrote us? The doctor conscripted helpers from among those who had survived the disease. A good chance they would not get the illness twice. So is the rumor. I did not speak my fear at the time. . . . I've been a servant of this house since before Master El'azar was born. Your brother was never ill as a boy. Never."

Marta closed her eyes. "We don't know he's got it. . . ." Her expression clouded. "Do we? Do we?" She glared at the letter as though it was a betrayal of blessings.

The gatekeeper nodded solemnly. "If your brother has taken ill, none but Tavita and Miryam can assist. Those two . . . they can pull Master El'azar through. He's strong. Lady Miryam is strong. Tavita is old and tough. She won't die until she's ready, eh?"

It was early the next morning when we placed hands on each boy's brow and prayed for God's blessing in the name of Yeshua.

As Miryam kissed the lads good-bye, many cried and asked her not to leave.

"I can't stay," she explained. "But I'll pray for you to grow stronger every day. Remember where your true strength comes from."

Finally El'azar, in a hoarse voice, quietly admonished each Sparrow to recall something: No matter what ben Dives claimed, the miracle of healing had been accomplished in their lives by prayers offered in the name of Yeshua of Nazareth.

All had survived! Not one had been lost! Who had ever heard of such a thing?

Trumpets announced the arrival of ben Dives. Outside the entrance to the warehouse he prayed loudly as a crowd gathered. "Consider our righteousness, O Adonai! You see our good deeds for these Sparrows, who are the lowest of humanity! We thank you, O Adonai, that we are more righteous than others! Consider the charity we have offered to restore their health! Reward our righteous deeds and grant our nation and the House of Lord Caiaphas continued prosperity!"

18

It was I who opened the gate for El'azar.

"It's good to be back home again," El'azar said.

I tried to count the days of our absence but could not make the sums add up properly. We had been away two Sabbaths . . . or was it three?

Despite the warmth of the sun heating the still air, El'azar was chilled. I saw how pale he was. He dismissed his weakness as the result of weeks without sleep. He told me rest was what he needed to put him right. A few nights of uninterrupted sleep and regular meals, and his strength would quickly return.

El'azar admitted to us he had no hunger. In fact, the sight and smell of food made his throat constrict. He refused to be worried by that fact and trusted it would soon change. He told us that with one day of meals prepared to his liking from his own kitchen, his usual hearty appetite would come roaring back.

I watched El'azar touch his fingertips to the swelling beneath the line of his jaw, then quickly drop his hand lest Miryam see the gesture and make more of it than it implied. Not ill, just weary. The slight soreness at the back of his throat; the need to harrumph before speaking—none of these irritations suggested anything serious. Not really.

Moving into the vacant vintner's cottage was merely a proper precaution for the sake of all the young ones who sheltered at the house. Besides, it would be quieter there. So much bustle of mothers and children around the manor house; he would rest better with a little more seclusion. Moreover, El'azar did not want to be a bother, did not want to interrupt the daily routine. What he hoped was that the flow of life in Bethany would quickly return to normal, before the diphtheria so disrupted their lives.

Tavita and I hurried ahead of the siblings. Marta and a row of servants had gathered to welcome El'azar back.

"Please," El'azar said. His voice sounded weaker than he intended. He tried again, louder and with greater force: "Please clear a path for me. I've been exposed to a dangerous disease. There is no fear of infection from Miryam or Tavita, but I . . . I must ask all of you to be careful and not come near me."

"Dear brother!" Marta cried, stepping forward.

El'azar's hand shot out, palm toward her. "No, Marta!" he enjoined harshly. Then more gently, "Marta? Is the cottage ready?"

Marta nodded, biting her lower lip.

"Good." El'azar tried to make his voice cheerful to overcome the hurt he saw in her eyes. "I'll sleep. Just for a bit. Tomorrow I'll be strong as ever. Don't worry. A few days only. We must stay on the safe side."

Miryam sat across the room from El'azar. While he dozed fitfully, she kept watch and prayed. I kept the fire roaring.

Tavita, carrying a basket of food, entered the vintner's cottage. "A hearty meal for you, love," she told Miryam. "You must keep up your strength, eh? True. Look at you! Wasting away as if you're also sick. Mistress Marta is frantic. She says she'll not be held back from seein' your poor brother."

"She mustn't come. She's never had diphtheria."

"Then you'll have to tell her yourself. Won't you take a break now? I'll stay with young Master El'azar. Go on now. Back to the house. Sleep awhile."

"No. Tavita, I won't leave him. I want to be here when he wakes up. Tell Marta . . . tell her when he begins to recover, then she may come."

"Ha! Tell Marta?" The old woman screwed up her face in a wrinkled protest. "As you say. But it doesn't seem to me that Master El'azar is recoverin' quite like the wee Sparrows in Yerushalayim." With a shrug and a sigh of resignation, she left the cottage.

El'azar groaned in his sleep, and instinctively Miryam rose and went to his side, placing her palm on his forehead. She said to me, "It's hot—not terribly so, but fevered." Miryam bit her lip.

El'azar appeared to me exactly like the Sparrows in the early stages of diphtheria.

Her touch, light as it was, woke him.

Red-rimmed eyes regarded her and the room without recognition for a moment. Then El'azar coughed twice and endeavored to sit up.

"Sorry . . . sorry," Miryam said. "Didn't mean to disturb you."

"Have you . . ." El'azar put his hand to his throat and grimaced. Shaking his head as if to deny the soreness, he croaked, ". . . been here long? No need. Just sleeping."

Miryam did not deny her concern but shrugged and handed him a carved wooden mug of water. He swallowed in tiny sips. After El'azar drained the cup, he handed it back to her with a sigh. "Don't worry about me," he protested. "Tired. Not enough sleep."

Miryam nodded sympathetically. "All the same, I added lemon to the kettle." She pointed to the cook fire, where a lazy curlicue of steam carried the tang of citrus. "It will help you rest."

"Just . . ." El'azar's voice rasped and Miryam saw a stab of pain cross his eyes. ". . . a winter cold. Don't worry. Two days, I'll be good as—" He coughed and his hand went to his throat again.

We did not speak the words, but the thought was in our minds: *If only Yeshua were here!* El'azar would be well in an instant. Of that I was confident.

As it was, Miryam straightened her brother's bedclothes and plumped up a pillow behind his head. "Cook made broth. Tavita just brought it fresh. Would you like some?"

El'azar shook his head. "Rest first." His head sagged wearily.

Confidently, Miryam prayed, "O Adonai Elohim, in the name of Yeshua, please heal my brother. He's a good man. Quickly restore his health. We saw a true miracle with the Sparrows. So many little boys alive because El'azar cared. I know you won't deny the same for El'azar. I know you'll make him well."

I made my bed in a lean-to shelter off the rear of the cottage. When I emerged, the midwinter sun set early beyond the Mount of Olives. A dun sky promised a cold night but offered no rain.

Miryam dozed in the chair beside the fire. I wondered if she dreamed of a younger El'azar with curly russet and gold hair . . . without any gray in his beard.

The distant barking of a dog did not fully rouse her. Vaguely, I considered if foxes were after Marta's chickens again. Marta was an implacable foe to anything that disturbed the orderliness of her household.

The barking grew louder, more insistent.

Miryam sat up with a start. I turned around in alarm. The hacking croup came from El'azar! The room was dimly lit by the fading gleam of the coals. There was no lamp burning as yet.

In the pale orange light Miryam saw her brother raised up and leaning on one elbow. His eyes were wide and staring, and his face was flushed. He was strangling!

Miryam surged out of her chair. "El'azar! I'm here! Try to be calm!"

There was a bottle of oil of camphor on a shelf above the bed. I fetched it for Miryam. She doused a rag with the pungent liquid and thrust it under his nose.

El'azar gasped for air. Every other breath was punctuated with a sharp, forceful cough with an almost metallic-sounding ring.

"Adonai! In the name of Yeshua, help!" Miryam cried aloud.

The choking fit subsided. El'azar's breathing deepened, then slowed, as the airways reopened and his terror decreased.

Miryam lit a pair of lamps and I stoked the fire. She hummed a bit of Psalm 91 as she worked.

"Miryam? Is that you?" El'azar inquired, though she was in plain sight.

Struggling to control her sudden apprehension at such an odd question, Miryam replied calmly, "Yes, of course! I've been right here. Was it a bad dream?"

"Yes . . . no . . . I can't see well. Everything's blurry."

Swallowing hard, Miryam employed as light a tone as she could manage: "It's the light. I'll light the lamp!"

"I ache . . . I ache all over. Poor lads! So . . . small . . ." A mercifully short paroxysm interrupted El'azar's expression of sympathy.

"All the boys got well!" Miryam reminded herself as well as her brother. "The Almighty's help in the name of Yeshua made them well. Tonight you're hurting, but tomorrow morning you'll be better. Now here, let me get you some broth."

"It seems your plan did not work out as expected," High Priest Caiaphas observed to Ra'nabel ben Dives as the two men met in the courtyard of Caiaphas' home. "Yeshua of Nazareth did not return to come to the aid of the Yerushalayim beggars."

"True, my lord. But your own generosity is widely praised. You are being proclaimed 'healer of the people.'"

Caiaphas sniffed. "Exactly the title I told them to spread around. But that was not the point! Everyone is claiming some part in the charity. It's even still being said that prayers in Yeshua's name effected the cure . . . or at least warded off the spread of the disease."

Ben Dives' eyes glittered and his head tilted to the side as he smiled. "There is later news still more to the point."

"Make it quick then," Caiaphas said with a shrug. "I have important guests coming for supper."

"I have received a report from one of my agents that El'azar of Bethany is himself ill. Very ill, it is said. Likely he has the leather-hide disease himself."

Caiaphas turned from examining one of his potted pomegranate trees. "Go on."

Boyish charm exuded from ben Dives as he explained. "You understand, my lord, that this El'azar is a close friend of Yeshua. Now the situation is even better than before. Either Yeshua will return and we will seize him, or he will stay away. If he does not come back, he will be thought a coward or perhaps afraid to suffer exposure as a fraud. And if El'azar should die . . ."

"Then Yeshua could not even save a close friend, and his name and power will be recognized as useless!" Caiaphas concluded.

"Just so, my lord."

Caiaphas nodded judiciously. "Keep me informed, ben Dives. Why don't you come to supper after next Sabbath?"

A bright yellow sun shone cheerfully. As if in gratitude, the almond trees at the corners of the Bethany estate were crowned with sprays of pinkish-white blossoms. Miryam gestured out the window at the showy display, but El'azar merely grunted in reply, then fell into a fit of feeble coughing.

I had just brought a steaming tureen of soup from the villa. Miryam inhaled appreciatively. She acted aware of her own hunger. After seeing to El'azar's meal she would feed herself, I knew.

The warmth, the almond blossoms, the renewed appreciation of good food—all these signals combined to reinforce our certainty that Master El'azar was on the mend. Today the world showed every sign of shaking off its winter depression. Surely now El'azar would shake off the last of his lethargy and the aftereffects of the illness.

This is the day we see the power of Yeshua's name, I thought. *Today our prayers and El'azar's kind heart are rewarded.*

Tavita ladled broth into a clay bowl, handing it to Miryam along with a wooden spoon. The old woman cast unhappy glances at El'azar. From Tavita's expression I knew that she saw the same decline that concerned Miryam.

Drawing a stool beside his bed, Miryam offered soup to her brother. Despite the ample warmth of the room, El'azar had the blankets drawn up under his chin. His eyes blinked at the spoon, and he shivered and shook his head.

"But you must eat to recover your strength," Miryam urged. "If you take nourishment, you'll be up and around by this time tomorrow."

El'azar turned his face toward the window. "Thro . . . hurrrs," he managed to growl. "Mebbe eat lay-er."

Miryam seemed surprised that El'azar's words were slurred. Clearly she had expected her own buoyant emotion to be shared.

"Let me try, dove," Tavita offered. "I nursed your brother when he was a tiny lad. Come now, El'azar, old Tavita is here. Miryam, there's also a bowl there for you. I know you must be famished."

Trading places with Miryam, Tavita leaned across the patient. She waved the spoonful of soup under his nose to tempt him with the aroma. "Now, Master El'azar," she coaxed as if he were a child, "try a bit of this. Open wide."

His face to the sunshine streaming in the window, El'azar dutifully opened his mouth. Light illuminated his cheeks, shrunken from not eating and gray with fatigue.

Miryam hummed with approval even though we could all see El'azar grimace as he swallowed. Then Tavita stiffened suddenly before squaring her shoulders. "That's it, Master El'azar," the servant crooned. "Good for what ails you. Try another."

El'azar managed to ingest a half dozen dribbles of broth. Then he waved Tavita away with a jerk of his chin. "S'nuff! Don' wan' more."

Tavita stood abruptly. She said brightly, "Well done, Master El'azar! I can tell you're getting better." Gesturing for Miryam and me to follow, she said, "I need to ask your sister a question about . . . about some supplies. It'll just take a moment."

A question about supplies? Addressed to Miryam? Marta handled all those details!

As soon as we were outside the cottage and the door shut, Miryam demanded, "What? What is it? You saw him eat. It hurt him, but he's getting better, right?"

The serving maid tucked her chin. Then she shook her head decisively once. "He has the white patches . . . in his throat. The back of his throat has two thin, white places, each about the size of a penny."

Miryam refused to take the information as an ominous sign. "But he's getting well," she argued again. "Maybe that's a sign of his healing. Maybe those places are where the illness has been, but is no longer. Like a scar."

Tavita sniffed dubiously but said nothing further.

Miryam both suggested and affirmed her own conclusions. "That's it, of course. Peniel! You saw him eating! Go tell Marta. Poor dear, I'm sure she's worried sick! Tell her our brother has eaten and is better."

"And the way he talks?" Tavita queried. "And he's seeing no clearer either. Perhaps we should send Peniel to fetch back the Master?"

"Yeshua loves El'azar. But he can't come back to Judea. Of course the illness has to clear itself out!" Miryam returned sharply, angry at Tavita's doubts. "You'll see. He's on the mend now! We've prayed. We have faith. All will be well. We must just hold on to our faith. Pray he gets his strength back quickly."

19

One night only Miryam allowed Tavita and me to stay with El'azar. A full eight hours of sleep restored Miryam's energy. She hurried to the vintner's cottage.

We emerged from El'azar's sickroom just as Miryam approached. Tavita's face was drawn and troubled. "I-I heard you coming, mistress. I want . . . before you see . . ."

Miryam did not appear to understand. Impatiently she suggested, "He's sitting up and asking for food? Tavita, I know you like surprises, but this is no time for games!"

"Mistress," Tavita said firmly, grasping Miryam's shoulders. "We must send for Yeshua. Today. Now!"

I agreed with the old woman's conclusion.

Incredulous, Miryam shrugged out of Tavita's grasp and pushed past her into the cottage.

El'azar's breathing was labored: gasping intake; shuddering, rasping exhale. His mouth hung open in his sleep. His beard and pillow were crusted with dried mucus. A thin trickle of blood seeped from one nostril.

Tavita slipped up beside Miryam in the room. "You see?" she whispered. "We must send Peniel for the Master at once."

"But El'azar absolutely forbids it," Miryam protested.

The two women retreated into a corner of the room, but I overheard their conversation. "He said Yeshua would be in danger if he returned to Judea now." Miryam hesitated. "No. Of course my brother looks bad, unwashed as he is. He's never stayed in bed this many days in his life! But let him sleep. When he wakes, I'll sponge him and feed him. You'll see. It's not like you to be easily frightened, Tavita. Not like you at all! You're acting more like my sister. Now go on. I'll take over here. In the name of Yeshua of Nazareth, my brother is getting well!"

I had vowed to only be a servant as Master El'azar lay in his sickbed. I observed the confidence of his sister waver, then strengthen. I watched and prayed, saying little, but I was afraid.

El'azar slept fitfully, ragged breaths punctuated with deep sighs. Miryam stirred the embers, then, wrapping her shawl around her shoulders, stepped out into the cool, moonless night.

Sinking down on the stone bench beside the door, Miryam fixed her gaze on the constellation rising in the east. Orion, The Hunter—*Chesil*, the Coming Forth as Light—climbed above the mountains of Moab. He carried his broad shoulders at a confident angle as he strode across the heavens. The glowing sheath of his mighty sword hung from his star-studded belt.

Was Yeshua also watching the turning wheel of night from beyond the Jordan? Could He sense all was not well with His friends in Bethany?

Did Yeshua know that Miryam prayed in His name before the throne of the Eternal Father? that again and again she had claimed God's healing for El'azar?

Even so, the heavens remained silent. The name of Yeshua had not healed Miryam's brother. Her faith had not healed him, nor had expectation changed the circumstance.

El'azar coughed, then moaned in his sleep, shattering the serenity of the night. Miryam sighed and stared toward the faint glow of Jerusalem that outlined the Mount of Olives.

O Lord, how long until you call your angels and defeat our enemies?

Miryam prayed. *Your Word teaches a time of joy and perfection is coming. How long until there is no more sickness or sorrow or death?*

𐤟

Yeshua was safe in Perea. Surrounded by His followers at some cheerful fireside, He no doubt taught them great and mighty truths:

> *"I, even I, am He who comforts you. . . . You have forgotten the Lord your Maker, who stretched out the heavens and laid the foundations of the earth."*[38]

Yeshua's words were Truth, but what did the heavens and the foundations of the earth have to do with El'azar's health? When there was no crisis it was easy to consider who had created the universe. Psalms about the faithfulness of the Almighty were reassuring enough when the need belonged to someone else.

Though we did not speak of it, Miryam seemed to suspect that El'azar was dying. Dying!

She needed more than pretty platitudes about the power of God. The facts in Bethany were grim—indisputably, unrelievedly grim. In spite of loving care and much prayer, El'azar declined hour by hour!

The mighty Eternal God by His word stretched out the heavens and set the stars in place. But did He really care whether El'azar lived or died? Why had He not answered their prayers?

Yeshua, at whose name demons had fled and every sickness had been healed, could not return. Yeshua, in danger of losing His life, could not come back to Judea to heal El'azar!

Miryam gazed up at the cold, unfeeling stars. I heard her pray: "Blessed are you, O Adonai, who heals all our diseases. Blessed are you. But . . . have you not heard our hearts? Oh, Lord! If only Yeshua were here! Then my brother would get well. If only!"

𐤟

Outside the Chamber of Hewn Stone, Gamaliel plucked at Ra'nabel ben Dives' sleeve as the scribe trailed in the wake of Caiaphas. "What news of our brother El'azar of Bethany?" the Pharisee inquired.

"Why ask me?" ben Dives responded, good-natured bewilderment playing across his tawny features.

"You are too modest. Surely nothing in the Holy City or its environs escapes your notice."

Ben Dives' chin rose slightly at the seeming praise, though he kept his eyes modestly downcast. "As it happens, I have received word from Bethany that El'azar is ill. Dangerously so. But he is being attended by an excellent physician, so we won't give up hope."

"No, we won't," Gamaliel responded. "And Yeshua of Nazareth? What news of him?"

"Why, nothing, Reb Gamaliel . . . unless perhaps you have received word yourself?"

Gamaliel made no reply. He attempted to look into ben Dives' eyes, but the scribe's gaze only briefly made contact before skittering away.

Evidently Caiaphas had only just noticed his secretary was missing from his entourage. The high priest made a peremptory gesture of summons and ben Dives bobbed his head with agreement. Over his shoulder he added to Gamaliel, "As to El'azar, we hope he has not waited too long to seek help—or that his hope for help is misplaced! Death is so . . . final."

"So you say, Sadducee. So you say. And perhaps you should hope you're right."

I waited beside the door to carry the message when needed. There was no longer any self-deception in Miryam's thoughts: Her brother was not well; he was not getting well. In fact, he was growing worse.

El'azar could barely swallow. Clear soup or water was all he could manage, and no more than a few drops. Any more made him gag and choke.

When Miryam tried to force him to take more than he wanted, El'azar flung his arm and knocked the spoon from her hand.

The white patches at the back of his throat had grown larger until they merged into a single mass. Without any hope of a positive change, Miryam checked yet again. The membrane appeared even thicker. It had darkened to an ominous gray. "Leather-hide" was how the name of the disease translated. There was no longer any denying that El'azar had the dread condition.

Moreover, El'azar was visibly dropping weight as if shedding extra clothing. His eyes were sunk in his head. His cheekbones protruded. And his hands! Miryam paid particular attention to El'azar's hands. From being strong, smooth, and youthful, now they were an old man's hands: veined and wrinkled. They fidgeted constantly. Even in his sleep they plucked at his throat and at the bedclothes. Miryam could gauge the suffering El'azar experienced in his throat by watching his hands: It was most intense when he wrung them together and clenched them into tight fists.

Almost with a start she noticed El'azar staring at her. She had not even known he was awake. His eyes scanned her features from hairline to chin. Was he trying to say something, or did he not even recognize her?

"Would you like some water?"

A shake of the head.

"Soup, then?"

This question produced only an exhausted tilt of the chin and a clamping shut of his mouth.

"El'azar," Miryam said softly, "I think . . . we mustn't wait any longer. We should call for the Master. Peniel will go to Yerushalayim. Marcus will ride. We need Yeshua—soon! He'll come if we send for him; I know he will!"

With a reserve of strength Miryam did not know El'azar possessed, her brother raised his head and shoulders from the pillow. "No!" he barked. "Naw safe. Naw hav' it!"

"But he's your friend! He should be told. He can decide for him—"

"No! They'd know. Trap him."

We knew whom El'azar meant by "they": Ra'nabel ben Dives and others of the high priest's cadre. There might be spies from Herod Antipas lurking about as well.

El'azar collapsed back on the bed with a spasm of coughing so forceful I thought his eyes would truly pop from his head. When the episode finally subsided El'azar drilled his sister with his gaze. "Promizz me," he ordered through teeth gritted with pain. "Prom's!"

Thinking furiously, Miryam nodded. "Since you ask it," she said, "I won't send for him today."

El'azar's body seemed to collapse into the mattress as if the protest had exhausted another measure of his remaining strength—strength that could not be replaced.

Except in his hands: Knotting and unknotting, grabbing handfuls of beard and clutching at his neck, they resumed their ceaseless motion.

We heard Marta's voice the instant she emerged from the main house. "He's my brother too," Marta shrilled. "You can't keep me away. I must and I will see him!"

A glance at El'azar confirmed he was still sleeping. "Stay here, Peniel," Miryam commanded me. She hurriedly left the cottage to meet Marta and Tavita beside one of the almond trees.

"Mistress, I tried to explain," Tavita said apologetically.

Marta evidently expected Miryam to prevent her from seeing El'azar, for she launched an immediate attack. "You can't keep me out! 'He's better.' 'He's not better.' 'He's much worse!' Something different every time! I must see for myself."

Miryam was too weary to argue and merely stepped aside.

As Marta rushed into the cottage I heard her sharp intake of breath. Even when El'azar's condition had been described, nothing prepared one for his altered appearance.

Miryam stood beside her sister, gravely gazing down at El'azar. His neck, grotesquely swollen from beneath his chin down both sides of his throat, was bull-like in form. It contrasted sharply with the shrunken appearance of his features, as if the throat ailment was growing bigger and more powerful at the expense of the man.

El'azar had been plucking at his beard. In moments of extreme agony his nails had torn his face in long gouges. These fresh scars were red and scaly.

Marta clutched her apron to her face and held it to her mouth as though using it to ward off the horrific vision on the bed. "Why didn't you tell me?" she scolded. "Why!? We must send for Yeshua at once."

"He made me promise. . . ."

"You can't bind me by such a foolish oath!" Marta announced. She backed abruptly from the room to keep El'azar from overhearing and preventing her resolution. "I'll send for that Greek doctor too. Now, who can find Yeshua? And who can we trust to bring him in a hurry?"

"Marcus," Miryam said immediately. "Send Peniel to Yerushalayim for the doctor and for Marcus at the same time."

I found the doctor at a tavern and compelled him to go to Bethany.

Sosthenes stood beside El'azar's bed. The Greek physician tugged his beard and frowned. "You say he was showing signs of this when he returned home from Yerushalayim? Why wasn't I informed? Why did you keep such facts from me?"

Tavita shook her head in misery. "Master El'azar said he was only tired and in need of rest and food. Later he said it was just a little sore throat—just a winter congestion of the lungs, he said—then this!"

"Then this, indeed!" Sosthenes repeated with a scowl. "I smell the lemon oil and the camphor. . . . Has he had the phytolaccas?"

Tavita nodded before the question was complete. "Regular as the dawn and dusk," she vowed. "We gave him twice the dose as the Sparrows got, seeing's how he's a man grown and not a boy."

"Should have been four times the dose," Sosthenes grumbled. "And did you not think to send for me sooner? that there might be more powerful weapons in my arsenal?"

"But we treated him just as you ordered for the Sparrows!"

"The Sparrows, the Sparrows! Street rats! Beggars, that's the fact of it. If they died, who would miss them? Why waste more expensive preparations on them? Besides, they showed improvement right away, so there was no need . . . but this!"

"You mean there is other medicine?"

But Sosthenes was not finished scolding. "Do you see how he gulps for each breath? Like he's trying to swallow a fish? See it? That's because the muscles supporting his lungs are affected. Not helping. He has to seize each bit of air and force it down. Bad, this is—very bad—and that's absolute fact."

Beaten with remorse, Tavita urged, "You said . . . other medicine? Do you have it?"

Raising one bushy eyebrow, Sosthenes finally relented a little. "The fact is, I can make no promises, but . . . oil of ailanthus. From the Orient. 'Ointment of the Celestial Tree,' in their incomprehensible tongue. His throat—I shudder to check there—his throat must be painted with the oil three—no, four times a day. And put six drops in each spoonful of wine and make him swallow it four times a day as well."

"And then, I mean, how will we know if . . . ?"

"Right now he's fevered. His body is still trying to fight back. But if his urine turns dark and strong . . . if his skin becomes pale and damp and you can't wake him, then . . ."

"Then?" Tavita inquired desperately.

Sosthenes shrugged. "Then you called for me too late."

The dismal forecast wrung from the servant a question she had not meant to ask: "What if we send for the Healer? for Yeshua?"

"That charlatan?" Sosthenes laughed. "Physicians like myself deal in facts not false hope. Now no more time to waste. Tell your mistress the ailanthus oil is very expensive. Because I admire and respect Lord El'azar, I can let you have it for twenty drachmae a bottle. I'll leave the first here today and return with another tomorrow. But I'll need forty drachmae then. Is that clear?"

Marcus arrived just as the doctor was leaving. He closed his eyes as Miryam buried her face in his chest and wept.

"They say . . . rumors in the palaces of Jerusalem are that Yeshua is in Perea. Openly teaching. Healing the sick. Thousands are traveling there. Can you take your brother there? Litter bearers?"

Miryam searched his eyes and shook her head. "We should have done it. Should have taken him there. The illness acts so quickly. El'azar wouldn't hear of it. He feared spreading the disease among the people. I never thought it would go so far. Every day we hoped . . . prayed . . . believed . . . that he would get well."

"Miryam, listen! If you carry El'azar to Yeshua, the danger would not be so great. They—the Herodians and the high priest—are waiting and hoping for Yeshua to return to Judea."

"My brother would die before we traveled a mile. The steam and camphor help him breathe. Oh, Marcus! We've done everything! Prayed . . . believed. Remembered other miracles . . . prayed . . . waited. Why have our prayers of faith been unanswered? Please . . . go tell Yeshua! We need him to come!"

The stench of El'azar's illness drifted out from the cottage. "Yes. Yes. Then Peniel and I'll ride to Perea now. Even from there Yeshua can restore your brother with a single word! They say . . . I've heard he heals all who come to him. So many . . . there in Perea."

"Tell him El'azar is near the brink. We'll do what we can . . . wait and pray for Yeshua to arrive in time! Or, if he can't come, the Father in Heaven will hear Yeshua if he asks for the life of our brother to be saved. Go, Marcus! Peniel, go beg Yeshua! Not a minute to delay."

CHAPTER 20

As I followed close on the heels of Marcus' great horse, the last acts of El'azar's tragedy were being played out. Sosthenes bent over the unconscious form. El'azar's breathing was torturous. Each gasp wheezed both in and out. His shoulders struggled up in his effort to clutch at a morsel of air . . . just like a man being crucified, Miryam thought.

Beside the bed Miryam prayed silently. Marta scurried about, pouring boiling water into clay pots that she placed in each corner of the room. That done, she swept the hearth and added exactly three lumps of charcoal to the fire. Withdrawing a rag from her apron pocket, she scoured an already gleaming empty soup bowl and peered at it with a critical eye.

"Woman," Sosthenes said gruffly, "be still!"

Marta bristled at the rebuke. Miryam thought rage would follow, but instead Marta sighed, clasped her hands, and sat down.

"I will bleed him again," Sosthenes observed to himself.

"Oh, please, no," Miryam countered. "He's so pale and weak now. Surely no more. Besides, his poor arms!"

El'azar's arms were covered with scratches where he had scored himself in his agony. Several of these wounds bristled with gray, sticky material, just like the evil thing in his throat.

Squeezing El'azar just above the elbow not only produced no reaction, it also raised no vein. "Perhaps you're right," the doctor admitted. "What is his urine like today?"

Marta answered. "There has been none. Yesterday it was brown. But since midnight . . . none."

Sosthenes grunted and touched the back of his hand to El'azar's forehead. "Skin damp and cool. Heart fluttery." He poked his thumb into El'azar's eye, drawing an exclamation from Marta but no response from her brother.

Prying El'azar's cracked lips apart, Sosthenes ordered Miryam, "Bring the lamp here. Hold it where I can see." From a leather pouch he withdrew a pair of brass tweezers. "If I can remove some of the membrane he will breathe easier." Beads of sweat stood on the doctor's brow as he manipulated the tools. But the growth, like an evil beast, resisted Sosthenes' attempt to dislodge it.

With a jerk of his chin toward Marta he brusquely demanded, "My bag. Get the long, thin-bladed knife."

Miryam averted her eyes as Sosthenes introduced both knife and tweezers into El'azar's throat. "Mind the light!" he barked.

Suddenly El'azar choked and coughed, spraying blood from his mouth as Sosthenes jerked out of the way.

"It's no good," the physician said, shrugging. "Too ingrown. He will choke on his own blood before I can remove the membrane." Turning away from El'azar, he added, "I'm sorry."

"And what will you try now?" Marta asked.

Sosthenes dropped his instruments back into the pouch. "You misunderstand. There's nothing further to be done . . . nothing at all."

"But the ailanthus oil! The other medicine!"

"By all means, use it all," Sosthenes allowed. "It won't . . . it won't do any harm. Now he's in the hands of the gods."

When the Greek had left the Bethany estate, the sisters clung to each other in the tiny cottage. "If only Yeshua would come," Marta repeated over and over. "Then El'azar would get well. If only . . ."

"He will come," Miryam said with assurance in her voice but none in her heart. "Marcus said he could reach Yeshua in only one day and

bring the Master back. Tomorrow or the next day at the latest. El'azar
can hang on until then. He must!"

The rocks and sand of the dry wadi were disturbed as though a great
herd of cattle had passed through not long ago. Pavor's long stride,
accompanied by me loping alongside, gobbled the distance between
Bethany and Perea in a day.

It was warm as a spring day, the kind of day when children take off
their shoes and splash in mud puddles, I thought as I urged myself to hurry.
My musings returned to the rasping wheeze of Miryam's brother.

As Marcus said, he had seen death approach many times before—
both in battle and after. El'azar was locked in a battle for his life.

"Come on, boy. That's it." Pavor eased into a gentle trot. The horse
and I would both deserve and need good fodder and a night's rest.

I heard what I thought was the chatter of a flock of geese ahead.

As I listened it took on an almost human tone. A copse of willow
trees became thicker, and Marcus guessed we were near the river.

The sun was high as we emerged from the ravine at the edge of the
stream. Boulders on the other side were covered with laundry. There
were no geese at the water's edge. Twoscore women crouched upon
the stones and chatted as they washed their clothes. A flock of children
played around them, barefoot and happy, squealing as they splashed in
the water.

Perhaps these were a part of the band that now followed Yeshua,
I reasoned. At the very least someone among them would be able to
give us information about Him.

Marcus scouted the current, judging that this would be a good place
to ford. Remembering the mud Pavor would stir up and the possibility
of spoiling the wash, he eyed a deeper place twenty yards downstream.

Suddenly one small child perched atop a stone and waving a pretend
sword at his companions spotted Marcus and me.

The triumphant expression of a make-believe warrior faded and
terror filled his eyes. He raised the wooden sword slowly to point at
Marcus, still in his winter uniform.

"Ma . . . ," the child croaked.

At the horror in his face his comrades turned toward us with one unified motion. "A Roman! Mama, a soldier!" a little girl screamed and ran to her mother.

Marcus called, "I've come seeking—"

Women on the banks scrambled to their feet and, abandoning their wash, rushed to snap up their little ones and run away.

"We've come seeking—," I tried.

"It's a Roman!"

"An officer!"

If these human geese had possessed wings, they would have flown away. Instead they vanished behind a copse of trees. I heard their cries of alarm. "A company of soldiers!"

Marcus called to their backs, "No! I'm searching for Yeshua of Nazareth! I need your help."

But they had all fled.

❦

Marta jumped up and flew to the door with the night bird's cry. "He's come! The Master's come!" Her heart raced. She peered out the door into the darkness.

Silence. Nothing stirred. Behind her El'azar groaned.

"No," Miryam whispered. "You were dreaming, Marta."

"If only!" Marta wrung her hands. "If only he would come."

It was just past midnight. Miryam was suddenly overcome with the certainty that Yeshua would not arrive in time. No matter how much Marta rushed about, the result was now inevitable.

It was a deathwatch they were keeping, even if Marta did not yet admit it.

El'azar's eyes were buried in his head. His lips were drawn back from parted teeth as if already gripped by death. His hands, so clutching and tearing in his pain, now lay quiet at his sides.

His breaths came so infrequently that Miryam had already given him up more than once.

In her mind she saw the youthful, strong El'azar. She saw him as the young, hopeful heir to the estate, full of plans for the future.

She also saw the bitter man. The one who had never married after their mother killed herself. El'azar feared his mother's madness would be inherited by his children.

Miryam saw the changed man. The one who had knelt at Yeshua's feet. The scholar who searched the Scriptures diligently for all the proofs that Yeshua of Nazareth was indeed the Messiah of Israel.

She saw the handsome, confident man at Yeshua's side, absorbing the Master's teaching in great, thirsty draughts, and being witness to countless miracles of healing.

Where is the miracle for him? Miryam thought yet again. *Yeshua saved me from being stoned to death . . . set me free from the demons that bound me. Would I not trade my life for my brother's? If Yeshua demanded it, would I not agree?*

If only Yeshua would come! Even now, it wasn't too late. The daughter of the man in Capernaum. She had been already dead! Marcus' servant Carta, now in Antioch . . . as good as dead!

If only Yeshua would come!

Tears trickled down her cheeks as she woke from her reverie and saw again the ruin of her brother.

And then, abruptly, she noticed he had stopped breathing. His shoulders lay still and untroubled. No more wheezing disturbed the quiet of the cottage. His head lay turned gently to the side on the pillow.

"Marta," Miryam said softly.

Just the use of her name was enough. Startled by the silence, Marta sat bolt upright. "Oh, El'azar! My brother! My brother." Great, wrenching sobs overflowed from the cottage.

So death had won a final victory.

Marcus and I finally reached Yeshua's camp outside a village named Salim. It was near the place where Yeshua's cousin, Yochanan, had done much of his baptizing some years earlier. Marcus, who had gone to see Yochanan before he ever met Yeshua, told me of the wild-haired, leather-robed prophet.

Without Marcus telling me I already knew that Yochanan had been killed by Herod Antipas . . . beheaded at the whim of Antipas' wife.

The association between that tragedy and this place was not a good one. I knew Tetrarch Antipas was even more afraid of Yeshua's power than he had been of Yochanan's. To what danger were we about to lure Yeshua back?

But I set aside such gloomy thoughts at the joy of seeing Yeshua again, and when I remembered the urgency of our errand. While we were still some distance away Yeshua spotted us and raised His hand in greeting. A crowd of several hundred gathered around Him turned at the gesture and stared.

I caused no remark, but many fingers were pointed at the sight of Marcus' uniform. Many more in the audience whispered behind their hands.

A few slipped away from the gathering, fading into the brush on the opposite side from our approach. Hopping down from the tree stump that had been the bema for His teaching, Yeshua came to us and embraced us each in turn.

Before Marcus spoke I saw something in Yeshua's eyes that I can only describe as instant comprehension. It was not just that He realized something important drove us to seek Him; anyone might have guessed as much. What I mean is, I think He knew all about our mission . . . about El'azar . . . and about what would happen later.

But what it all meant I had no clue at the time.

With military precision Marcus delivered his message in clipped sentences. "Rabbi, Miryam of Bethany sends word: 'The one you love is sick.'"[39] Then the Roman centurion relaxed his bearing enough to add, "El'azar is gravely ill. He has diphtheria."

Those close enough to overhear the exchange gasped. Like a rock dropped into a pond, the message spread outward from the center.

"Master," I added, "El'azar spent his money and all his strength helping the Sparrows of Yerushalayim when almost all of them contracted the disease. Now that he has it himself, it may cost him the coin of his life unless you help."

"They cannot expect the Master to return to Judea," I heard one of the talmidim remark. "It isn't safe."

Eyeing Marcus' tunic and the centurion's swagger stick he carried, another disciple muttered, "Even this place isn't far enough away from Yerushalayim."

"What if it's a trap?" Thomas inquired aloud.

"I assure you, this is real and very serious," Marcus corrected. "It took us longer to find you than I expected, and he was very ill before they sent us."

"But they can't expect the Master to thrust his head into a noose by returning!" Thomas refused to be reassured.

"In point of fact they did not ask him to return. The message is: 'The one you love is sick.'"

Suddenly the implication of that remark sank in. It was not necessary for Yeshua to go to Bethany or anywhere near Jerusalem for El'azar to be healed. Like the time Marcus' servant Carta was healed without Yeshua ever setting foot in his house, the same could be true now. All that was required was for Yeshua to be aware of the need.

In the next moment Yeshua Himself seemed to confirm this answer by saying, "El'azar's sickness will not end in death. No, it is for the glory of God. I, the Son of God, will receive glory from this."[40]

Was it a test of our faith?

It was of mine. Yeshua had such high regard for El'azar. With the Sparrows, El'azar had so completely demonstrated true righteousness. If anyone was worthy of a miracle, it was he. Even knowing El'azar would get well, did it not seem like cowardice, or a lack of compassion, not to go to him at once, no matter what the risk?

And what did "receive glory from this" mean?

PART VII

ABRAHAM'S SEVENFOLD BLESSING

I will make you into a great nation

and I will bless you;

I will make your name great,

and you will be a blessing.

I will bless those who bless you,

and whoever curses you I will curse;

and all peoples on earth

will be blessed through you.

GENESIS 12:2-3

21

C H A P T E R

ℳ iryam and Marta sat silently on the floor beside El'azar's bed.
Strange how in death and free of pain, he seemed so young.
A boy again, thought Miryam as she gazed at his face. *Beautiful
and peaceful, untroubled by our grief.*

His body had been washed, his hair combed back. Dark curls
unfurled on the pillow. The shroud lay still folded on the foot of the
bed. Seventy pounds of embalming spices were in jars along the wall.
For the first time in days the air in the cottage smelled clean and fresh
from the fragrant balm.

A crowd of mourners waited outside in the cold for the announcement.

Tavita shuffled around the room, straightening, cleaning. At last she
asked, "When, Lady Marta? When? Miryam, my dove?"

The sisters answered almost in unison. "Not yet!"

"Yeshua might come!"

"A while longer. Even from over Jordan Yeshua could speak one
word and . . ."

"A command . . ."

"One word from Yeshua . . ."

"And our brother will wake up. . . ."

Tavita brushed away a tear. "If only the Lord could have been here!" *Too late now*, her expression seemed to say. *Too late for El'azar.*

In an inner room beside his office in the tower of Nicanor Gate, High Priest Caiaphas was having his hair and beard anointed with perfume. He leaned back in his chair with a blissful expression as the servant drizzled warm oil and massaged it into his scalp. He barely opened one eye at the knock on his door.

"What is it?" he demanded with a hint of impatience.

"Ben Dives, my lord. I have important news."

When the scribe entered he glanced sharply at the attendant. The implication was not lost on Caiaphas, who dismissed the barber with a curt "Wait outside." Then to his secretary: "Important?"

"El'azar of Bethany has died, lord. He succumbed to the diphtheria. The fact is, there was never any hope. Once the disease progressed past a certain point, he was as good as dead already."

"And Yeshua of Nazareth?"

"Never returned. I am told messengers from El'azar's sisters seek him, but . . ."

"And now everyone will say there is no power in the name of Yeshua . . . no virtue in him, if he cannot even save a close friend."

"That is the fact of the matter, my lord."

Caiaphas rubbed his beard and smoothed the oil into his mustache. "Perhaps the Galilean was hoping El'azar would live, but stayed away, hoping his absence would protect his reputation as a healer."

Ben Dives grasped his left elbow with his right hand. He frowned, then responded thoughtfully, "Nothing is more ruinous to a reputation than a dead friend."

"And we're certain El'azar is truly dead?" Caiaphas retorted with a sudden raising of his eyebrows. "We want no fake miracles."

"Horribly and completely dead, my lord. Burial today."

"Send my barber in to me as you go," Caiaphas ordered. "You've done well, ben Dives. Very well indeed."

"Thank you, my lord. With my lord's permission I will be absent a few days now. A Sabbath day's journey tomorrow, then I'm going to my property near Jericho. My harvests have done so well this past year I need to build bigger barns."

"Truly HaShem has blessed you. Go in peace."

"Thank you, my lord."

The lavender sky of twilight reflected in the ripples of the Jordan River. Marcus, helmet beside him on the boulder, searched for the first evening star. My father sat close beside me. I did not speak, though I shared Marcus' concerns.

"Shabbat Shalom." Zadok joined us as the evening prayers drifted through the window of the stone house nearby. "You're mighty glum," he remarked.

"It's almost Sabbath," the centurion replied. "From sundown tonight till sundown tomorrow. Peter says Yeshua won't come with me."

"Aye," Zadok answered. "'Tis right."

Marcus ran a weary hand over the stubble on his cheek. "Sabbath. Now. Even if I convinced him to go, Yeshua won't start his journey back to Bethany tonight."

I sighed. "Yeshua says . . . he says the illness won't end in death."

"Well then—" Marcus spread his hands—"it's just . . . El'azar hovered at the brink even as we rode from Bethany. His sisters, so frantic with worry. Urged me to make all the haste I could. Now this . . . delay."

Zadok suggested, "Yeshua can save El'azar's life even from this distance. Eh? With a single word. You of all people know this, man. Marcus? Here are the facts. Didn't your servant, Carta, lay dyin' in Capernaum?"

I gazed into the sky. The first star gleamed above the rugged hills.

"Yes," Marcus admitted. "Near death. I knelt before the Lord and knew he was a king. I said to him, 'When I send an order, it is obeyed. . . . How much more true is that of you?' And by Yeshua's command, I knew Carta would be healed . . . *was* healed. Even though the boy was such a distance from Yeshua, still I had no doubt. And the truth is, when Yeshua spoke the words, Carta *was* healed.[41] But this time Yeshua didn't say the word. At least I didn't hear him."

Zadok sniffed. "And y' think he must pronounce somethin' aloud for it t' happen? He who can call forth lightnin' and calm storms?" The old shepherd thumped Marcus on his back. "All will be well. You'll see."

"Miryam sent me. I traveled two days here to find him. It's Sabbath Eve, and he won't begin the journey. And now with Sabbath upon us, Yeshua will not leave tomorrow. Sabbath doesn't end until sunset tomorrow. He won't travel in the dark tomorrow night. Another day gone before Yeshua could set out."

"Aye. Those are the facts. You have stated it fairly." The old man turned to me. "Lad, tell us the facts of your former circumstance. What state were y' in when first y' laid eyes on Yeshua? That is, so t' speak."

I closed my eyes. "The fact is, I was blind. Stone blind. Born blind."

My father chimed in: "I heard the Sanhedrin say it: 'Never in the history of the world has anyone ever opened the eyes of a man born blind.' Not Elijah the Prophet. Not Mosheh the Lawgiver. And yet . . ."

I resumed: "Those are the facts. And the truth is, now I can see."

Zadok beckoned for Emet to join us. "Here comes my wee lad, Emet!"

"Papa! Almost suppertime. Shabbat Shalom!" The boy's words were cheerful. With one glance at Marcus his face clouded. "Oh, Marcus! Shabbat Shalom! It's Shabbat—glorious, wonderful Shabbat! Why are you sad?"

"Shabbat Shalom," Marcus replied, mussing Emet's fair hair. "I am sad because—not sad . . . worried about a friend."

Emet smiled broadly. "We don't worry in this place. Yeshua is with us. We are learning Torah."

Zadok laughed. "Aye! Such lessons my lads are learnin'. Taught by the Master himself! That's right, Emet." He nudged Marcus. "Emet. Tell Marcus the meanin' of your name."

Emet put a hand on Marcus' arm and gazed up at him with somber brown eyes. "Emet means 'Truth.'"

"Aye," Zadok concurred. "Truth now can speak. And the fact is, Truth is a stronger force than fact. Fact is, Emet here could not speak last year. Couldn't utter a sound or hear the birds' chorus or know the chatter of the water in the river. But Truth is, Yeshua opened the ears of Emet so he could hear Truth. And Yeshua gave Truth a voice to speak. Listen, Marcus, to the lessons Truth has been learnin' in Torah school."

Marcus, seeming to shake off his disappointment and anxiety, nodded and fixed his attention on Emet.

Zadok queried, "So, Emet. Here's a *fact* from the *Book of Beginnings:* Father Avraham was a very old man without a son. He wanted a son, but his wife, Sarai, was also very old. Now what is the *truth?*"

Emet shifted his weight and stared heavenward. "Truth is . . . God said Avraham would have a son through Sarai. Baby Isaac was born."

Zadok cheered him on. "Very good, Emet! Now once more. Tell your father the answer t' this . . . fact. Joseph the Dreamer, great-grandson of Avraham, was sold into slavery by his brothers, unjustly accused, and imprisoned. What is the truth of this story?"

Emet furrowed his brow in thought. "Truth: Joseph became a great leader in Egypt. His brothers bowed down to him and he saved the whole family of Israel."

Zadok squared his shoulders, clearly proud of his son's knowledge. "Aye! There's my clever lad!"

"Another one, Papa?"

Zadok sighed. "Aye. Here's a difficult one for you, Emet. And also for me, when I think on it. Fact: Pharaoh ordered all the baby boys of the Hebrews t' be slaughtered because he feared their numbers."

I considered the terrible story I had heard about the loss of Zadok's baby boys in Beth-lehem over thirty years earlier. Like Pharaoh, Herod had slaughtered the innocent in his attempt to destroy the Messiah and nullify the promises of God. Surely the link between Moses and the slaughter of the babies in Beth-lehem still burned in Zadok's memory.

Emet laid his head against Zadok's chest and answered quietly. "Papa, you remember. The truth: Baby Mosheh was saved when he was placed into a basket and set adrift on the Nile River. He was rescued by Pharaoh's daughter, nursed by his own mother, and grew up to be a prince of Egypt and the deliverer of Israel." Emet kissed Zadok's cheek. "Even so, Papa, I think the other papas who lost their boys were very sad."

"Aye, lad. Sometimes the truth that God holds all things in his hand does not quench the pain of sufferin' in this life. So we who do not understand it all . . . we need courage t' go on. T' believe the truth even when the facts seem very sad, eh? Even if truth doesn't seem t' be what we want, in the end we know God's Truth is greater than circumstance, eh?"

"Aye, Papa. One more true thing, Papa? Shall we recite one more, Papa?"

Zadok seemed to scour his memory, searching for some familiar lesson Emet could recite. "Here it is, then. Fact: On their journey from Egypt, the former Hebrew slaves were trapped between the Red Sea and the approachin' chariots of Pharaoh. Now, Emet, tell us if you can. What is the truth?"

Emet eagerly declared, "God parted the waters of the sea, the Hebrews crossed over on dry land, and then the waters closed over the heads of the Egyptian pursuers and drowned them. Israel escaped and became a great nation." He bowed as we applauded. "May I go now? Shabbat is beginning."

"Well spoken, lad. Go on, then. We will follow after."

I watched the boy dash toward the house. I remembered the slaughter of Zadok's children. Not even the presence of baby Yeshua had saved the children of Beth-lehem. Sometimes the terrible circumstance of evil remained unchanged by goodness. Death was mankind's great enemy. Could it be that the good soul of El'azar was meant to fly away?

"Zadok," Marcus began, "your point is well taken. The fact is that Emet was deaf and dumb . . . and no one could heal him. The truth is, he now speaks. It is proof. But I tell you, I can't see how El'azar can remain alive. As he was near death when I left. Even now it may be too late."

"If that's the fact and he's dead, then there'll be some great truth even in his death. We'll find Truth shinin' in the darkness like a gem from Solomon's crown. Aye. Where there's unbearable facts in this life, Yeshua proves the Truth that the Eternal Father is not only Almighty, but that his love and mercy are forever. *Ha yada l'Yahweh. Kee tov, kee l'olam, chesed*," Zadok quoted from the hundred and thirty-sixth psalm. *Give thanks to the Lord, for He is good. His love and mercy endure forever.*[42]

"Still," Marcus mused, "if Yeshua won't return tonight, I don't believe El'azar will still be alive when he gets to Bethany. How can that be either love or mercy?"

At the call to the Shabbat meal, Marcus Longinus stood and placed his hand on my shoulder. "Peniel, you did well to follow so close on Pavor's heels. I'd recruit you if you didn't have more important battles to fight. Our journey didn't end as I expected. But you're safe now at any rate. Miryam's message delivered. So I'll ride out and camp at the mouth of the wadi and keep watch through the night."

Zadok, who never had a good word for a Roman until he met Marcus, instructed his boy, "Emet, go on. Fetch a loaf of fresh bread and some fish for this good fellow." Then he extended his hand to Marcus. "Your sword is welcome. Even though you remain unseen by those in the camp, I will tell the Master you're there. Aye. 'Tis a comfort t' me that you're there."

Moments later, Marcus, meal in hand, mounted his horse. It was just after sunset when he rode out from Yeshua's camp to keep silent vigil over us all.

The Shabbat candles were lit when Zadok and I entered the house, washed, and took our places at the far end of the Lord's table. Platters of food were laid out. There were thirty-six men gathered round. And twelve women honored to sit with us. The mother of the Lord sat at His right hand. Wives and relatives of the inner circle of supporters were there as well.

As we broke bread, Yeshua spoke the Torah portion from memory and then, without benefit of a scroll, He taught us from the words of Ezekiel the Prophet. "It is written and is the Truth of the Covenant forever:

"'I will give you a new heart and will put a new spirit within you; I will remove from you your heart of stone and give you a heart of flesh. And I will put My Spirit in you and move you to follow My decrees and be careful to keep My laws. You will live in the land I gave your fore-fathers. You will be My people, and I will be your God.'"[43]

Yeshua looked around the table, capturing each eye. "It is written:

"'I want you to know that I am not doing this for your sake,' declares the Sovereign Lord. 'Be ashamed and disgraced by your conduct, O Israel!' This is what the Sovereign Lord says."[44]

I closed my eyes, unable to bear the beautiful image of His face. Light reflected on His face . . . or was it from within Him? I wanted to shout "Hosannah!" and "Praise to him!" as He held up the bread to bless it.

Controlling myself, I squeezed my eyes tight and just listened to Him speak.

Suddenly, in perfect harmony, I heard another deeper voice:

On that day I cleanse you from all your sins. I will resettle your towns, and the ruins will be rebuilt. The desolate land will be cultivated instead of lying desolate in the sight of all who pass through it. . . . Then the nations around you that remain will know that I the Lord have rebuilt what was destroyed and have replanted what was desolate. I the Lord have spoken and I will do it.[45]

I scanned the room and leaned close to Zadok. "Did you hear it?" I whispered. "From *olam haba*?"

When the old man looked strangely at me, I knew that I alone at the table heard the Eternal echo.

Candles flickered. I wondered what had become of El'azar. How did he fare in his illness? Yeshua seemed unconcerned about His friend. Did that mean that I also should set aside my worries?

Yeshua continued to recite from the Book of the Prophet. Angels seemed to hum the passage as the words flowed easily from Yeshua's lips.

"The hand of the Lord was upon me, and He brought me out by the Spirit of the Lord and set me in the middle of a valley. It was filled with bones. . . . He asked me, 'Son of man, can these bones live?'"

Yeshua smiled directly into my eyes as if the question was for me. I blurted the answer Ezekiel had given so long ago, *"O Sovereign Lord, You alone know."*

Some turned in my direction, startled and disapproving that I had spoken. Then Yeshua and the heavenly voice continued. "Well spoken, Peniel. . . . *This is what the Sovereign Lord says to these bones: 'I will make breath enter you and you will come to life.'"*

In the far distance thunder rumbled. **Hear, O Israel!**

Yeshua continued the antiphonal recital of the ancient covenant of resurrection. *"I will attach tendons to you and . . . cover you with skin. I will put breath in you, and you will come to life. Then you will know that I am the Lord."*[46]

Hear, O Israel! The echo resonated in my chest.

Yeshua knew I could hear it. He said to me, *"These bones are the whole house of Israel."*[47]

I heard the name: **El'azar! Israel!**

"Israel says, 'Our bones are dried up, and our hope is gone; we are cut off.' This is what the Sovereign Lord says: 'O My people, I am going to open your graves and bring you up from them. I will bring you back to the land of Israel.'"[48]

The roaring in my ears drowned out every sound but the voice of Yeshua. **El'azar! The whole house of Israel!**

"Then you, My people, will know that I am the Lord, when I open your graves and bring you up from them. I will put My Spirit in you and you will live, and I will settle you in your own land. Then you will know that I the Lord have spoken, and I have done it, declares the Lord."[49]

Yeshua raised His eyes briefly and spoke the blessing over the food. "Blessed be the Name of the Lord."

I knew that tonight's Torah portion had something to do with El'azar of Bethany, but the full meaning of it was unclear to me.

I queried Yeshua without speaking. *Lord? Do we wait here in Perea because you fear Herod Antipas or the high priest? Is your dear friend El'azar already healed?*

Yeshua answered my question aloud for all of us to ponder, "You wonder about El'azar. I tell you again, his illness is not meant to end in death. Our dear friend El'azar has fallen asleep."[50]

Zadok sighed with relief. "Aye! Praise The Eternal! There's good news from a far land, eh, Lord?"

Thomas and Levi raised their cups. "Then here's to good El'azar! *L'Chaim!*" Others joined them as they toasted the health and life of good master El'azar.

Zadok expressed the relief we all felt. "Well then. Yeshua, Rabbi, if El'azar's asleep, then he'll recover. No need for you t' enter into danger, eh? No need t' return to the territory of Herod Antipas and his jackals."

Yeshua leaned forward. "Understand this, Zadok. It's *because* I love my dear friends, El'azar, Miryam, and Marta, that I'm staying here awhile longer. . . . For the sake of my love for them we will not return to Bethany yet. Because of love—*not* from fear of Herod."

Mary, the Lord's mother, asked her son, "Because you love them?"

He nodded, smiled, and lifted the cup to His lips. So. We had all heard Him correctly, but we still did not understand His meaning.

CHAPTER 22

Before Marta would allow her brother's body to be interred, she insisted his tomb be cleaned. The grave, hewn from solid rock many decades earlier, had never been used. Still, clean to Marta meant the sepulchre must be swept and dusted. Marta would not allow anyone to attend to the duty but herself and her sister.

Miryam accompanied Marta on the early morning errand. She was grateful to leave the keening of the hired mourners behind, at least for a time. As they traversed the unpaved path through fig orchard and olive grove, Miryam mused: *A hidden place. The place where the stones and outbuildings of our father's house were quarried. Not far now.*

Parting a curtain of vines overhanging a narrow space, Miryam topped a rise and gazed down as she waited for Marta to join her. A stone block, serving as a bench, overlooked the small, privately owned quarry. A few broken blocks were scattered in a limestone pit with stair-step ledges leading to an open cave three steps above the floor.

"It's there." Miryam raised her hand toward the hand-hewn entrance. "The last stones were taken from that cave the day El'azar was born, or so Father always said."

Marta observed, "Strange to think his grave has been waiting for him for his whole life. But then that's true of all of us, isn't it?"

Miryam remembered playing around the quarry when they were children. There had been no ominous thoughts in those days. *Brother's name comes from the name of the prophet Ezra. "God is my help." And Ezra is the man who helped build the Second Temple after Israel's exile in Babylon. Father, in gratitude for El'azar's birth, sent the blocks from that cave to Yerushalayim for the construction of the Temple buildings. Virgin stone, never exposed to the world since creation, Father said, until they were placed into the Temple in Yerushalayim. This was in the last days of old Herod, the Butcher King. Our family's stones were used to repair the steps of Solomon's Colonnade. El'azar can show—could have shown—you where our stones live in the Temple. Father always said . . .*

Memories of her father diverted Miryam's thoughts for a moment before she continued: *Father always said that cave here on our land—the place where Solomon's blocks were hewn—was meant for El'azar's tomb. Someday his bones would rest there. Father believed there was honor in that connection. For El'azar, like Ezra, to be returned in death to the stone womb in the very earth from which Solomon's Porch was given birth.*

Miryam scanned the quarry that showed evidence of her efforts to convert it into a garden. This time of year it brooded, dismal and depressing. There were no other open caves but the one. "Such a secret place."

"Come on, then," Marta insisted abruptly. "Cleaning to be done." She carefully descended the gravel path to the quarry floor. A flock of startled crows cawed and rose into the gray sky.

Miryam's pace quickened as she hurried to join her sister at the opening of the cave. Peering in, her hand went to her heart in great emotion.

"If only Yeshua had been here," she murmured. "If only . . ."

Though his route lay to the north and east of Jerusalem, ben Dives chose to exit the Holy City by the gate nearest his home. The Dung Gate was so named because it was the portal used to transport garbage out of the city.

Servants in the retinue accompanying ben Dives cleared the way ahead of him. They distributed pennies to the beggars and shooed the *am ha aretz* out of the important man's path. They later reported he had taken only one step outside the city before his face was transfixed as at a great and wholly unexpected sight. His hand, which had been rubbing his left shoulder, suddenly clutched at his chest as if he could not draw a deep breath.

Ben Dives pounded his fist over his heart even as he sagged to his knees.

His steward, believing his master had stumbled, hurried to raise him quickly. The servant knew he would be beaten if ben Dives' expensive brocade robe was soiled by the refuse in the sodden street.

"Let me help you, lord," the steward urged.

But Ra'nabel ben Dives was beyond help. His servants picked him up . . . dead.

The Shabbat morning lesson had not yet begun. A great crowd gathered in the plowed field stretching up from the riverbank. To the south and west, toward Jerusalem, storm clouds hovered over the mountains, but the sky was clear above us. The breeze in this rugged country was as warm as spring against our faces. We waited eagerly for Yeshua to speak the words that would bring us abundant life!

Yeshua invited Marcus to join us. The centurion, his threatening authority hidden with his armor in a clump of willows beside the river, sat on my left.

Zadok was at my right hand. His boys had joined a cadre of other children from the camp and had sped off to play beside the stream.

I spotted the faces of several wealthy Pharisees among the multitude of *am ha aretz*. They had come, no doubt, to trip Yeshua up, to twist His words into offenses they could report to the high priest and Herod.

A tiny brown sparrow flitted briefly around Yeshua's head as He walked toward a knoll. The bird fluttered off to perch on the branch of a scrubby sage as though to listen to the words of the great Rabbi.

Zadok scowled, inclining his head toward the side with the eye patch, as Yeshua stood before us and made the baracha. "Aye," the old shepherd said to me. "I feel it. Somethin's amiss, Peniel! See his expression!"

Indeed there was a sorrow in Yeshua's eyes—a weariness I had never seen in Him before this Shabbat morning. Always before, His stories had been suffused with forgiveness and grace. Even before He taught one word, His demeanor always exuded hope.

I had heard Him speak of the prodigal son who betrayed and left his father, only to repent and return. I had seen Him point to the pet sparrow belonging to Zadok's boys and heard Him spin tales about the Almighty's great care for every human. There were tales of seed sown in bad soil and parables of lost sheep who were found.

But this morning, when Yeshua studied the vast, silent congregation, He began to speak about death. "There was a certain rich man. He was clothed in purple and fine linen. Every day he had any sumptuous dish he wanted to eat."

Marcus, knowing the Latin word for wealthy, murmured, "Perhaps Yeshua speaks of ben Dives."

"And there was a certain beggar named El'azar. . . ."

I heard a gasp from Yeshua's mother.

Yeshua continued. "And El'azar the beggar, covered with sores, lay at the gate of the rich man. He wanted only to be fed, like the dogs, from the crumbs that fell from the rich man's table. But instead, the dogs of the rich man came out and licked the sores of El'azar."

Yeshua's eyes seemed to bore into my soul as He spoke the next phrase. "And it came to pass that El'azar, the beggar, died. He was immediately carried by the angels to Avraham's bosom."

Marcus stirred uneasily. I did not glance at him, but I knew he had the same question as I had. Had El'azar of Bethany died? Was Yeshua speaking prophecy, parable, or hinting a warning?

Yeshua's use of the beggar's name in this parable was unusual. Ordinarily He would have referred to the poor man as He did the rich one: "There was a certain beggar . . ."

But this beggar had a name, and it was a familiar one!

Yeshua fixed His gaze upon the Pharisees. "The rich man also died, and he was buried. In hell, and in great torment, he lifted his eyes. He saw Avraham far off, and El'azar the beggar in his bosom. And from his place in hell the rich man shrieked and begged, 'Father Avraham! Have mercy on me! Send El'azar, that he may dip the tip of his finger in water and cool my tongue! I am tormented by this flame!'"

I shuddered, suddenly aware that Yeshua always spoke the Truth. In these words we were being shown a terrible reality.

I considered ben Dives, arrogant and secure in his wealth and position. If El'azar had really died, then something must have also happened to ben Dives!

Yeshua paused only a moment as every mind considered the unquenchable thirst of hell and the eternal separation from hope in that terrible place.

"But Avraham said to the rich man, 'Son, remember in your lifetime you received all good things. And likewise El'azar evil things. But now El'azar is comforted and you are tormented. Between us and you there is a great gulf fixed. Those who long to pass from here to you cannot do so. Neither can you pass from hell to where we are.'"

Somewhere in the center of the crowd a woman began to weep. Was she crying for someone gone whom she knew could not be in heaven?

Yeshua's face also reflected sorrow as He continued the parable. "Then the rich man shouted across the gulf: 'I beg you, Father Avraham, send El'azar to my father's house. I have five brothers who live just as I lived my life. Let El'azar testify to them lest they also come into this place of torment!'

"But Avraham replied, 'Your five brothers have the five books of Mosheh and the Prophets. Let your brothers hear them!'

"The rich man in torment said, 'No! They won't pay attention to Mosheh or the prophets. But if someone went back to them from the dead, then they will repent!'"

Yeshua raised His voice so all in the multitude could hear the warning. "But Avraham replied, 'If they will not listen to Mosheh and the prophets, neither will they be persuaded . . . even if someone rises from the dead.'"[51]

I could hardly concentrate on the rest of the lesson. Just the night before this, Yeshua had recited to us Ezekiel's prophecy of Messiah and the resurrection of multitudes. Today's Shabbat lesson was certainly the exposition of what He had begun last night. Yet I was deeply troubled. Yeshua had used the name of His dear friend El'azar for the dead beggar. Why?

The crowd buzzed with Yeshua's words. A man of obvious wealth and position harrumphed loudly. He spoke of how ill-advised it was to curry favor with the poor by abusing those HaShem had blessed with property.

Another agreed, asking if Yeshua didn't know that all the sages agreed that wealth was a sign of righteousness and God's approval.

Among the *am ha aretz* the discussion was more about life and death. How if someone came back from the dead—someone who had really been dead—and spoke about heaven and hell, they would be believed.

And on the face of Yeshua's mother: unutterable pity and compassion.

A wealthy Pharisee who had come down from Jerusalem to argue precepts of the Law with Yeshua challenged, "Are you saying, Rabbi, that a rich man cannot enter Avraham's bosom?"

Yeshua simply turned and studied the man, who shrunk away from gold-flecked eyes that knew the contents of his heart.

The lesson ended early that day. We returned to the shelter that had been the home of Yochanan the Baptizer. It was here Yeshua explained to us of the talmidim the deeper meaning of His parable.

"You have heard me say before that it's easier for a camel to pass through the eye of a needle than for a rich man to enter *olam haba*."[52]

Thomas asked, "Must we all start our journey to *olam haba* as leprous beggars? Must we be poor before we can enter the Kingdom?"

Yeshua smiled at the sarcasm in Thomas' voice. "Compared to the righteousness of the Father in Heaven every man is a leprous beggar . . . and poor. But the mercy and compassion of my Father in Heaven long to heal the wounds of every life. Listen to my words and search your heart! It is those who claim they have no sin and believe they have no need of mercy who will be turned away."

The Lord placed His hand on Thomas' head as if he were a small child. "Listen, Thomas. Hear and believe the word of the Lord to this generation of religious hypocrites. This is fact: There are many in this broken nation who teach their congregations that worldly prosperity and success are the sign a man is favored by my heavenly Father. Here is Truth: I am not rich as the world defines wealth, yet I offer treasure and joy beyond comprehension. Those who are wealthy by the world's standards are courted by the leaders of the synagogue and seated in places of honor. The righteous poor are asked to dig deeper and give more, then are shoved aside when the rich man enters.

"But I have today in this parable shown you Truth. The ruler who possessed great wealth was miserable every day of his life. He was bitter, angry, and consumed with hatred, pride, and envy against those who were deeply beloved by the Lord. The rich man had everything the flesh could wish for: good food, the clothing of a prince, honor among men. Yet this man detested anyone who did not bow low to him or bring him financial gain and honor. Here is Truth; think on it: This rich man died and passed immediately from the greatest comfort and ease of this world. He stepped suddenly and unexpectedly into the reality of hell's torment! After death, there was no place but hell for his soul to reside. His pride would have tried to push everyone else out of heaven. His pride still blames others that he is not in heaven."

Yeshua smiled, and we all understood the sort of man He was talking about. "This fellow has been rightly judged. He was always secretly a hypocrite and a liar. Though other men considered him to be a great religious success, he did not know or serve the merciful Father in Heaven who knows the hearts of all men. Money was the god of his idolatry. It was written long ago by the prophet Isaias that the religious offerings of a hypocrite are as detestable to the Lord as though the blood of a pig had been offered on the altar."

Yeshua shook His head from side to side as though He could see a multitude. "This world judges the Lord's favor wrongly—by the standard of financial success and even outward religious piety. The Lord judges the heart of a man.[53] A hypocrite is one who lies to his fellow men. But he cannot hide his sin or lie to the Lord of Heaven." Yeshua searched every face in the field.

Thad dropped his eyes. Philip's pale skin flushed. I noticed that Judas stared fixedly toward a corner of the ceiling. His mouth was clamped shut.

"According to Torah," Yeshua continued, "do you keep your vows? Do you sign your name to a covenant with your fellow men and break your promise? Are you envious and critical of the Lord's anointed? Do you seek to destroy the lives and work of those you can't control? These are the questions every man must ask himself now, while he still lives and breathes. One moment after your last heartbeat will be too late. Repent now!

"My Father in Heaven is full of mercy and unending compassion for all who call upon him in truth! Here is my warning: Hell is a real place that I have told you about. There will come a time when it is too late to repent and be received in friendship in heaven. There are some here among us who will not believe, though they will see a dead man return to life from death. Though all will come to pass according to the sign written about by the prophet Ezekiel, still many will reject the Truth and deny the Lord. As Avraham said to the rich man in hell, 'If they do not believe Mosheh and the prophets, they will not believe even if one returns from the dead.'"[54]

23

It was the second day after Marcus and I brought the news of El'azar's illness to Yeshua's camp. There was no longer any buzz among the talmidim about Yeshua's action, or rather, the lack of any. After all, when He said that El'azar's sickness would not end in death, that satisfied almost everyone. Since all of us had seen the Master perform miracles, none of us had any reason to doubt His words.

Marcus still chafed at being kept away from fulfilling his errand, but even he admitted that El'azar's return to health would remove any urgency felt by El'azar's sisters.

Further, among those who feared for Yeshua's own safety, it seemed sensible to stay in Perea. The catalog of villains in the Holy City grew with each encounter there, but never shrank. Jealous Pharisees, angry Temple authorities, guilty Herodians, and frustrated Romans all combined to lend an air of danger to even the slightest thought of being in Jerusalem. A journey back to that neighborhood was not to be contemplated.

The memory of Yeshua's near stoning at the Temple portico was still fresh in everyone's mind. I had only to touch the still tender place on my scalp to be reminded of the reality of the threat.

So Yeshua produced instant consternation among His followers when over a breakfast of bread and dried fish He announced, "Let's go to Judea again."

Silence reigned throughout the encampment. In the absolute quiet I heard Philip finish chewing a morsel of barley loaf, heard him swallow. Brushing crumbs from his beard and coughing into his fist, he argued, "But you said—"

And the silence was shattered.

"Just a few days ago . . ."

"The Pharisees want . . ."

"The Temple authorities will try to kill you."

Thomas summed up the babble by asking, "And you're going there again?"

Marcus, whose timely intervention had prevented further injury on the last occasion, said nothing. Perhaps, being a Roman and a Gentile, he thought he had no place in this discussion. Perhaps he wanted to wait and see if others could sway Yeshua before advising Him privately. I don't know. All I knew for certain was that there was danger for Yeshua in Jerusalem . . . and for the rest of us.

Here's what the Master said: "There are twelve hours of daylight every day. As long as it is light, people can walk safely. They can see because they have the light of this world. Only at night is there danger of stumbling because there is no light."

There was some whispering among the talmidim at this.

"What does he mean?"

"What's his point?"

Levi leaned over toward me and quoted, "'*Your word is a lamp to my feet and a light to my path.*'[55] That's what he's saying. He has a duty to perform, and nothing will keep him from it."

Then Marcus surprised us both by leaning across from the other side to offer, "But that's not all he means. Don't you recall what he said at the Feast of Tabernacles? 'I am the light of the world. If you follow me you won't be stumbling in darkness, because you have the light that leads to life.'"[56]

The light that leads to life—that part sounded positive. But if Yeshua was the Light, why did He mention a time when there was no light?

Like the rest of His followers, I was so busy pondering what He meant that I almost missed hearing His next remark: "Our friend El'azar has fallen asleep, but now I will go and wake him up."

Thaddeus was the first to argue. "But he's been sick."

Then the others took up the refrain: "He's been sick. He needs to sleep."

"We're going all the way back to Bethany to wake him up?"

Philip suggested, "Lord, if he's sleeping peacefully, doesn't that mean he's getting better?" Hidden within his words was a repetition of the earlier argument: *Surely it's too dangerous for you to go there now.*

It was then that my eye fell on young Abel, who had been brought back from the dead and was now sitting beside his mother across the campfire from me. Instead of confusion on his face I saw sober understanding. Bending his head close to his mother, he whispered in her ear and got a sorrowful nod in reply.

What Abel knew and what I came to guess at was confirmed when Yeshua said, "Let me tell you plainly: El'azar is dead. And for your sake I am glad I wasn't there because this will give you another opportunity to believe in me. Come, let's go see him."

Dead? Already dead? Days ago Yeshua promised that El'azar's sickness would not end in death. Moments ago He said El'azar was asleep.

What was happening?

And still the fear of returning so near to Jerusalem was strong—stronger even than Yeshua's promise of "another opportunity to believe."

Yeshua stood and began to roll His blanket and stuff His few possessions into a pouch, in preparation for leaving.

While Abel nodded with confidence, most of the group shared a resigned sigh.

Thomas was the one who spoke, but he was not alone in his opinion. "So, let's all go . . . and die with him."[57]

⚲

Marcus and I were sent ahead of Yeshua and the talmidim to alert the sisters to His coming. Even before the Bethany house was in sight I could hear the rustle and chatter of a great throng of people. Hundreds were gathered outside the gates with at least another hundred crowded into the courtyard. Pavor and Marcus' uniform parted the crowd like a ship pushes aside the waves.

Though having heard Yeshua's words we already knew the answer, Marcus asked, "What's happened here? Why are all these people gathered?"

Perhaps Marcus hoped Yeshua had been wrong; perhaps he hoped we had misunderstood His words, though He said plainly, "El'azar is dead." Perhaps we hoped something had changed yet again during the time of our return from Perea.

Yet the reply was exactly what we expected and feared: "Shalom, Centurion. This is a house of mourning. El'azar of Bethany has died and indeed is in the grave four days already. He was such a righteous and kind man! I am his neighbor here in Bethany, but many mourners have come from Yerushalayim to pay their respects to his sisters."

Drawing me aside, Marcus said, "It may cause trouble if I go inside the house. You go tell Miryam that Yeshua is approaching. I'll ride back to Yeshua and tell him . . . tell him what to expect."

I nodded and entered the house. Miryam and her sister were seated there. With dull, unseeing eyes and expressionless faces they received the condolences of the people.

Tavita recognized me at once and came to me. "Did he come?" she asked, seeing agreement and sorrow mingled on my face. Gnawing on her lip, Tavita was engaging in some inner debate about what to say or how to say it to her mistress when Marta looked up and saw me, then faced Tavita. The servant mouthed the words, "The Master has come."

Immediately Marta rose. She whispered briefly in Miryam's ear, who shook her head. No, she would remain where she was.

It was in my mind that Miryam of Magdala was praying—clinging desperately to a hope. If Yeshua still denied her request, her last hope was gone.

So I escorted Marta back outside. *Escorted* is a polite expression. The reality was that Marta rushed ahead of me, continually urging me to greater speed. Footsore and weary as I was, I found it difficult to keep up.

When the moving mass of the talmidim came into view, Marta abandoned me altogether and raced forward. The disciples parted to let her reach Yeshua.

She dropped to her knees at His feet. "Lord," she said bitterly. "Lord, if you had only been here, my brother would not have died."

I suppose it was impossible for her to keep the reproach out of her tone. More than just a statement of fact, her words were a complaint.

How could you let us down so badly? Perhaps recognizing the harsh criticism in her expression, Marta belatedly added, "Even now I-I know . . . God will give you whatever you ask." Such faithful words.

Such a desperate plea!

Instead of rebuking her for lack of faith, or even raising her to her feet, Yeshua chose instead to kneel in front of her. Putting His hands on her shoulders, He stated, "Marta. Your brother will rise again."

"Yes, Lord," Marta said fiercely, wiping her eyes with the backs of her hands as if to deny any grief. "I know he will, when everyone else does, at the last day." Her final words were spoken with bitterness.

"Marta," Yeshua said gently. "I AM the resurrection AND the life."

In His words I heard no simple platitude, but a ringing, threefold declaration of Truth.

The fact was, El'azar was dead.

The greater Truth is that Yeshua is the I AM, the Mighty God, the Everlasting Father. Not only does He have the power to raise the dead. No! He IS that power. Not only can He give life, He created life! He sustains life. In Truth, there is no life apart from Him.

All this I understood in an instant, as if a great voice shouted it from heaven into my soul.

But how? What?

But Yeshua was not through speaking. "Marta, those who believe in me, even though they die like everyone else, will live again. They are given eternal life for believing in me and will never perish."

With a kind touch He raised her chin so her eyes met His. "Do you believe this, Marta?"

I saw her shoulders square and her back straighten as her spirit reasserted itself. "Yes," she said firmly. "You are the Messiah, the Son of God. The One who came into the world from God."

Some words passed between them that I could not hear. Perhaps He instructed her to fetch her sister while He awaited them there. Marta rose then and headed back toward the house.

In the interval between Marta's departure and Miryam's arrival, Yeshua did not move; neither did He speak. The talmidim milled around Him, and there was much whispered conversation.

What was he doing?

After having come all this way, why did he not go to the house?

Yeshua had never shown regard for the opinions of others when it came to His ability to work miracles or comments about His reputation. Had that suddenly changed? Did He want to meet Miryam away from the public criticism of His failure?

Much sooner than I thought possible Miryam approached. Even from a distance you could see the hurry she was in, running as rapidly as her robe and sandals permitted. Behind her was Marta, and behind her, clearly baffled at her rush from the house, came a crowd of mourners.

Tavita later told me that when Marta whispered to her sister that Yeshua was asking for her, Miryam leapt up and left without explanation. The rest of the crowd imagined Miryam to be overcome with grief and rushing off to El'azar's tomb.

Arriving in front of Yeshua, Miryam fell on her knees like Marta had, but she also embraced Yeshua's feet. Her hair, unbound by running, was a wild mane about her tear-streaked face. "Lord," she said, her voice choked with emotion, "if you had been here, my brother would not have died. He wouldn't have died!"

Despite the similarity of the words spoken, I heard in Miryam's voice something different than in her sister's. Where Marta's speech had been tinged with reproach, Miryam's was altogether a statement of faith. Even when she said, "If you had *been* here," her expression said, "If *you* had been here." What's more, Miryam's haste in coming at Yeshua's summons suggested she knew He would not have called for her without a reason.

In her grief, she could add nothing further but wept even harder than before. Her shoulders shook and her hands were clenched until her knuckles turned white.

Kneeling in front of her, Yeshua brushed a lock of hair out of her eyes, then laid His palm on her forehead in blessing. When He stood He gave a great groan, as if He saw embodied in Miryam all the grief of all the bereavement of all the world.

Surveying the curious faces and spotting El'azar's elderly gatekeeper, Yeshua asked, "Where have you buried him?"

Tugging his forelock, the porter replied, "It's not far, sir. Not far at all. Come and see."

It was then I noticed how Yeshua's face was also wet with tears. He made no move to hide them or wipe them away; He gave no sign that grief was somehow unspiritual or avoidable.

No, I'm convinced Yeshua's compassion for His friends, for all of us, made Him share in all our sorrows, all our griefs.

How could He not weep, when He had to carry it all?

Someone behind me whispered, "See how much he loved El'azar?"

And someone else—a Pharisee of Jerusalem who clearly recognized me—said with deliberate cruelty, "He opened the eyes of a blind beggar. But he couldn't save the life of his friend?"

Such scorn and derision heaped into those few words!

Yeshua's purposeful strides proved He ignored all distractions as He followed the porter to the abandoned quarry and the tomb.

A great flat, round stone the size of a dining table sealed the entrance to the grave. All the onlookers hung back, uncertain what was to come and wary of intruding on great sorrow. Yeshua advanced directly to the stone and laid His hands on it, upraised above His shoulders, the way the priests pray.

Then in a commanding voice Yeshua ordered, "Roll the stone out of the way!"

There was a stunned silence while the crowd, uncertain they had heard correctly, paused a beat. Then they began to mutter and whisper among themselves.

"What can Yeshua be thinking?"

"No good can come of this, I tell you!"

"He's going to make their grief ten times worse."

Marta—practical Marta, anxious-everything-be-proper Marta—stepped to Yeshua's side and plucked His sleeve. "Lord," she said. Her eyes scanned the crowd to see if anyone would assist her, would relieve her of this terrible thing she felt compelled to say.

No one did.

"Lord, it's been . . . he's been dead four days. It . . . the smell . . . will be terrible."

In the trembling of her voice you could hear the unspoken plea: *Don't put me through this! I saw him dead, and it was horrible enough! But now! Not now!*

Kindly but firmly, Yeshua drew her aside. With a gesture He

summoned Miryam to join them. Then He said, "Didn't I tell you that you'll see God's glory, if you believe?"

In that instance Yeshua's teaching from Ezekiel flashed into my thoughts: *This is what the Sovereign Lord says—"I am going to breathe into you and make you live again!"*[58]

In that instant I saw Ya'ir's daughter, Deborah, and Eve's son, Abel! I had never met them—either one—until *after* each had been dead and raised to life again by Yeshua!

But four days dead? Dead, stinking dead?

And this is what rumbled from heaven, though perhaps no one else in the whole assembly heard it except me: **Don't ever again confuse facts with Truth! That Israel was trapped between Pharaoh's chariots and the Red Sea was fact . . . but not Truth! That a virgin could never conceive and bear a son was fact . . . but not Truth! Watch and see Truth!**

And like The Lord of All the Angel Armies issuing an order, Yeshua repeated, "Roll the stone away!"

The old porter summoned three attendants and they did so, moving the barrier aside with a chunk of limestone wedged under it.

Then they backed away.

The crowd was deathly still . . . and I use the word very deliberately.

Lifting his face toward the brilliant blue sky, Yeshua said, "Father, I thank you for hearing me. You always hear me, but I said this out loud for the sake of all these people standing here, so they will believe you sent me."

Because I love them!

In the rumble within my mind I heard an echo of what I had overheard on the Mountain Set Apart: **This is my Son, my chosen one. Listen to him!**

And then before the last of Yeshua's words had finished rolling around in my head, He suddenly shouted, "El'azar! Come forth!"

Yeshua never shouted, seldom lifted His voice. But I believe His cry that day could be heard in Jerusalem.

There was a rustling from within the shadow. A figure detached itself from a stone slab and stood upright. Then El'azar, shuffling because of the layers of cloth with which his arms and legs were bound, stepped blinking into the sunlight.

He could not speak because of the cloth wrapping his jaw tightly to his head, but his eyes said, *Where am I? What is this crowd doing here?*

And Yeshua, with a great smile of incredible joy, gestured for El'azar's sisters and the attendants. "Well? What are you waiting for? Unwrap him and let him go!"[59]

24

CHAPTER

iryam gave a shout of joy rivaling Yeshua's call across the gulf between this world and the next. Darting forward, she flung herself around her brother's neck. She yanked the cloth from his face and tore at the winding sheet.

Marta tottered and would have fallen over backwards if my father and Nakdimon had not been perfectly placed to prop her up. One man on either side assisting, she advanced toward her brother. As soon as one of El'azar's hands was unbound, she pressed it to her cheek.

The crowd of onlookers was a mass of confusion. When El'azar emerged from the tomb, some tumbled away and many more pressed forward. All babbled with astonishment. Many a man asked his neighbor if his eyes were deceiving him.

The very same Jerusalem Pharisee who had been so snide and dismissive about my new eyes now grasped me eagerly. He sought my confirmation of what we both had witnessed!

El'azar was surrounded by willing helpers, eager to remove the trappings of the grave. Marcus stood apart from the throng but was the first to offer his cloak for El'azar to use.

Miryam stroked her brother's face; her eyes bored into his. Over and over she proclaimed, "Glory to God! Glory to God!"

Marta was rooted in place, but trembling. Without releasing her grip on her brother, her gaze swiveled between him and Yeshua. At each pivot toward the Master she proclaimed, "Thank you! Thank you!"

When El'azar was unfettered and clothed again, he approached Yeshua. Dropping to his knees, he grasped both Yeshua's fists in his. Then El'azar bowed his forehead until it rested on their clasped hands.

Finally El'azar stood. My father and I, Nakdimon, and Marcus were the next ring about him after his sisters and Yeshua. I reached out and grasped his shoulder. I was not surprised to see each of the other men do the same.

Here is something I want to make clear: Unlike even Marta's trembling or the shaky sensation I had in my knees, El'azar appeared perfectly sound. This was not a man risen from a sickbed, weak and infirm after a long illness.

Yeshua had not merely restored El'azar to life; He had returned him to complete and perfect health and strength.

And more than that, El'azar's countenance was transfixed. He had the face of one still basking in a view of great beauty and wonder and mystery: a glorious sunset, a father's newborn baby, a bridegroom marveling at the beauty of his bride.

Even though no one had yet asked him to describe it, El'azar murmured, "There are no words, Lord. Lord, you know, but I can't explain it, can I? Bright colors! Flowers! Such fragrance! Music! Air full of psalms sparkling with every shade of gold and crimson and sapphire and brilliant green. Stars singing together that I heard in my chest. The most amazing garden. A chorus of voices in the stream: *Praise the Lord, O my soul!* And people. Father Avraham. I knew him at once! And then . . . your voice, Lord. As clearly as I hear myself speaking now, I heard you call me and . . . here I am. I'll never forget it—never! I'll never be afraid again. But I'll never be able to describe it either."

Then home we went. I could not help dancing and singing.

Many in the crowd stayed until well past dark. Though all had seen the same occurrence, they still did not cease reviewing each detail over and over.

Some rushed off to spread the news in Jerusalem. Some were eager to share the extraordinary event with friends and family in Bethany. Others, I'm sorry to report, scurried away to carry the tale to Caiaphas.

And the only sorrow in my recollections of that day are the words of the Lord's parable that replayed continually in my mind: *Even if one returned from the dead, they still will not believe.*

All the rest is purest joy and wonder.

And I saw it all, with my own eyes.

Nor was the raising of El'azar to life from death witnessed by a mere handful of biased onlookers. No, rather it was seen by over a hundred men and women. Some were people of position, others of notable reputation, and a fair number were reported to be scrupulously honest.

In other words, from the crowd present that day there were many excellent, reliable witnesses. All could attest to the reality of the occurrence: El'azar was dead . . . stinking dead . . . four days dead. And then he was alive again, at Yeshua's call.

In *olam haba*, the world to come, El'azar had heard Yeshua's Voice and returned to this earth. He came not to warn us about the terrors of hell, but to woo us with true tales of heaven . . . the world the Father has prepared for those who love Him!

Not to warn, but to woo!

And I am now convinced that if anyone had even one glimpse into heaven, nothing on earth would keep them from running to Yeshua.

What's more, this most significant of all Yeshua's miracles did not happen in some backwater village of the Galil or Perea. Bethany was within a Sabbath day's journey of one of the major cities of the world. Hundreds of thousands of people lived in Jerusalem.

It is not an exaggeration to assert that most of them heard of the raising of El'azar within a day or two at most of the event.

And what was the result, you ask?

In part, it's as you would expect. A great many came to believe in Yeshua as the Messiah of Israel. Because of that one demonstration of His power and authority, great hope spread throughout the Holy City and all over Judea.

"The Holy One has come! The time of which the prophets Ezekiel and Dani'el wrote has come to us! Now! In our day!"

But this resurgence of hope was not universal, as hard as that is for me to believe and to record.

There were those among the circle around Caiaphas and the

Sanhedrin who chose not to believe, or to ignore the evidence. They had a greater fear of losing their prestige and power than they had reverence for what they had witnessed. They were more concerned about their position than about the fact that Immanu'el—God-with-us—had conclusively demonstrated the validity of that title.

In truth, this Bethany event so terrified Caiaphas and others that they actively sought ways not merely to silence Yeshua, but to kill Him.

And they hated El'azar enough to want him dead as well.

It was said by John bar Zebedee, when he wrote of the Master's life, that there are certain signs to be tallied as evidence of Yeshua's authority. The day Yeshua changed the water into wine is one such;[60] the day He healed a nobleman's son is another.[61] Restoring the crippled man by the Pool of Bethesda is listed.[62] So is feeding five thousand with five barley loaves and two dried fish.[63] Yeshua proved His ability to create fishers of men by first demonstrating a miraculous catch of fish.[64] That event was another noteworthy occurrence. Creating eyes for a man born blind—for me—was a particularly significant day![65]

Now John noted that "if all the things Yeshua said and did were written down, not all the books in the world could contain them."[66] And that is true. There were many healings, many demons cast out, many broken lives restored, which were never recorded, except in the hearts of those touched by Yeshua's mercy.

But John recorded seven specific signs of Yeshua's power and authority. He made special note of seven occasions when Yeshua showed irrefutably that He was indeed who He claimed to be—that He was and is the Son of God.

And the day on which El'azar of Bethany was raised was the seventh of these . . . the seventh day.

What did I learn from what I witnessed in those weeks that I traveled with Yeshua?

I learned to never confuse facts with Truth.

The fact is, El'azar was dead.

The greater Truth is that Yeshua is the Resurrection and the Life.

I learned that sometimes we do not understand how The Lord of All the Angel Armies is working for our benefit.

The greater Truth is that He *always* cares and provides for us. Even if He delays, it is *because* He loves us.

I learned that Yeshua cried. He shed tears of grief for what El'azar suffered.[67] He shed tears of compassion for the pain of Miryam and Marta's loss.

He shed tears of longing for all creation to be restored, for death to be abolished, because that day was not just about El'azar. Everyone present that day had a grave awaiting them.

But the greater Truth is that Yeshua wept because for all His love, compassion, and longing, for all His sacrifice, some will still refuse His gift. Out of arrogance or pride, some will die as Ra'nabel ben Dives died . . . and Yeshua was weeping for him and for all like him who leave this world outside the friendship of God.

Finally I learned the true meaning of the Sabbath. Six days are appointed for us to work, to labor for the Kingdom. Six days we will face turmoil and deal with grief. Six days we will long for Yeshua's return. *"Lord, if you had only been here . . ."*

But the greater Truth is that the Seventh Day *is* coming. The Lord of the Sabbath, The Lord of the Seventh Day, is returning.

May it be today!

Epilogue

The air of the cavern was suffused with the aroma of lavender. Alfie said, "Your papa told me, 'Give this scroll to Shimon when he needs it most.' That's what your papa told me."

Shimon raised his eyes and slowly rolled up the scroll and replaced it in the ancient jar. "Papa was right. It's as though death has no power anymore. I almost expect to meet them all here in the cavern. You know? Expect to hear them speak to me. El'azar—Lazarus they call him now. But anyway, I half expect he'll just step into the cavern and come and join us at the table, you know, Alfie?"

The old man's massive head bobbed in agreement. "Sure. Sure! I know. Just what your papa said the first time we read the book—1948 it were. Like yesterday. Time don't mean nothing beneath the Temple Mount in Jerusalem. Everything waiting till Yeshua comes back. Waiting. Time don't mean nothing here."

Alfie grinned back at Shimon with childlike delight. He waved his big paw over the scrap of linen Shimon guessed must have come from a shroud. "Four days El'azar were dead," Alfie continued. "Four. Don't matter four days or forty years or four hundred. Or a thousand or two thousand. It don't matter none about how long. God is the God of the living, not the dead. Time don't mean nothing to God. That's the point. That's what your papa wanted you to know at the end of seven days' mourning. See? It don't matter how long, Shimon. Your papa wanted you to know that especially today."

"The seventh day. That's what it means. Shabbat Shalom. Peace. The end of mourning," Shimon whispered. The painted stars above their heads shimmered with ethereal light. "Alfie? What happened to El'azar after that? Is it written down somewhere? In some scroll?" Shimon stroked the cool clay of the second jar. "Is there some account of how long El'azar lived after that?"

Alfie did not reply for a long time. His eyes shone with amusement at Shimon's question. "You mean, where is El'azar of Bethany now?" He raised his finger to his lips. "Ah, Shimon . . . can't you hear? Make your mind be still and listen."

The faint tinkle of bells, like a wind chime in a gentle breeze, echoed from some distant place. And behind the bells was a melody—angelic voices singing a song without words.

Shimon shivered and managed a hoarse whisper. "Alfie? Do you hear that?"

Alfie inhaled with deep satisfaction. He closed his eyes and nodded once. "Sure, Shimon, sure. I hear them always."

Jesus said to her,

"I am the resurrection and the life.

He who believes in Me will live,

even though he dies;

and whoever lives and believes in Me

will never die.

Do you believe this?"

JOHN 11:25-26

Digging Deeper into
SEVENTH DAY

Dear Reader,

Have you ever waited so long for something that you couldn't believe it when it finally happened?

The people of Nazareth had waited a long time for the Messiah of prophecy to rescue them from the reign of the Romans, who crushed their spirits, their bodies, and their finances. The people had waited so long, in fact, that they were rather cynical about anyone who made messiah claims. So many men had come to Israel and declared themselves messiah, but most had either faded away or had died under a Roman sword.

But Yeshua was different. When He touched people, their bodies were healed. Their hearts were healed. Hope was reborn. Though the Sanhedrin had the authority to judge and condemn men, Yeshua had the far greater authority to heal men's souls and bodies. He called them back to God from the far exile of sin and proclaimed mercy and forgiveness in the name of His Father.

El'azar of Bethany was a different man. Witnessing Deborah's death and return to life had changed the young landowner forever. He had come to the Galil with Nakdimon as an arrogant, opinionated, bitter young man. Together the friends had moved from suspicion and ambiguity to the belief that Yeshua was at the very least a great prophet. . . . But was there more to Him than even that?

Who was Yeshua? By what authority did He speak? Where did His mysterious power come from?

Through the written records of Peniel, Shimon Sachar was confronted with the Truth about who Yeshua is. And Shimon experienced an emotional, spiritual miracle:

> "I read the scrolls and saw myself for the first time. I knew I was blind like Peniel. I was a leper like Lily. Bitter like Alexander. Afraid like Yosef. And then, Yeshua was born in my heart. Now when I'm outside, I walk through the streets in a different century. I go to the Pool of Siloam, where Peniel washed clay from his eyes and gained his vision. I search the faces of everyone as I pass by, thinking I'll see Peniel. Hoping I will round a corner and find Yeshua teaching his talmidim. I drink a cup of coffee at Starbucks—and count the hours. Can't wait to come back here. To read. To learn. To know Yeshua better."
>
> —SHIMON TO ALFIE (P. XI)

In *Seventh Day*, El'azar himself experienced a physical miracle: Yeshua raised him from the dead—when he had been four days dead, no less. And Yeshua not only raised him but restored him to full health!

What kind of miracle do you long for today? Physical health? The healing of a relationship? Calm for a mind clouded with worry? Do you feel guilt over the past? Do you fear the future? Do you wonder, like Shimon did after losing his wife and baby, if life is worth living anymore? Come to Yeshua! Come to know the Truth! Read, learn, and get to know Him better.

Following are six studies. You may wish to delve into them on your own or share them with a friend or a discussion group. They are designed to take you deeper into the answers to questions such as:

- Could a man walking the earth really be God?
- How can you handle personal suffering?
- Are miracles real—or made-up, dramatic stories?
- What is your life story, and what do stories from the Bible have to do with it?
- What's the difference between the facts of your life situation and God's ultimate Truth . . . and how can you bridge the gap?
- What do you think heaven—or the afterlife—will be like?

Through *Seventh Day*, may the promised Messiah come alive to you . . . in more brilliance than ever before.

1 | THE MAN NEXT DOOR

"The baby in the manger's grown up. A man."
—ALFIE (P. XIII)

Yeshua, who created everything seen and unseen, came to dwell among men in the time appointed. Conceived in the womb of a virgin in Nazareth, He was born in Beth-lehem and grew to be a great teacher and miracle worker known by all the world.
—JOURNAL OF PENIEL (P. 3)

If you heard stories that your neighbor was performing miracles in your local community, what would your first reaction be? Why?

_____

_____

_____

What would you do next?

- Call another neighbor to find out if he/she had heard the same thing?
- Check out the facts for yourself with someone who had been "healed"?
- Talk to the supposed miracle worker?
- Shake your head and call all your neighbors crazy for even thinking such a common person could work miracles?

Why? What does your response have to do with your own background and experiences?

_____

_____

_____

Nazareth was a peaceful little village. The people there were relatively untouched by King Herod's maniacal rage and the deadly politics of Jerusalem and Rome. They lived fairly uneventful lives. Among them was Yeshua, the son of a carpenter, who left the village after He had grown. But His return caused a great stir. . . .

READ

It was some time after the death of Yosef, His earthly father, that Yeshua returned to Nazareth to reveal the secret—to plainly share the testimony of His true paternity, as prophesied in Torah.

Though certain they had known Him all their lives, the people of Nazareth had no idea who Yeshua was or where He had come from. Nor could they imagine the eons that had passed since this moment of divine revelation had been planned.

Despite the fact that every detail of Messiah's life and mission was revealed within the text of ancient law and prophets, the good people of Nazareth did not comprehend.

Not surprising.

After all, could Messiah live next door?

"Yeshua, my mother wonders, please, could she borrow two eggs?"

Was it possible that The Lord of All the Angel Armies, El Olam, and Ancient of Days, had descended to earth from His throne and was singing in the carpenter's workshop?

Could the descendant of David—Prophet, Priest, and King—be more than a metaphor? Could He truly be Immanu'el, God-with-us?

They had heard of Yeshua's miracles, yes, but even then, few in Nazareth believed.

—PP. 7–8

ASK

If you were one of the people in Nazareth—Yeshua's neighbors—would you immediately believe that He, the little boy you'd seen grow up as an ordinary carpenter's son, could perform miracles? Why or why not?

_____

_____

_____

What sign would you require in order to believe that Yeshua was a miracle worker? Why that sign in particular?

_____

_____

_____

If you were going to research Yeshua's claim, what source would you turn to first?

READ

Written record:

Ben Dives turned the pages of the journal he had acquired from the archives under the Temple Mount. . . .

The journal recounted how prophecies about the promised descendant of David had been fulfilled thirty-three or so years previous, or around the time of the conflagration. According to Eliyahu, a whole sequence of miraculous events began when an angel appeared to an aged priest named Zachariah, promising that he and his equally ancient wife would have a son. This baby was said to be the forerunner of the Messiah, as spoken of by the prophet Malachi. King Herod, disliking any reference to someone other than himself as "king of the Jews," sought the parents but could not find them.

Then, the record continued, about a year and a few months after the first angelic announcement, Jerusalem was again disturbed by astounding news. A group of Levite shepherds, Beth-lehemites, were said to have also had angelic visitors. Rabbi Eliyahu claimed that he had been with the shepherds when the angels appeared. At their direction, he and the shepherds found an infant whom Eliyahu believed to be the promised Messiah . . . newly born in a lambing cave and lying in a manger.

Ben Dives raised his head, frowned, and bit his lower lip. Not an auspicious beginning for the Anointed One. Maybe the rabbi was crazy, or maybe he was trying to cover something up. . . .

After the prescribed forty days, the child was presented in the Temple. This occurrence was said to be witnessed by many, including an ancient holy man called Simeon the Elder. . . .

Eliyahu wrote that King Herod, taking no chances with any baby's claim to his throne, ordered the slaughter of all the two-year-old and younger males in Beth-lehem. This command, carried out in a single night's slaughter, eliminated all such children, including Eliyahu's own son. . . .

Then the scroll added a startling, cryptic, and final note. In a firmer hand it stated: *But he escaped.*

The child, the messianic pretender, escaped that destruction? And today He would be . . . thirty-two. How old was Yeshua? It could be Him, ben Dives mused. It could be. . . .

—PP. 47–48

Eyewitnesses:

"Thirty years ago angels spoke in the Temple to an old priest named Zachariah. The father of the Baptizer. Shortly afterward the signs in the heavens declared a King had been born in Israel. Angels showed themselves to Temple shepherds on the same night the prophet Haggai promised. The echoes of their shouts are still in the memory of the people. No baby is ever born already ruling as a king. First the baby must be a prince. But those who saw the signs knew that the one born in Beth-lehem in the time of the Feast of Dedication was, according to the prophecies of Haggai and Micah, the true King of the Jews. Wise men, who had studied the weeks of years spoken of by Dani'el, came from distant lands to worship this new King. My grandfather—Reb Gamaliel's father, Simeon the Elder—actually met the promised infant when he was brought to the Temple for his dedication." . . .

Nakdimon continued, "Old Herod feared this prophecy above all others and ordered the children of the City of David murdered." . . .

Gamaliel finished, "Each year at this time, the people recall the prophecy of Haggai. They wonder if the Son of David, grown to manhood, will come to the Temple."

Nakdimon added, "Herod Antipas, the son of the old Butcher King, now sits on his father's throne. He fears the same prophecy. He killed the Baptizer, succeeding where his father failed. Antipas fears that maybe the butchery of that long-ago night in Beth-lehem did *not* kill the promised King Messiah. And he is right, eh?"

El'azar concurred. "Yes. It is Yeshua. I've heard the story myself from the lips of old Zadok the Shepherd, who saw the angels. He whose own baby boys were murdered. The Feast of Dedication comes soon again. The shepherds of the Temple flocks in Beth-lehem say this is when the angels told them to seek a baby in the lambing cave."

Gamaliel pondered the statement. "And was that baby Yeshua? High Priest Caiaphas and his minion ben Dives dread that Yeshua *is* the child the shepherds found. They fear he escaped the slaughter and that he may come to the Temple on that date."

El'azar counted the remaining days. "The twenty-fourth day of Kislev."

Nakdimon stared hard at the book of Haggai. "As Haggai predicted. The Feast of Dedication."

—PP. 55–56

Yeshua Himself:

> "*Today you are standing, all of you, in the presence of Adonai, your God . . . in order to enter into a covenant with Adonai, your God; a covenant Adonai is making with you today and sealing with an oath.*" (Deut. 29:10-12)

Taken literally, the verse informed the congregation plainly that they were in the presence of the Lord, that He was physically there.

Yet the hearers did not hear.

Those who saw Him did not see.

Another read:

> "*But I am not making this covenant and this oath only with you. Rather I am making it both with him who is standing here with us today before Adonai our God and also with him who is not here with us today; those of future generations. . . .*" (Deut. 29:14-15)

The truth of the message escaped them. After all, Scripture was just Scripture. Familiar. Boring. An obligation. They studied it, read a different Parashah every week, memorized it, and talked about it all the time. It never meant anything literal, did it?

That the Lord Himself was standing in their midst?

—P. 8

Scripture:

The scroll of the prophet Isaias was presented to Him. Unrolling it, He found the appointed place and began to read:

"The Spirit of Adonai is upon Me, because He has anointed Me to preach good news to the poor. He has sent Me to bind up the brokenhearted, to proclaim freedom for the prisoners and recovery of sight for the blind, to release the oppressed, to proclaim the year of the favor of Adonai." (Isa. 61:1-2)

Yeshua rolled up the scroll, gave it back to the shammash, and sat down. The eyes of everyone were fastened on Him, and He said to them, "Today this passage of the Tanakh is fulfilled in your hearing."

—P. 9

ASK

If you were to believe that Yeshua was the promised Messiah, which evidence would you find most compelling?

- Written record (journals)
- Eyewitnesses
- Yeshua Himself
- Scripture

Why?

_____

_____

_____

If you read the above evidence, what would your conclusion be about who the man next door is?

_____

_____

_____

If you did believe Yeshua was the Messiah, what, if anything, about your life would change? If you don't believe He's the Messiah, what are your reasons? Do any past experiences, beliefs, or philosophies hold you back from trusting that Yeshua is who He says He is? If so, which ones—and why?

_____

_____

_____

READ
"What?"
"Fulfilled?"
"You don't say?"
The congregants eyed each other in consternation.
Yeshua's earthly father was dead, His mother left a widow.
"If you are truly the Messiah, why did Yosef die?"
Broken hearts in Nazareth were still broken. The poor were still poor. Blind were still blind. The oppressed were still burdened. If Yeshua *was* Messiah, He had not done them any favors!
"Today the Scripture is fulfilled, he said? Who does he think he is?"
"Isn't this Yosef's son?" an old man asked. . . .
If only they had opened their hearts, they might have understood that Yeshua was The One Sent from heaven to lavish Yahweh's endless *chesed,* mercy, on all who called out to Him.
If only!
But the people of His hometown were in no mood to listen.
"He's a nobody, this son of a carpenter!"
"Yet now he declares he meets the criteria to be Messiah!"

"*Heal the sick and raise the dead? To cleanse the Temple of corruption and set up a kingdom? And bring the exiles home?*"

"*Yeshua claims he is the fulfillment of all the writings of Torah and the prophets?*"

"*He's a madman! Or worse!*"

It was a mob comprised of old friends and good neighbors who dragged Him outside the town with the goal of hurtling Him over a cliff.

The Sovereign Lord of the Universe, the Anointed Messiah promised by the prophets, had indeed lived next door. And they drove Him away.

The Parashah proclaimed, *Listen! Today you stand before Adonai! He has come to you personally to seal the covenant He made with Abraham, Isaac, and Jacob! Choose life!*

They chose, instead, to try to kill Him.

Yeshua never returned to Nazareth. Not ever. There were other towns, other needs, others who hoped He would come to them.

—PP. 9–10

Gamaliel rubbed a hand over his brow and muttered, "What a time we live in. If he is who we believe, can it be?"

"We should warn him." El'azar's brow wrinkled with worry.

Gamaliel sighed and sat down heavily. "Warn? Yes. By all means. We should send a delegation . . . or a messenger into the Galil. And they'll bring the saddest tidings in the history of Israel's rebellion against the Lord's Anointed. 'So, Yeshua,' they'll say. 'Don't come to Yerushalayim. Don't reveal yourself to your people now, though we know who you are already. The rulers of Israel are sold out to the Romans. They will kill you. Plunge a dagger into the heart of your blessed mother. Do not come down to the Festival of Lights this year . . . although you alone carry the light of God within you.'"

Nakdimon stood slowly. "I'll travel north. Find him. Warn him of danger." . . .

"You'll have to leave without being seen. The chief priest and his contingent have hired assassins. We know that. You'll have to leave Yerushalayim quietly."

—PP. 56–57

One of Gamaliel's talmidim openly heckled, "Tell us again, Rabbi! Who are you? This time in plain language!"

Yeshua did not falter. He fixed His gaze on ben Dives and then past him to where the bulk of High Priest Caiaphas stood framed in the doorway of a dressing chamber. "The proof is what I do in the name of my Father."

There was a ripple, then a roar from the scribes and Pharisees. "Your *father*!"

At the hatred and scorn poured into the word, I jumped as if stung. I moved toward Yeshua, wanting to be a shield for the man who had given me eyes . . . and sonship. . . .

"Do you mean the Holy One, blessed be he forever, is YOUR father?" a Levite challenged Yeshua. "You claim to be the Son and Heir? You claim that what you do is from the Holy One?"

"Your *father*?" one of the Pharisees bellowed at the Teacher. "You are the Son of the Almighty? Blessed be he, and cursed is your blasphemy of HaShem today!"

—P. 93

But Yeshua was widely known as being from the Galil, even called Yeshua the Nazarene—not that being from Nazareth was anything of which to be proud!

Ben Dives chuckled and it became a snort of derision.

Still . . .

This would bear closer examination. Not that ben Dives believed Yeshua's claims . . . not for a minute. But if He was the same as this fortunate surviving infant, might He not use that circumstance to advance His claim?

And ben Dives would be able to turn that news to his own advantage.

—PP. 48–49

ASK

How did these people respond to Yeshua's claim to be Messiah?

- The townspeople of Nazareth
- Nakdimon, Gamaliel, El'azar
- The religious leaders
- Ben Dives

_____

_____

_____

Explain why you think these groups responded differently. What did each have to gain—or lose—if Yeshua's claims were true?

_____

_____

_____

WONDER . . .

The rejection of the power of the Holy Spirit and the salvation of Yeshua the Messiah began long ago. The rejection of Yeshua's gift of mercy began with those among whom He had grown up.

I, Peniel, man born blind, scribe of the Way, record these memories for generations who will be born after us.

Is it still true in your day that those who should trust Him with the faithfulness of a child are instead the very ones who deny the glory, might, and power of The One Sent to open the eyes of the blind?

—JOURNAL OF PENIEL (PP. 4–5)

How could they accuse Yeshua of blasphemy when clearly the miracles were proof of His goodness? . . . I raised my fingers to my eyes, remembering my darkness. I thought of the shadowed quiet of the Holy Place, where prayers were recited day after day. I considered how in the interior of that sacred building men spoke in hushed whispers as they breathed air thick with the incense of half a thousand years. And yet! Had none of the holiness of the place entered their souls? How could those who lived and breathed the worship of the Almighty be so insensitive to the fragrance of Messiah? . . .

Yeshua raised His fingers slightly as if to draw in the clamor and hold it in His palm. "You don't believe me because you're not part of my flock." Then embracing with His eyes all those who had risked everything to follow Him, He continued, "My sheep know my voice. I know them and they follow me. I give them eternal life, and they will never perish."

—PP. 93–94

What do you believe about the man next door? Is your heart sensitive to the presence of the Messiah? Do you know His voice and follow Him? Why or why not?

2 | THE SUBSTANCE OF HOPE

His name was Abel. Abel begins with *alef*, the first letter of the alphabet. He was Eve's first and only son—her miracle, her joy. He was her life. He was everything . . . the substance of every hope.

—P. 10

Who or what is your everything . . . the substance of your hope? Why?

_____

_____

_____

If you suddenly lost that person or thing, how would you respond?

_____

_____

_____

Eve was the daughter of an innkeeper. She was kind, but not the first chosen to be a wife since she was rather homely. Still, she longed for love and marriage. Finally she was married off to a childless older scribe after his second wife died. When she became pregnant, her world swirled with hope. . . .

READ

Like Isaac, the baby was a miracle child—a gift from God, his father, Absalom, said. So they named him Abel, meaning "God is my Father."

Circumcised into the covenant of Abraham at eight days, Abel was the lone offspring of Eve and Absalom the Scribe.

Perhaps her dreams for him were unrealistic, her love for him too extravagant. Much later the people of Nain would say she should have known better, should have been more cautious with her love.

After all, nothing ever turns out the way it should. . . .

Almost from the beginning Abel's hold on life was tenuous. He could not run and play like other boys in the village of Nain. When the winds blew in from the fields and orchards, he was put to bed and ordered not to venture out. The boy sat beside his aged father in the doorway and wheezed worse than the old man as they watched the world pass by.

Though Abel did not have the breath to sing, his mother sang to him constantly. He knew and loved the psalms and could write the words by heart before he was seven.

Abel was only eight when his father suddenly died. And just that suddenly the boy was the lone remaining joy in his mother's life. She clung to him and thanked Adonai that at least she had this one reason for living, so her life was not over!

Even then people whispered that she should hold something back—be cautious in her dreams. After all, nothing ever turned out the way it should . . . not on this side of *olam haba*, the world to come.

Abel mourned for his old father seven days. In the silence of his grief it was as though the boy was old and wise beyond his years. When he rose from the ashes, he whispered aloud a thought that was surely a prophecy about his future.

He told Adonai how very much he longed to be with his father one day. When Abel became very ill, he told Adonai he wouldn't mind dying, except for the fact that his mother needed him.

He was only thirteen years old when the life that had begun with such joy moved inexorably toward its end.

—PP. 10–12

ASK

If you were Eve, how would you respond to having a chronically ill child? What would your feelings be toward your child? toward God?

_____

_____

_____

What if, as you were dealing with your sick son on a day-to-day basis, suddenly your husband died? What would you think then?

_____

_____

_____

READ

Eve, the wife of Absalom, had only one son. Abel was neither strong nor healthy. Even so, his mother widely proclaimed that Abel was better to her than ten sons. She thanked Adonai daily for the gift of Abel's life. . . .

Much later, perhaps, Eve would say she knew all along there was something greater, something eternally necessary, some purpose more important than the suffering she endured for the sake of loving her child.

But not now. . . .

Not as she sat helpless at his bed and bargained with a silent God for the life of the only one who loved her in all the world.

Please! My life for his!

Not as she held her son in her arms and watched him die. . . .

Vain hopes for his healing had killed him. She was responsible.

She would have to live with that guilt.

If only. If only we had stayed home. If only we had not set out in search of a miracle! If only! . . .

It was not supposed to be like this. It was unnatural in the order of life. A mother was not meant to outlive her child. No, not ever. Such a tragedy would crack the still-beating heart of any woman into so many pieces that it would never properly heal.

She reminded the One God of Israel of this fact as the doctor toiled to save the boy that afternoon.

Take my life instead. Anything! Please. Only let him live.

—PP. 11–13, 16

ASK

Have you ever bargained with God for anything? If so, what? What was
the result?

_____

_____

_____

Have you ever felt guilty or responsible for something bad that has happened
to someone else? What happened? How have you come to terms with your _if
only_?

_____

_____

_____

READ

She did not call out for help or rend the fabric of her garment as finally she
accepted his death. No. A few hours more of this night and the women from
the synagogue would come . . . and carry him away from her forever.

Forever!

For now, only in these last few hours before their parting, he still
belonged to her. Her boy. Her only . . . only son. The one true treasure.

She lay her cheek against his head and silently rocked him. Sleeping in
her arms for this last time, he was once again her baby, toddler, little boy,
youth, young man. . . .

Maybe one day she would be content to live only with memories of
her son's unfinished life. Perhaps in a time to come she would think of Abel
singing in heaven and be comforted by songs she could not hear.

But not now. Not tonight. No.

As if he could hear her whisper, she rehearsed details of his short life
and thanked him, _thanked him,_ for the love he had given her.

—P. 20

ASK

Have you lost someone close to you? If so, how did you respond to that loss then . . . and now?

_____

_____

_____

In what way(s) is your response similar to or different from Eve's?

_____

_____

_____

How could you "rehearse the details" of your loved one's life—and thank that person for the love he or she gave you?

_____

_____

_____

READ

"Last night. It's Abel! Last night . . . he's . . . flown away. Gone. Oh, help me! Yahweh has turned his back on me. My son . . . my boy is dead!"

With that admission, every action was beyond her control. A child was sent to the synagogue with the news. Within minutes the solemn blast of the shofar announced to all that death had visited their congregation.

The who and the how and the why of it spread through the community like a fire.

"They were on their way to find Yeshua!"

"They hoped he would be healed!"

"The doctor commanded her to keep him in bed!"

"She was so full of hope when they set out!"

—P. 21

The unspoken question foremost in every mind asked how the widow would survive her own advancing years without at least one child to support her. Who would marry a woman on whom The Eternal had frowned twice with such severity?

"Her husband taken. She has no other living relatives. Now the only son cut off."

Surely this was a judgment of Adonai against some hidden sin in her life.

—P. 22

"Poor creature. She loved him, though he was always a burden."

"Aye. Poor thing. But she's better off now he's gone. Maybe now she can sell herself as a bondservant. Have a roof over her head and food to eat. Couldn't do that as long as he was alive."

"It was meant to be. They're both better off now he's gone. Suffering ended. Better off, they are."

"Aye. Anyone could see by looking what a sickly boy he was."

"And as for him ever giving her grandchildren? He never would have married anyway."

"Cursed by poverty and illness. Who would marry such a one?"

"And what did she expect? They say Yeshua and his talmidim often steal away to the hills or across the waters to escape the crowds. Many have gone in search of him and he's not there."

"Take the lad twenty-five miles to find a miracle worker? What was she thinking?"

"Blessed are they who do not hope, for they shall never be disappointed."

—P. 25

ASK

How did the townspeople respond to Eve's pain? Have similar comments been made to or about you when you were hurting? Or have you said things like these in light of others' pain? In what situation(s)?

_____

_____

_____

"Blessed are they who do not hope, for they shall never be disappointed." Has that ever been a mantra of yours? If so, what happened to make you believe that?

_____

_____

_____

And then Eve meets Yeshua on the way to bury her son. . . .

READ

Yeshua? Now? Why has he come today? her heart challenged. *Why not yesterday, when it mattered?*

If only!

What could the miracle worker offer her now but empty platitudes and sympathy?

Yeshua's appearance with the mob of followers and eager supplicants only served to remind Eve that Abel might still be alive today if they hadn't gone in search of a miracle.

—P. 28

Yeshua stepped into the center of the road and blocked the procession. He strode past Rabbi D'varim and came toward Eve as though He had always known her.

When He lifted her chin from staring at the dusty path, she took in

His sweat-stained robe and brown beard. Sad brown eyes flecked with gold regarded her.

Quietly, privately, as if for her ears alone, He said, "Shalom. Peace. Woman, *don't* cry." . . .

Eve's heart rebelled at His callousness. How could she not weep? Who was this to give such a command?

—PP. 28–29

Yeshua's eyes brimmed with compassion. With His right thumb He brushed a tear from her cheek. "Don't cry." His earnest gaze steadied her. "*Hazak!* Be strong!"

Leaving her, He approached the body. He stood too near death to remain undefiled. Gazing down into the ashen face as though He knew the boy, Yeshua touched the bier. Closing His eyes, He lifted His face toward heaven. . . .

"Young man? I say to you, get up!"

An instant of stunned silence passed. . . .

The flutter of Abel's lashes moved the coins on his lids.

Hazak! Be strong!

And then in a barely audible whisper the boy began to recite the first words of the Amidah as he had every night and every morning in the months before his bar mitzvah: "*Adonai, open my lips, that my mouth may declare your praise*" (Psalm 51:15). . . .

The world spun around Eve. Her knees buckled and she fell. "Abel?"

—PP. 29–30

ASK

Put yourself in Eve's place. What emotions and thoughts would you experience in each of the three portions of the story above?

_____

_____

_____

_____

If you saw a loved one rise from death to life, would you believe these words to be true or not? If not, what would it take to convince you?

"Your name is Yeshua, Salvation! Holy are you, and your name is revered; there is no god like you. Blessed are you, Adonai, the holy God."
—P. 30

WONDER . . .

Mired in hopelessness before Yeshua came, the *am ha aretz*, the common folk, were resigned to suffering. Bitterness was a kind of opiate that numbed the pain of living and the inevitability of death. Beaten down by unrelieved despair, they accepted the fact that life was brutal and unmerciful, and they made the best of it.

Then rumors stirred the watch fires of Israel. The quiet whisper was passed from one to another as water was drawn from the village wells.

"They say the Deliverer is alive! His name is Yeshua!"

Hadn't Yeshua healed someone who knew someone who told someone who told everyone?

Yeshua, a descendant of King David, restored health to the sick, gave galaxies and sunsets to the blind!

Poetry and song poured from the throats of the mute!

Music and laughter tickled the ears of the deaf!

Cripples danced at the Temple gates!

Lepers were made whole again!

There was free bread for all who were hungry!

Messiah!

Tenuous roots of possibility sank deep into hearts and minds with every new report. Then suddenly it was not enough simply to hear about Him anymore. Those who were most desperate for an answer lay in bed and stared into the darkness at night.

If only!
—P. 13

"King, Helper, Savior, and Shield! Blessed are You, O Eternal! Reviving the dead; You are all powerful to save! He sustains the living in mercy, and reanimates the dead in abundant compassion; supports the fallen, heals the sick, releases those who are bound! Who is like You, Lord of mighty deeds?"
—PP. 8–9

In what way(s) are you in need of healing? in need of answers? in need of hope? Explain.

_____

_____

_____

Yeshua is waiting, with arms spread wide, for you to turn to Him.

3 | MIRACULOUS HAPPENINGS . . . OR PROOF?

"Unless you people see miraculous signs and wonders," Jesus told him, "you will never believe."
—JOHN 4:48

"Papa told me each scroll represents a life. An event. A miracle. So much more Yeshua did. So much never recorded. All the books in all the world can't hold everything."
—SHIMON (P. XII)

Do you believe that miracles can occur today? Or were they just something that happened way back, ages ago? Explain.

_____

_____

_____

If you could be granted one miracle in your lifetime, what would you choose? Why?

_____

_____

_____

When the apostle John wrote about Yeshua's life, he said that there were certain signs that could be tallied as evidence of Yeshua's authority. And these signs were at the heart of Yeshua's miracles.

READ

The wedding at Cana (read the whole story in John 2:1-11):

While Yeshua was at a wedding in Cana, His mother told Him that they had run out of celebratory wine. So Yeshua asked the servants to fill the jars with water, then told them to draw some out and take it to the master of the banquet.

They did so, and the master of the banquet tasted the water that had been turned into wine. He did not realize where it had come from, though the servants who had drawn the water knew. Then he called the bridegroom aside and said, "Everyone brings out the choice wine first and then the cheaper wine after the guests have had too much to drink; but you have saved the best till now."

This, the first of His miraculous signs, Yeshua performed at Cana in Galilee. He thus revealed His glory, and His disciples put their faith in Him.

The nobleman's son (read the whole story in John 4:43-54):

Yeshua left Nazareth, because He was not honored in His own country. When He arrived in Galilee, the people there welcomed Him. They had seen all that He had done in Jerusalem at the Passover Feast, for they had also been there. When Yeshua visited Cana again (the same location where He'd turned the water into wine), a royal official came to Him, told Him about his sick son, and begged Him to come heal his son, who was close to death.

Yeshua replied, "You may go. Your son will live."

The man took Yeshua at His word and departed. While he was still on the way, his servants met him with the news that the boy was living. When he inquired as to the time when his son got better, they said to him, "The fever left him yesterday at the seventh hour."

Then the father realized that this was the exact time at which Yeshua had said to him, "Your son will live." So he and all his household believed.

This was the second miraculous sign that Yeshua performed, having come from Judea to Galilee.

The crippled man (read the whole story in John 5:1-15):

While Yeshua was in Jerusalem for a feast of the Jews, He visited the pool of Bethesda, where a great number of disabled people used to lie. One had been an invalid for thirty-eight years.

When Yeshua saw him lying there and learned that he had been in this condition for a long time, He asked him, "Do you want to get well?"

"Sir," the invalid replied, "I have no one to help me into the pool when the water is stirred. While I am trying to get in, someone else goes down ahead of me."

Then Yeshua said to him, "Get up! Pick up your mat and walk." At once the man was cured; he picked up his mat and walked.

The feeding of the five thousand (read the whole story in John 6:1-15):
Yeshua crossed to the far shore of the Sea of Galilee and a great crowd followed Him because they had seen the miraculous signs He had performed on the sick. When Yeshua saw the huge crowd, He asked Philip, one of His disciples, "Where can we buy bread for these people to eat?" (He said that only to test Philip, since He already knew what He was going to do.)

Philip was the first to speak, and he was a naysayer about the costs of feeding such a group.

Then Andrew spoke up. "Here is a boy with five small barley loaves and two small fish, but how far will they go among so many?"

Yeshua said, "Have the people sit down." He then took the loaves, gave thanks, and distributed to those who were seated as much as they wanted. He did the same with the fish.

When they had all had enough to eat, He said to His disciples, "Gather the pieces that are left over. Let nothing be wasted." So they gathered them and filled twelve baskets with the pieces of the five barley loaves left over by those they had eaten.

After the people saw the miraculous sign that Yeshua did, they began to say, "Surely this is the Prophet who is to come into the world." Yeshua, knowing that they intended to come and make him king by force, withdrew again to a mountain by Himself.

The catch of fish (read the whole story in John 21:1-14):
Some of Yeshua's disciples were fishing by the Sea of Tiberias and not having much luck. Early in the morning, a man on the shore (they didn't recognize that it was Yeshua) called out to them, "Friends, haven't you any fish?"

"No," they answered.

He said, "Throw your net on the right side of the boat and you will find some." When they did, they were unable to haul the net in because of the large number of fish. Simon Peter dragged the net ashore. It was full of large fish, 153, but even with so many the net was not torn.

The man born blind (read the whole story in John 9:1-41):

In Jerusalem I sat in darkness, incomplete, unable to comprehend the glory of The One who created the stars. And though I heard the psalms that spoke of the beauty HaShem had created, I could not understand.

One day Yeshua saw me in the Temple Gate, and His compassion was warmed for me. Then He who is the Great Potter, forming all creation with His hand, knelt beside me. He spit into the dust of stones King Solomon had raised. He made clay from the dust of Israel's fallen greatness. This dust of Jerusalem, beloved by God, still bears witness to the covenant power of HaShem to forgive and heal the land and the people.

The truth of God's love and mercy is recorded in Torah, the Prophets, and the Writings. Everything in Scripture means something. Every story written about an individual or the whole nation of Israel is meant to teach us to trust God. Even my blindness, such a grief to my father and mother, was meant to prove to Israel that "nothing is impossible for God!"

In my darkness I longed for The Light of the World, as did all of Israel.

Yeshua, The One Sent from Olam Haba, anointed my unformed eyes with the clay of glory He made. Then the Anointed One sent me to wash in the pool called "Sent." When I washed, I could see as well as any man born with vision. In this way Yeshua created eyes for me to receive the light.

I was blind and now I see. By this miracle God strove to prove the identity of His Son and awaken faith in the hearts of His beloved people.

I am only one among a multitude who have been forever changed by a touch or a word from Yeshua. There are miracles beyond counting in the lives of men and women I know well.

—JOURNAL OF PENIEL (PP. 3–4)

The death and raising of Lazarus (read the whole story in John 11:1-57):

On His arrival in Bethany, Yeshua found out that El'azar (Lazarus) had already been in the tomb for four days.

"Lord," Martha said to Yeshua, "if you had been here, my brother would not have died. But I know that even now God will give you whatever you ask."

Yeshua said to her, "Your brother will rise again."

Martha answered, "I know he will rise again in the resurrection at the last day."

Yeshua said to her, "I am the resurrection and the life. He who believes in me will live, even though he dies; and whoever lives and believes in me will never die. Do you believe this?"

"Yes, Lord," she told Him, "I believe that you are the Christ, the Son of God, who was to come into the world."

Yet later Martha tries to dissuade Yeshua from entering the tomb, because the dead body would, by now, have a bad odor.

Yeshua said, "Did I not tell you that if you believed, you would see the glory of God?"

So they took away the stone. Then Yeshua looked up and said, "Father, I thank you that you have heard me. I knew that you always hear me, but I said this for the benefit of the people standing here, that they may believe that you sent me."

When He had said this, Yeshua called in a loud voice, "Lazarus, come out!" The dead man came out, his hands and feet wrapped with strips of linen, and a cloth around his face.

Yeshua said to them, "Take off the grave clothes and let him go."

ASK

How might each of these miracles show Yeshua's authority as the Son of God?

- The wedding at Cana
- The nobleman's son
- The crippled man
- The feeding of the five thousand
- The catch of fish
- The man born blind
- The death and raising of Lazarus

_____

_____

_____

READ

The villages of the Galil—Capernaum, Chorazin, and Bethsaida—profited economically during the times Yeshua lived and taught in the nearby fields and by the shores of the lake. Food enough to meet the needs of thousands, sales of shoes and clothing—all boosted the village economy. The inns were crowded to overflowing. Spare rooms in homes were rented. Miracles in Capernaum were altogether good for business. When Yeshua traveled, however, the crowds of *am ha aretz* thinned and the financial benefits dwindled.

There remained some, like me, who longed to see Yeshua's return not for monetary gain, but because He had loved us first. In tonight's gathering of forty at the Capernaum synagogue were men, women, and children who had experienced a life-transforming miracle at the hand of Yeshua.

—PP. 31–32

After all, was there anyone—anyone—in Galilee and Judea who had not heard about Yeshua, the wonder worker of Nazareth? . . .

With trembling hands they constructed an image of their savior out of the very stones that weighed them down. But it was a false image, nothing like the truth of Who and What He Was and Is.

They plotted ways they might meet Him personally. Imagining themselves close enough to touch Him, they rehearsed what they would say to Him if only.

If only . . .

"You are the Messiah? I've been waiting for you to come. You see, I want a lot! But I've heard you can do everything for me. Health, first of all. Yes. You haven't got anything if you don't have your health. Heal me. And after you make me healthy, please make me be happy always! I heard you can arrange everything. I want to be loved. I want my children always content around me, appreciating me, honoring me. I want my problem solved right now. You can do it if you're really the Messiah. I want to be right, and I want everyone to know how right I am. I want to win. I want those who hurt me to be punished. I want guaranteed success. Prosperity for my business. Always. I want you to thank me for being so righteous. I want . . . I want . . . I want. . . ."

Everyone wanted something. Few made the journey simply to meet Yeshua face-to-face. Tens of thousands of the *am ha aretz* took up the pilgrim staff, drawn to Him as the baker of endless bread, the panacea for every problem. Searching, longing for a personal miracle, they swept in like the tide.

—PP. 13–14

ASK

There are all kinds of reasons that people want a messiah. What different motives are revealed in the passages above?

_____

_____

_____

Which motives most closely resemble yours, and why?

_____

_____

_____

READ

When the Sparrows, the orphans of Jerusalem fell ill, no one in leadership did anything about them. It took the tenaciousness of Marcus, a Roman soldier; El'azar; his sister Miryam; their servant Tavita; and Peniel to attempt what looked impossible: to keep the ailing boys alive.

But after two weeks without another death, it became clear something wonderful had happened in the olive oil warehouse. Not one more Sparrow's soul had flown away! The children grew stronger every day.

Even with the repudiation of miracles by the high priest, the *am ha aretz* were stirred by the story of so many ragged boys surviving such a great and terrible plague. How had this been accomplished if it was not a miracle wrought by the disciples of the great Rabbi Himself? . . .

Two weeks and a day had passed when ben Dives himself, not wishing to be outshone by a farmer from Bethany, paraded through the streets of Jerusalem with a train of donkeys laden with supplies. Trumpets announced his arrival. There followed a retinue of servants wearing the livery of Jerusalem's wealthiest merchants. These were sent to assist in two twelve-hour shifts. The epidemic feared by the authorities of Jerusalem had been halted. They declared hard work had accomplished the feat. It was no true miracle, they said.

"My medicine," declared the Greek physician as he strode through the hospital and peered down the gullets of those children he had expected to be long gone.

In the souks of the city, the wonder was discussed and credit for the good deed advertised and put to use peddling merchandise.

"My charcoal," boasted the charcoal contractor to all who passed his booth.

"My blankets." The wool merchant held up the cheap fabric, much thinner than that which El'azar had purchased to cover the sick Sparrows.

"My barley." The grain merchant let the grain thinned with sand sift through his fingers. He went on to extol the miraculous advantages of barley grown near the seacoast.

"My bread," declared the baker, waving a thick, crusted loaf of tough, gritty bread. He guaranteed the healthful benefit of his product.

"Our righteousness," proclaimed the religious leaders of the nation. "Our prayers! Our ritual! Our strict observance of the Law! Not any doing of that charlatan Yeshua!"

—PP. 139–140

"And ben Dives," Caiaphas added, "I want you to take personal charge of the infirmary. Send El'azar and his people home. And warn them I don't want anyone spreading nonsense around Yerushalayim that the name of that country preacher has any power. See to it."

—P. 142

Ben Dives' smile hardened. He lowered his voice. "Hear me, El'azar, for I speak with the voice of Caiaphas. You are commanded to return to your own home and your own place. It has been reported that an incantation of magic has been used in the treatment of the boys. The link boys are all beggars under the care of the Sanhedrin and the Temple authorities. You are relieved of this . . . task."

"But, sir," Miryam began to protest, "the boys are getting on well. The danger is past. May we not—"

Ben Dives' lip curled with disdain, silencing her. His eyes glinted with cold fury. "You, madam. It seems you have led your esteemed brother astray about the Nazarene. A dangerous deception. In his mercy, Lord Caiaphas allows you to remain free . . . in spite of the fact that you are an open supporter of Yeshua. But now you indoctrinate these innocent boys with your blasphemy. It is reported you practiced some witchcraft over them,

calling upon the name of Yeshua, whom we all know is a servant of the Evil
One. You and your brother are to gather your things and return to your
home . . . by tomorrow."

—PP. 144–145

Finally El'azar, in a hoarse voice, quietly admonished each Sparrow to recall
something: No matter what ben Dives claimed, the miracle of healing had
been accomplished in their lives by prayers offered in the name of Yeshua of
Nazareth.

All had survived! Not one had been lost! Who had ever heard of such a
thing?

Trumpets announced the arrival of ben Dives. Outside the entrance
to the warehouse he prayed loudly as a crowd gathered. "Consider our
righteousness, O Adonai! You see our good deeds for these Sparrows, who
are the lowest of humanity! We thank you, O Adonai, that we are more
righteous than others! Consider the charity we have offered to restore their
health! Reward our righteous deeds and grant our nation and the House of
Lord Caiaphas continued prosperity!"

—P. 148

"I have received a report from one of my agents that El'azar of Bethany
is himself ill. Very ill, it is said. Likely he has the leather-hide disease
himself."

Caiaphas turned from examining one of his potted pomegranate trees.
"Go on."

Boyish charm exuded from ben Dives as he explained. "You understand, my lord, that this El'azar is a close friend of Yeshua. Now the
situation is even better than before. Either Yeshua will return and we will
seize him, or he will stay away. If he does not come back, he will be thought
a coward or perhaps afraid to suffer exposure as a fraud. And if El'azar
should die . . ."

"Then Yeshua could not even save a close friend, and his name and
power will be recognized as useless!" Caiaphas concluded.

"Just so, my lord."

—PP. 153–154

ASK

Contrast the way El'azar and Miryam treat the Sparrows with ben Dives' view of the Sparrows.

_____

_____

_____

What motives did ben Dives have for acting as he did? What about Caiaphas?

_____

_____

_____

Do you find yourself eager to believe in miracles? wanting to take credit for miracles? tearing down the possibility of miracles? Why? What do miracles have to do with the proof of who Yeshua is? Who, in the end, are the miracles pointing toward?

_____

_____

_____

Consider, too, this contrast: The scheming and pompous ben Dives (who looked so good on the outside) was exiting the Dung Gate, where garbage was taken out of the city, and fell down dead. Whereas El'azar, who was known for his kind, compassionate actions, was raised from the dead to live again.

What does this say about God's justice in the long-term?

_____

_____

_____

READ
Reread the revealing story Yeshua tells of Lazarus and the rich man on pages 190–193.

"This world judges the Lord's favor wrongly—by the standard of financial success and even outward religious piety. The Lord judges the heart of a man (1 Sam. 16:7). A hypocrite is one who lies to his fellow men. But he cannot hide his sin or lie to the Lord of Heaven." Yeshua searched every face in the field. . . .

"Do you keep your vows? Do you sign your name to a covenant with your fellow men and break your promise? Are you envious and critical of the Lord's anointed? Do you seek to destroy the lives and work of those you can't control? These are the questions every man must ask himself now, while he still lives and breathes. One moment after your last heartbeat will be too late. Repent now!

"My Father in Heaven is full of mercy and unending compassion for all who call upon him in truth! Here is my warning: Hell is a real place that I have told you about. There will come a time when it is too late to repent and be received in friendship in heaven. There are some here among us who will not believe, though they will see a dead man return to life from death. Though all will come to pass according to the sign written about by the prophet Ezekiel, still many will reject the Truth and deny the Lord. As Avraham said to the rich man in hell, 'If they do not believe Mosheh and the prophets, they will not believe even if one returns from the dead'" (Luke 16:31).

—PP. 193–194

ASK
Contrast the lives of the two men in Yeshua's story on earth—and after death.

_____

_____

_____

_____

Do you think of heaven as a real place? of hell as a real place? Why or why not?

_____

_____

_____

What warning does Yeshua give about rejecting the Truth? What will happen as a result?

_____

_____

_____

What questions do you need to ask yourself, based on the passage above?

_____

_____

_____

WONDER . . .

I am Peniel the Scribe. Once I was blind, but now I have seen His face and The Light shines brightly in my heart.

Even so, there were those who witnessed my miracle with their own eyes who refused to believe Yeshua gave me sight. Instead they sought to dishonor and kill The One who is my Light, The Light of Israel.

Yeshua, The Light of the World.

Yeshua, proof that God's covenant promises are Truth.

There was a time at the campfire in Perea when I looked at His face and saw that His heart was consumed with grief at their rejection of God's mercy. Unbelief betrayed Him.

"This is not meant to end in death. . . . You will yet see the glory and power of God."

Even now He grieves for those who will not trust Him.

"Only believe me and you will see. . . ."

—JOURNAL OF PENIEL (P. 4)

Innumerable eyewitnesses have recorded the miracles of Yeshua . . . not just as stories, but as proof of who Yeshua is—the Son of God, sent to deliver us from our sins. The burden of proof is very heavy . . . and irrefutable. Will you deny the miracles and The One Sent from God Himself, as ben Dives did? Or will you accept these miracles as truth, proof of who Yeshua is, and revealing the glory of God? If you accept them as proof of God's authority, what things need to change in your life?

4 | MORE THAN JUST NAMES IN A STORY

"They were real, these people. More than just names in a story, eh?"
—Shimon (p. xii)

Think about the people you know, people whose lives intersect with yours. Do any of them (maybe it's you!) have a powerful story of overcoming seemingly insurmountable obstacles? If so, tell the story!

_____

_____

_____

How did the experience change their (or your) personality or actions after that point?

_____

_____

_____

Why does going through a crisis clarify your life's path?

_____

_____

_____

The Bible was written many, many years ago. But its characters were real people very much like us today. They had real wounds—physical, emotional, and mental. And many of them experienced a personal miracle. They were touched by Yeshua.

READ

Beside me, Peniel, was old Zadok, former Chief Shepherd of the flocks of Migdal Eder. Zadok had lost three sons thirty years before in Beth-lehem at the hand of the Butcher King. Tonight he nestled three adopted sons: Twelve-year-old Ha-or Tov had been blind. Six-year-old Emet, deaf and dumb. Ten-year-old Avel had nearly died of a broken heart. Yeshua had healed them all, then sent them to heal Zadok's wounded soul.

I spotted others who had lived without hope but were now restored to full health. Blind, deaf, lame, demon-possessed, dying of cancer or consumed by leprosy, oppressed by drink . . . too many stories for anyone to tell in a lifetime. Every life a story with a happy ending, as rewritten by Yeshua.

—P. 32

"You are right in the details. He was blind from birth. A beggar at Nicanor Gate in the Temple. Then one day: a miracle! Yeshua of Nazareth came, spit in the dirt, and made clay like a potter. He put it on the blind eyes of my boy and commanded him to wash in the Pool of Siloam. So Peniel did. And when the clay on the blind eyes of the potter's son was washed away, there were eyes where *nothing* had been before.

"I tell you, Yeshua is the True Potter sent from heaven, for he alone ever made eyes for a boy blind from birth. And all Yerushalayim knew it. Peniel, his new eyes shining, gave testimony before the Council of what Yeshua had done. And his mother and I just pretending nothing important had happened. 'He's of age,' we said. . . . 'Ask him yourself!' So Peniel is thrown out for . . . for being *healed* by the great Rabbi Yeshua. I was too afraid to speak up. Because of my cowardice, my son was sent away by the synagogue authorities. Ah, that I could see his face now and ask his forgiveness!"

I covered my eyes with my hand. Tears brimmed, spilling down my cheeks and onto my beard. At last I stepped into the light. "Papa? Don't you know me?"

Papa's face paled. His jaw dropped. Rising slowly, he turned his head suspiciously to the side as though examining a clay pot just off the wheel.

He studied me through one eye. His expression registered but could not reconcile recognition and disbelief at the transformation from ragged beggar to full-grown man. "Peniel? Son? Is it you?"

"Yes, Papa. I'm Peniel. You know me. Came to find you. To tell you . . . no, to *show* you the rest of the story. Papa! Yeshua has returned to Yerushalayim for the Feast of Dedication. Or rather, I have returned with Yeshua. I wanted to—"

"Oh, my son!" Papa replied with a ragged sob. He reached out and grasped me, pulling me tight in an embrace. "My son! My son! Oh, Peniel! My son! You've come home!"

—PP. 85–86

"But along with the old sayings, the true things, he adds this: Even if we die, if we believe in him, we will live. Do *you* believe him, El'azar?" Miryam turned her deep brown eyes full on her brother's face.

"I believe it, when I see it myself. The daughter of Ya'ir raised from death in Capernaum. The son of the widow in Nain. Lepers healed. Blind. Deaf. Can I doubt it when I hear you tell of what he did—healing so many in the Galil?"

Miryam leaned against the wall and remembered the condemnation she had faced in Jerusalem. "And in my own life. He raised me from a kind of living death. Called me from the grave of my sin."

El'azar studied his sister for a long moment as though he had forgotten what Yeshua had done for her. "You are someone else now."

"It is written that he fills the house of the barren woman with children." Miryam smiled as the groans and chatter of waking children sounded from the courtyard. "That's the point, isn't it? Yeshua takes the mess we make of our lives and makes us new and alive again. Fills our lives with his great love and heals us with his mercy and forgiveness. And then he tells us to give away the best of what we have. These little ones are the life he gave me."

El'azar embraced her. "Yes. Yes. I believe him. Gold and rubies and lapis shoes are nothing compared to the face of God that smiles in our home."

—P. 113

A Roman centurion and a Jewish landowner. Could there ever be two such unlikely allies? Yet Marcus and El'azar were united in purpose. That night I began to fully comprehend that Yeshua had come to confirm a new covenant with us.

It is written in the scroll of the prophet Ezekiel:

A new heart also I will give you, and a new spirit will I put within you; and I will take away your stony heart out of your flesh, and I will give you a heart of flesh. And I will put My Spirit within you and cause you to walk in My statutes, and you shall keep My judgments and do them. Moreover I will make a covenant of peace with them; it shall be an everlating covenant with them. (Ezek. 36:26-27; 37:26).

Though unlikely allies, Marcus of Rome and El'azar of Bethany had both been transformed by Yeshua. Hearts of stone had been cut away and replaced with hearts of compassion.

—PP. 121-122

ASK

What miracles took place in each story?

- Zadok
- Ha-or Tov
- Emet
- Avel
- Peniel
- Peniel's papa
- The daughter of Yai'r
- The son of the widow in Nain
- Miryam
- Marcus and El'azar

_____

_____

_____

_____

Which of the stories above is most compelling to you? Why? What kind of healing do you long for in your own life? Explain.

_____

_____

_____

_____

READ

But we did not send word to Yeshua. Had He not anointed us to pray in His name? to ask of our Father and expect God to answer?

And so we prayed in Yeshua's name and worked among the Sparrows as if Yeshua were there with us.

Like stewards representing a king, we spoke the name of Yeshua and the demons trembled.

And as those who would be great in the Kingdom must be the servants of all, as Yeshua taught us, there was much work for us to do.

—P. 128

We have different gifts, according to the grace given us.
If a man's gift is prophesying, let him use it in proportion to his faith.
If it is serving, let him serve;
if it is teaching, let him teach;
if it is encouraging, let him encourage;
if it is contributing to the needs of others, let him give generously;
if it is leadership, let him govern diligently;
if it is showing mercy, let him do it cheerfully.
—ROMANS 12:6-8

ASK

How might you become part of a miracle—small or large—in someone else's life?

_____

_____

_____

In what ways can you go about your daily life "as if Yeshua were there" with you?

_____

_____

_____

WONDER . . .

These are stories beyond counting, as the great disciple John says. Your own life is a story written by the very hand of the Lord. Every event in your life is meant to teach you to trust that God loves you. Perhaps it is easier to believe what God has done for others.
— JOURNAL OF PENIEL (P. 4)

> *I will sprinkle clean water on you, and you will be clean;*
> *I will cleanse you from all your impurities. . . .*
> *I will give you a new heart and put a new spirit in you;*
> *I will remove from you your heart of stone and give you a heart of flesh.*
> *I will put My Spirit in you and move you to follow My decrees.*
> — EZEKIEL 36:25-27

What is your story?

5 | FACTS OR TRUTH?

What is truth, men ask today? Is there truth anywhere?
   —CHESED TO PENIEL (P. 102)

"Yeshua brings heaven's Truth to Israel. Truth that, when revealed, condemns liars and phonies," El'azar mused. "Darkness hates light because it reveals lies for what they are."

   "He is the Truth."

   "Truth is different than I imagined it to be. No armies or clashing swords. Not even an excess of words. He asks us so many questions about ourselves. What do we think? He waits for us to answer. We reply with old clichés. He nods once when we get it right and says to us, 'It's so simple. I am the way, the truth and the life,' he says" (John 14:6).
   —EL'AZAR AND MIRYAM (PP. 112–113)

"If Yeshua can indeed raise the dead to life, then his claims must be given serious consideration."

   "Never happen," the senior Sadducee concluded. "The fact is, no one can raise the dead! Dead is dead! There is no more basic fact than that!"
   —BEN DIVES AND CAIAPHAS (P. 61)

Do you think it's possible for someone to come back to life after he or she is dead? Why or why not?

_____

_____

_____

El'azar, a treasured friend of Yeshua, was very sick. El'azar was a good man. A man who cared about the sick and dying orphans of Jerusalem and actively worked to save them. As a result, he became ill himself. His sisters, Miryam and Marta, were desperate to save him . . . but their hope was dying in the light of the hard fact that his throat was closing. Breath was hard to come by. Would Yeshua come in time? With each passing minute, they wondered. . . .

READ

Sinking down on the stone bench beside the door, Miryam fixed her gaze on the constellation rising in the east. Orion, The Hunter—*Chesil*, the Coming Forth as Light—climbed above the mountains of Moab. He carried his broad shoulders at a confident angle as he strode across the heavens. The glowing sheath of his mighty sword hung from his star-studded belt.

Was Yeshua also watching the turning wheel of night from beyond the Jordan? Could He sense all was not well with His friends in Bethany?

Did Yeshua know that Miryam prayed in His name before the throne of the Eternal Father? that again and again she had claimed God's healing for El'azar?

Even so, the heavens remained silent. The name of Yeshua had not healed Miryam's brother. Her faith had not healed him, nor had expectation changed the circumstance.

—P. 158

Yeshua was safe in Perea. Surrounded by His followers at some cheerful fireside, He no doubt taught them great and mighty truths:

> *"I, even I, am He who comforts you. . . . You have forgotten the Lord your Maker, who stretched out the heavens and laid the foundations of the earth."* (Isa. 51:12-13)

Yeshua's words were Truth, but what did the heavens and the foundations of the earth have to do with El'azar's health? When there was no crisis it was easy to consider who had created the universe. Psalms about the faithfulness of the Almighty were reassuring enough when the need belonged to someone else.

Though we did not speak of it, Miryam seemed to suspect that El'azar was dying. Dying!

She needed more than pretty platitudes about the power of God. The facts in Bethany were grim—indisputably, unrelievedly grim. In spite of loving care and much prayer, El'azar declined hour by hour!

The mighty Eternal God by His word stretched out the heavens and set the stars in place. But did He really care whether El'azar lived or died? Why had He not answered their prayers?

—P. 159

ASK

Is it more difficult for you to suffer or to watch someone you love suffer? Why?

_____

_____

_____

Have you ever felt like Miryam—that God is silent and not answering your prayers? If so, when?

_____

_____

_____

READ

Yeshua, at whose name demons had fled and every sickness had been healed, could not return. Yeshua, in danger of losing His life, could not come back to Judea to heal El'azar!

Miryam gazed up at the cold, unfeeling stars. I heard her pray: "Blessed are you, O Adonai, who heals all our diseases. Blessed are you. But . . . have you not heard our hearts? Oh, Lord! If only Yeshua were here! Then my brother would get well. If only!"

—P. 159

Zadok suggested, "Yeshua can save El'azar's life even from this distance. Eh? With a single word. You of all people know this, man. Marcus? Here are the facts. Didn't your servant, Carta, lay dyin' in Capernaum?" . . .

"Yes," Marcus admitted. "Near death. I knelt before the Lord and knew he was a king. I said to him, 'When I send an order, it is obeyed. . . . How much more true is that of you?' And by Yeshua's command, I knew Carta would be healed . . . *was* healed. Even though the boy was such a distance from Yeshua, still I had no doubt. And the truth is, when Yeshua spoke the words, Carta *was* healed. But this time Yeshua didn't say the word. At least I didn't hear him."

Zadok sniffed. "And y' think he must pronounce somethin' aloud for it t' happen? He who can call forth lightnin' and calm storms?" The old shepherd thumped Marcus on his back. "All will be well. You'll see."

"Miryam sent me. I traveled two days here to find him. It's Sabbath Eve, and he won't begin the journey. And now with Sabbath upon us, Yeshua will not leave tomorrow. Sabbath doesn't end until sunset tomorrow. He won't travel in the dark tomorrow night. Another day gone before Yeshua could set out."

"Aye. Those are the facts. You have stated it fairly."

—PP. 179–180

ASK

What are the differences between Miryam's and Marcus' thinking and Zadok's thinking?

_____

_____

_____

Do you tend to believe more in what you can see and touch (like Miryam and also Marcus) or in what you know to be true in your head and heart (like Zadok)? Explain. How does this perspective influence your actions day to day?

_____

_____

_____

When Marcus desperately needed proof that God would act, Zadok first turned to personal experience—two people Marcus could see and touch.

"Lad, tell us the facts of your former circumstance. What state were y' in when first y' laid eyes on Yeshua? That is, so t' speak."

I closed my eyes. "The fact is, I was blind. Stone blind. Born blind."

My father chimed in: "I heard the Sanhedrin say it: 'Never in the history of the world has anyone ever opened the eyes of a man born blind.' Not Elijah the Prophet. Not Mosheh the Lawgiver. And yet . . .'"

I resumed: "Those are the facts. And the truth is, now I can see."

—ZADOK, PENIEL, AND PENIEL'S PAPA (P. 180)

"Emet. Tell Marcus the meanin' of your name."

Emet put a hand on Marcus' arm and gazed up at him with somber brown eyes. "Emet means 'Truth.'"

"Aye," Zadok concurred. "Truth now can speak. And the fact is, Truth is a stronger force than fact. Fact is, Emet here could not speak last year. Couldn't utter a sound or hear the birds' chorus or know the chatter of the water in the river. But Truth is, Yeshua opened the ears of Emet so he could hear Truth. And Yeshua gave Truth a voice to speak. Listen, Marcus, to the lessons Truth has been learnin'."

—P. 180

ASK

What were the facts and the truth to Peniel? Is there a difference between them? If so, what?

_____

_____

_____

To Emet?

_____

_____

_____

Next, Zadok turned to the truths recorded in the Bible.

READ

Zadok queried, "So, Emet. Here's a *fact* from the *Book of Beginnings:* Father Avraham was a very old man without a son. He wanted a son, but his wife, Sarai, was also very old. Now what is the *truth*?"

Emet shifted his weight and stared heavenward. "Truth is . . . God said Avraham would have a son through Sarai. Baby Isaac was born."

Zadok cheered him on. "Very good, Emet! Now once more. Tell your father the answer t' this . . . fact. Joseph the Dreamer, great-grandson of Avraham, was sold into slavery by his brothers, unjustly accused, and imprisoned. What is the truth of this story?"

Emet furrowed his brow in thought. "Truth: Joseph became a great leader in Egypt. His brothers bowed down to him and he saved the whole family of Israel." . . .

Zadok sighed. "Aye. Here's a difficult one for you, Emet. And also for me, when I think on it. Fact: Pharaoh ordered all the baby boys of the Hebrews t' be slaughtered because he feared their numbers."

I considered the terrible story I had heard about the loss of Zadok's baby boys in Beth-lehem over thirty years earlier. Like Pharaoh, Herod had slaughtered the innocent in his attempt to destroy the Messiah and nullify the promises of God. Surely the link between Moses and the slaughter of the babies in Beth-lehem still burned in Zadok's memory.

Emet laid his head against Zadok's chest and answered quietly. "Papa, you remember. The truth: Baby Mosheh was saved when he was placed into a basket and set adrift on the Nile River. He was rescued by Pharaoh's daughter, nursed by his own mother, and grew up to be a prince of Egypt and the deliverer of Israel. . . .

"Aye, Papa. One more true thing, Papa? Shall we recite one more, Papa?"

Zadok seemed to scour his memory, searching for some familiar lesson Emet could recite. "Here it is, then. Fact: On their journey from Egypt, the former Hebrew slaves were trapped between the Red Sea and the approachin' chariots of Pharaoh. Now, Emet, tell us if you can. What is the truth?"

Emet eagerly declared, "God parted the waters of the sea, the Hebrews crossed over on dry land, and then the waters closed over the heads of the Egyptian pursuers and drowned them. Israel escaped and became a great nation."

—PP. 181–182

ASK

Make a list of the facts and the truth from the events above, chronicled in the Bible:

Avraham and Sarai
- Facts:

_____

_____

_____

- Truth:

_____

_____

_____

Joseph
- Facts:

_____

_____

_____

- Truth:

_____

_____

_____

Moses and the Hebrew children
- Facts:

_____

_____

_____

- Truth:

_____

_____

_____

The slaves and the Red Sea
- Facts:

_____

_____

_____

- Truth:

_____

_____

_____

How could Zadok be so confident of God's ultimate Truth, even in the face of the facts of life? Because Zadok himself had experienced the glory of seeing the angels sing around the Messiah's birth . . . and also the horror of the death of his three young boys, who were slaughtered by Herod's soldiers as they searched for the young Messiah. Yet in God's mercy, He brought Zadok three new sons.

READ

I watched the boy dash toward the house. I remembered the slaughter of Zadok's children. Not even the presence of baby Yeshua had saved the children of Beth-lehem. Sometimes the terrible circumstance of evil remained unchanged by goodness. Death was mankind's great enemy. Could it be that the good soul of El'azar was meant to fly away?

"Zadok," Marcus began, "your point is well taken. The fact is that Emet was deaf and dumb . . . and no one could heal him. The truth is, he now speaks. It is proof. But I tell you, I can't see how El'azar can remain alive. As he was near death when I left. Even now it may be too late."

"If that's the fact and he's dead, then there'll be some great truth even in his death. We'll find Truth shinin' in the darkness like a gem from Solomon's crown. Aye. Where there's unbearable facts in this life, Yeshua proves the Truth that the Eternal Father is not only Almighty, but that his love and mercy are forever. *Ha yada l'Yahweh. Kee tov, kee l'olam, chesed,*" Zadok quoted from the hundred and thirty-sixth psalm. *Give thanks to the Lord, for He is good. His love and mercy endure forever*" (Ps. 136:1).

"Still," Marcus mused, "if Yeshua won't return tonight, I don't believe El'azar will still be alive when he gets to Bethany. How can that be either love or mercy?"

—p. 182

ASK

How do Zadok's and Marcus' life philosophies differ? Why do you think this is so?

_____

_____

_____

Have you ever wondered if God is loving or merciful? In what situation?

_____

_____

_____

READ

Kindly but firmly, Yeshua drew her aside. With a gesture He summoned Miryam to join them. Then He said, "Didn't I tell you that you'll see God's glory, if you believe?"

In that instance Yeshua's teaching from Ezekiel flashed into my thoughts: *This is what the Sovereign Lord says—"I am going to breathe into you and make you live again!" (Ezek. 37:5).*

In that instant I saw Ya'ir's daughter, Deborah, and Eve's son, Abel! I had never met them—either one—until *after* each had been dead and raised to life again by Yeshua!

But four days dead? Dead, stinking dead?

And this is what rumbled from heaven, though perhaps no one else in the whole assembly heard it except me: **Don't ever again confuse facts with Truth! That Israel was trapped between Pharaoh's chariots and the Red Sea was fact . . . but not Truth! That a virgin could never conceive and bear a son was fact . . . but not Truth! Watch and see Truth!**

And like The Lord of All the Angel Armies issuing an order, Yeshua repeated, "Roll the stone away!"

The old porter summoned three attendants and they did so, moving the barrier aside with a chunk of limestone wedged under it.

Then they backed away.

The crowd was deathly still . . . and I use the word very deliberately.

Lifting his face toward the brilliant blue sky, Yeshua said, "Father, I thank you for hearing me. You always hear me, but I said this out loud for the sake of all these people standing here, so they will believe you sent me."

Because I love them!

In the rumble within my mind I heard an echo of what I had overheard on the Mountain Set Apart: **This is my Son, my chosen one. Listen to him!**

And then before the last of Yeshua's words had finished rolling around in my head, He suddenly shouted, "El'azar! Come forth!"

Yeshua never shouted, seldom lifted His voice. But I believe His cry that day could be heard in Jerusalem.

There was a rustling from within the shadow. A figure detached itself from a stone slab and stood upright. Then El'azar, shuffling because of the layers of cloth with which his arms and legs were bound, stepped blinking into the sunlight.

He could not speak because of the cloth wrapping his jaw tightly to his head, but his eyes said, *Where am I? What is this crowd doing here?*

And Yeshua, with a great smile of incredible joy, gestured for El'azar's sisters and the attendants. "Well? What are you waiting for? Unwrap him and let him go!"

—PP. 201–203

ASK

Imagine that you were standing in the crowd, watching this event. What would you be thinking? What would you be feeling?

_____

_____

_____

When you were confronted with the facts—that El'azar was dead—then saw the truth with your own eyes—that El'azar was now alive—what would your response be? Would there be any doubt in your mind that Yeshua was who He said He was? Explain.

_____

_____

_____

READ

"In point of fact they did not ask him to return. The message is: 'The one you love is sick.'"

Suddenly the implication of that remark sank in. It was not necessary for Yeshua to go to Bethany or anywhere near Jerusalem for El'azar to be healed. Like the time Marcus' servant Carta was healed without Yeshua ever setting foot in his house, the same could be true now. All that was required was for Yeshua to be aware of the need.

In the next moment Yeshua Himself seemed to confirm this answer by saying, "El'azar's sickness will not end in death. No, it is for the glory of God. I, the Son of God, will receive glory from this."

Was it a test of our faith?

It was of mine. Yeshua had such high regard for El'azar. With the Sparrows, El'azar had so completely demonstrated true righteousness. If anyone was worthy of a miracle, it was he. Even knowing El'azar would get well, did it not seem like cowardice, or a lack of compassion, not to go to him at once, no matter what the risk?

And what did "receive glory from this" mean?

—P. 173

ASK

Do you believe that God allows suffering to test our faith? Why or why not?

_____

_____

_____

Think back to the toughest moment in your life. Did it harden your heart toward spiritual things or soften your heart? Explain.

_____

_____

_____

How could you allow God to "receive glory" from that life-changing moment?

_____

_____

_____

WONDER . . .

What did I learn from what I witnessed in those weeks that I traveled with Yeshua?

I learned to never confuse facts with Truth.

The fact is, El'azar was dead.

The greater Truth is that Yeshua is the Resurrection and the Life.

I learned that sometimes we do not understand how The Lord of All the Angel Armies is working for our benefit.

The greater Truth is that He *always* cares and provides for us. Even if He delays, it is *because* He loves us.

I learned that Yeshua cried. He shed tears of grief for what El'azar suffered. He shed tears of compassion for the pain of Miryam and Marta's loss.

He shed tears of longing for all creation to be restored, for death to be abolished, because that day was not just about El'azar. Everyone present that day had a grave awaiting them.

But the greater Truth is that Yeshua wept because for all His love, compassion, and longing, for all His sacrifice, some will still refuse His gift. Out of arrogance or pride, some will die as Ra'nabel ben Dives died . . . and Yeshua was weeping for him and for all like him who leave this world outside the friendship of God.

Finally I learned the true meaning of the Sabbath. Six days are appointed for us to work, to labor for the Kingdom. Six days we will face turmoil and deal with grief. Six days we will long for Yeshua's return. *"Lord, if you had only been here . . ."*

But the greater Truth is that the Seventh Day *is* coming. The Lord of the Sabbath, The Lord of the Seventh Day, is returning.

May it be today!

—PP. 208–209

Is your heart tender toward God, even in the midst of suffering? How can knowing that Truth reigns over the facts give you a broader perspective?

> *"I will give you a new heart and will put a new spirit within you; I will remove from you your heart of stone and give you a heart of flesh. And I will put My Spirit in you and move you to follow My decrees and be careful to keep My laws. You will live in the land I gave your forefathers. You will be My people, and I will be your God."*
>
> —EZEKIEL 36:26-28

6 ANTICIPATING HEAVEN

> "Heaven is as real as Capernaum. We have seen *olam haba*. Those
> righteous loved ones you thought were dead are alive. Yeshua told me
> after death comes life. His words are true!"
> —ABEL (P. 32)

If you watch TV or read the newspaper, it's inevitable that you'll see
someone claiming that they experienced "life after death" and then were
returned to the earth to be given a second chance at life. Do you think there
is any truth to those stories? Why or why not?

_____

_____

_____

What do you envision "the afterlife" or "heaven" to be like? Describe the
picture in your mind.

_____

_____

_____

Thirteen-year-old Deborah and fourteen-year-old Abel didn't have to
wonder what heaven was like. They knew, because they had both died . . .
visited heaven . . . then been returned to life! Even more, they agreed on the
experience!

READ

Tonight the two young witnesses at the center of the congregation brought good news far greater than anything anyone living on earth had ever heard before! . . .

The heartbeat of hope pulsed within the room.

Thirteen-year-old Deborah, daughter of Ya'ir, the Capernaum cantor, sat beside Abel, fourteen-year-old son of Eve, the widow of Nain. Until tonight neither young person had met or spoken to the other, yet the details they shared were nearly identical. Both were adolescents. Both had suffered and *died* of terrible illness. Both had been prepared for burial. And, as many witnesses could attest, both Abel and Deborah, stone-cold dead, had returned to life at the word of Yeshua! . . .

Tonight in Capernaum there was a flood of friendly questions from those who had experienced the life-changing power of Yeshua. Where had Abel and Deborah gone the instant their souls had flown away?

Abel and Deborah recounted their journeys to *olam haba*.

The rabbi of Capernaum asked, "Children, please tell us—tell us old ones . . . say what you remember—were there others in *olam haba*? People you recognized?"

Abel frowned, then grinned, as his changing voice cracked. "Rabbi, Your Honor, there were many there who I knew must be from of old. Though I can't name them, they seemed as though I knew them from my Torah studies. My bar mitzvah. And some from my family. But the one I met first was my father. My father was there, waiting just on the other side, in the light. *Such light!* Golden. Shimmering! Waiting for me, I think, so I would not be afraid. Only he was very tall, young . . . without age . . . and strong. He called out my name in welcome. He embraced me. I clung to him and wept for joy for a very long time. I was so happy to see him, to be with him. Then I knew I was not finished here. I was needed here. My mother, you see . . ." Abel gestured toward his widowed mother, who sat beside the mother of Deborah. "It was so wonderful. I didn't want to come back. I would have stayed except for . . . Yeshua's voice."

The rabbi steepled his fingers. "Yeshua's voice? In *olam haba* you heard Yeshua speak to your soul? Though he is here on earth? You heard him?"

"Clearly."

—PP. 32–33

ASK

If you could peek through heaven's doors right now, who do you expect you'd see there? Why? What qualities make you think that person would be in heaven?

_____

_____

_____

What is the "dividing line" to you of who goes to heaven . . . and who does not?

_____

_____

_____

READ

"But this place—*olam haba*, the world to come—what was this place like? Where you saw your father?"

"A garden . . . such color!" Abel spread his arms wide as though color in heaven was a tangible thing to be embraced and not just experienced with the eyes.

Deborah bobbed her head in agreement. "Yes! I was in the same place. The garden. Flowers! Such fragrance! No thorns! Waterfalls so high I couldn't see the top. Rainbows. Hues so deep the air hummed with the music of color. I never knew color is music. Seven colors matched seven musical notes. But all with different shades and voices. Reds and blues and greens, a thousand pitches of every color. I can't explain it. I try, but I can't. . . . It's so . . ."

"And the stream!" Abel placed his hand on the girl's arm. "Deborah! Could you hear the voices singing in the waters?"

"The song! Yes. Oh!" Deborah shook her head in wonder as she answered him. Suddenly the two were speaking to one another as though no one else was in the room. "Was there ever such music?"

He laughed. "I dream of it."

"Remember?" Deborah lowered her chin and quietly hummed the first notes.

Abel brightened in recognition of the music. Though he had never sung before, Abel began to hum with her, testing his voice.

Thunder rumbled outside, rattling the nerves of those who listened to the description of heaven. What the eyes of the two children had seen was more . . . more . . . than anyone imagined! And these beloved children who had been dead, prepared for burial, had returned to tell about a place they knew was real! . . .

They ended their song at the same instant. Words and music of the hymn reverberated in the room. The flames of candles flickered in the breath of unseen angels.

And then, silence.

The rush of wind and rain outside the synagogue sounded like applause from a great amphitheater.

Deborah and Abel blinked at one another in relief. *Yes! The testimony of two witnesses. A boy and a girl. The testimony of two!*

They laughed and huddled with heads close together. They seemed to me like old friends meeting unexpectedly on a lonely and distant shore. They rejoiced as they remembered the familiar sights and sounds of their much-loved home.

In this case heaven was home. This *present* world was the strange and distant shore to which they had returned.

—PP. 33–35

ASK

How is your vision of heaven similar to, or different from, Deborah's and Abel's?

_____

_____

_____

_____

What do you look forward to in heaven? What do you worry about in regard to heaven?

_____

_____

_____

If you believed that heaven was your real home, how might you live your life differently? Explain.

_____

_____

_____

READ

The stories of Abel and Deborah were unlike any others. Deborah, only daughter of the cantor of Capernaum, dead for hours. Abel, only son of the widow of Nain, carried toward the grave the previous spring. Yet here they were—laughing, talking, singing, surrounded by friends and family! Abel and Deborah were two witnesses to the eternal life Yeshua promised those who followed Him. On the other side of this life was *LIFE*! They had personally experienced the joy of heaven!

And then Yeshua had called them back to live again: two witnesses, as required in court by the laws of Torah. Witnesses to resurrection! Yeshua had restored these only ones to full health and placed them again in the arms of grieving parents!

"After death comes life," Yeshua often told us.

I pondered the meaning of the Master's teaching. *After death?* LIFE! Here was the proof!

At the end of the evening it was Deborah who embraced her friends and family with a smile and summed up what it all meant. "We all have so much to look forward to. Everything he told us is true. And we never, ever, have to be afraid again!"

—P. 36

ASK

List all the ways the stories of Abel and Deborah were different from the other miracles that Yeshua performed.

_____

_____

_____

How might knowing that you have a secure place in heaven take away the fears you face in living on earth? How might it give you a different perspective on any hardships you are currently facing?

_____

_____

_____

WONDER . . .

"Marta, those who believe in me, even though they die like everyone else, will live again. They are given eternal life for believing in me and will never perish."

With a kind touch He raised her chin so her eyes met His. "Do you believe this, Marta?" . . .

"Yes," she said firmly. "You are the Messiah, the Son of God. The One who came into the world from God."

—P. 199

If Yeshua were to ask you today, "Do you believe this?" what would you say?

_____

_____

_____

Dear Reader,

You are so important to us. We have prayed for you as we wrote this book and also as we receive your letters and hear your soul cries. We hope that *Seventh Day* has encouraged you to go deeper. To get to know Yeshua better. To fill your soul hunger by examining Scripture's truths for yourself.

We are convinced that if you do so, you will find this promise true: *"If you seek Him, He will be found by you."*
— I CHRONICLES 28:9

Bodie & Brock Thoene

Scripture References

1 John 21:25
2 Luke 1:37
3 Deut. 29:10-12
4 Deut. 29:14-15; 30:15, 19
5 Isa. 61:1-2
6 Luke 4:23-26
7 Deut. 29:10-12; 30:15, 19
8 Deut. 6:4
9 Num. 6:24-25
10 Ps. 51:15
11 John 5:24
12 Ps. 103:1
13 Ps. 103:11
14 Ps. 103:17-18
15 Ps. 103:19-22
16 John 21:25
17 Hag. 2:18-19
18 Hag. 2:20-22
19 Mark 9:33
20 Mark 9:35
21 Mark 9:37
22 Mark 9:38-41
23 Matt. 18:6, 10
24 Luke 2:49

25 Luke 9:51-56
26 Read the story in
   John 10:22-30.
27 Read the story in
   John 10:31-39.
28 1 Kings 3:6-7, 9
29 1 Kings 3:18-22
30 1 Kings 3:25-27
31 Isa. 5:20-21, 24
32 John 14:6
33 John 11:25
34 Deut 30:6
35 Ezek. 36:26-27; 37:26
36 Matt. 5:13-14
37 Matt.10:29-31
38 Isa. 51:12-13
39 John 11:3
40 John 11:4
41 Luke 7:1-10
42 Ps. 136:1
43 Ezek. 36:26-28
44 Ezek. 36:32-33
45 Ezek. 36:33-36
46 Ezek. 37:1-6

47 Ezek. 37:11
48 Ezek. 37:11-12
49 Ezek. 37:13-14
50 John 11:11
51 Luke 16:19-31
52 Luke 18:25
53 1 Sam. 16:7
54 Luke 16:31
55 Ps. 119:105
56 John 8:12
57 John 11:16
58 Ezek. 37:5
59 Read the wonderful story of
   Lazarus in John 11:1-44.
60 John 2:1-11
61 John 4:43-54
62 John 5:1-15
63 John 6:1-15
64 John 21:1-14
65 John 9:1-41
66 John 21:25
67 John 11:35-36

Authors' Note

The following sources have been helpful in our research for this book.

- *The Complete Jewish Bible.* Translated by David H. Stern. Baltimore, MD: Jewish New Testament Publications, Inc., 1998.

- *iLumina*, a digitally animated Bible and encyclopedia suite. Carol Stream, IL: Tyndale House Publishers, 2002.

- *The International Standard Bible Encyclopaedia.* George Bromiley, ed. 5 vols. Grand Rapids, MI: Eerdmans, 1979.

- *The Life and Times of Jesus the Messiah.* Alfred Edersheim. Peabody, MA: Hendrickson Publishers, Inc., 1995.

- Starry Night™ Enthusiast Version 5.0, publishing by Imaginova™ Corp.

About the Authors

BODIE AND BROCK THOENE (pronounced *Tay-nee*) have written over 45 works of historical fiction. That these best sellers have sold more than 10 million copies and won eight ECPA Gold Medallion Awards affirms what millions of readers have already discovered—the Thoenes are not only master stylists but experts at capturing readers' minds and hearts.

In their timeless classic series about Israel (The Zion Chronicles, The Zion Covenant, and The Zion Legacy), the Thoenes' love for both story and research shines.

With The Shiloh Legacy and *Shiloh Autumn* (poignant portrayals of the American Depression), The Galway Chronicles (dramatic stories of the 1840s famine in Ireland), and the Legends of the West (gripping tales of adventure and danger in a land without law), the Thoenes have made their mark in modern history.

In the A.D. Chronicles they step seamlessly into the world of Jerusalem and Rome, in the days when Yeshua walked the earth and transformed lives with His touch.

Bodie began her writing career as a teen journalist for her local newspaper. Eventually her byline appeared in prestigious periodicals such as *U.S. News and World Report*, *The American West*, and *The Saturday Evening Post*. She also worked for John Wayne's Batjac Productions (she's best known as author of *The Fall Guy*) and ABC Circle Films as a writer and researcher. John Wayne described her as "a writer with talent that captures the people and the times!" She has degrees in journalism and communications.

Brock has often been described by Bodie as "an essential half of this writing team." With degrees in both history and education, Brock has, in his role as researcher and story-line consultant, added the vital dimension of historical accuracy. Due to such careful research, the Zion Covenant and Zion Chronicles series are recognized by the American Library Association, as well as Zionist libraries around the world, as classic historical novels and are used to teach history in college classrooms.

Bodie and Brock have four grown children—Rachel, Jake, Luke, and Ellie—and seven grandchildren. Their children are carrying on the Thoene family talent as the next generation of writers, and Luke produces the Thoene audiobooks. Bodie and Brock divide their time between London and Nevada.

For more information visit:
www.thoenebooks.com
www.familyaudiolibrary.com

THOENE FAMILY CLASSICS™

✪ ✪ ✪

THOENE FAMILY CLASSIC HISTORICALS
by Bodie and Brock Thoene

*Gold Medallion Winners**

THE ZION COVENANT
*Vienna Prelude**
Prague Counterpoint
Munich Signature
Jerusalem Interlude
Danzig Passage
*Warsaw Requiem**
London Refrain
Paris Encore
Dunkirk Crescendo

THE ZION CHRONICLES
*The Gates of Zion**
A Daughter of Zion
The Return to Zion
A Light in Zion
*The Key to Zion**

THE SHILOH LEGACY
*In My Father's House**
A Thousand Shall Fall
Say to This Mountain

SHILOH AUTUMN

THE GALWAY CHRONICLES
*Only the River Runs Free**
Of Men and of Angels
*Ashes of Remembrance**
All Rivers to the Sea

THE ZION LEGACY
Jerusalem Vigil
Thunder from Jerusalem
Jerusalem's Heart
Jerusalem Scrolls
Stones of Jerusalem
Jerusalem's Hope

A.D. CHRONICLES
First Light
Second Touch
Third Watch
Fourth Dawn
Fifth Seal
Sixth Covenant
Seventh Day
Eighth Shepherd
and more to come!

CP0064

THOENE FAMILY CLASSICS™

✪ ✪ ✪

THOENE FAMILY CLASSIC AMERICAN LEGENDS

LEGENDS OF THE WEST
by Bodie and Brock Thoene

Legends of the West, Volume One
Sequoia Scout
The Year of the Grizzly
Shooting Star
Legends of the West, Volume Two
Gold Rush Prodigal
Delta Passage
Hangtown Lawman
Legends of the West, Volume Three
Hope Valley War
The Legend of Storey County
Cumberland Crossing
Legends of the West, Volume Four
The Man from Shadow Ridge
Cannons of the Comstock
Riders of the Silver Rim

LEGENDS OF VALOR
by Luke Thoene

Sons of Valor
Brothers of Valor
Fathers of Valor

✪ ✪ ✪

THOENE CLASSIC NONFICTION
by Bodie and Brock Thoene

Writer-to-Writer

THOENE FAMILY CLASSIC SUSPENSE
by Jake Thoene

CHAPTER 16 SERIES
Shaiton's Fire
Firefly Blue
Fuel the Fire

✪ ✪ ✪

THOENE FAMILY CLASSICS FOR KIDS

BAKER STREET DETECTIVES
by Jake and Luke Thoene

The Mystery of the Yellow Hands
The Giant Rat of Sumatra
The Jeweled Peacock of Persia
The Thundering Underground

LAST CHANCE DETECTIVES
by Jake and Luke Thoene
Mystery Lights of Navajo Mesa
Legend of the Desert Bigfoot

THE VASE OF MANY COLORS
by Rachel Thoene (Illustrations by Christian Cinder)

✪ ✪ ✪

THOENE FAMILY CLASSIC AUDIOBOOKS

Available from
www.thoenebooks.com or
www.familyaudiolibrary.com

CP0064